# One For Sorrow
## A Sam Meredith Novel

John Gillick

For Letty.

# PROLOGUE

The Watcher observed the Whore as she left to go to work, rushing as usual for the train. It was the same every morning – why could she not get up a bit earlier? Why could she not get organised?

The Watcher hated people who were disorganised, who were always late; it was disrespectful and selfish. Sometimes the Watcher wondered if it was deliberate, if maybe they enjoyed it. Perhaps it was a form of protest against routine and order. Well, let her continue with her protest. The irony of it was that she was consistent in her disorganisation, which made her predictable.

And that would make it easier for the Watcher to plan what needed to be done, and when to do it; to ensure that the strategy and plan of action would be successful. Because one day the Watcher would be there waiting for her.

And the Watcher had all the time in the world and

was happy to wait until the time was right; until the right opportunity arose.

And the Watcher would not be late. The Watcher would be on time, even if the Whore was late.

And the Watcher would make sure that it was the last time she would ever be late – very, very late.

# CHAPTER 1

Sam stared disbelievingly at the screen and tried to make sense of what he was reading, or *trying* to read, because the page was a blur and the words seemed to have a life of their own. He couldn't seem to stop them from swimming around. It seemed like they weren't on the page, but inside his head. Surely this was some kind of twisted joke or wind up? Surely this could not really be happening to him. Things like this only happened in films, didn't they? Not to people like him. He was just an ordinary, working class nobody, who hadn't done anything to deserve this.

Had he?

He had only gone on to an adult dating site because he was curious, that was all. He hadn't had sex with anyone. He hadn't had an affair with anyone. OK, so he had messaged a few women, but that was mainly to see if he got any response; to see whether it actually did what it said on the tin and lived up to its slogan of; 'Have an Affair'. To see whether there were indeed women on the site that were not hookers; women who were just 'unhappily married' and were genuinely willing to meet up to have casual sex with complete strangers. That it wasn't all a front for prostitution or blackmail, as was being suggested by certain investigative journalists.

As it turned out, he had received several responses, but they weren't from women who were gagging to jump into no-strings, unconditional sex.

No, the pattern was that initially they would respond in a quite flirtatious, playful way, but stopped short of agreeing to meet up, ultimately always giving some reason why they couldn't. He remembered wondering what he would have done in the event of somebody agreeing to get together. It was while he was wondering this that he got his answer, because one of the women he had messaged responded by asking him to contact her on her email address, rather than on the site. Because of his naivety, he still hadn't worked out what the deal was, and he needed to know if somebody was actually going to go through with it and take it all the way.

So, he contacted her, and after some fairly inconsequential flirtatious chit chat, and her forwarding him some mildly risqué snaps, she informed him that she was an escort and was happy to meet up with him for sex, at a cost of £150 a time. That was when he realised that he was the one looking for an excuse to get himself off the hook. Fortunately for him, she only did 'out calls', which gave him his out: he lied that he was living with a partner and wasn't in a position to access hotel rooms without jeopardising his relationship. Which was true, well, partly. He was in his second marriage– his first wife having died of cancer some years previously – of almost 20 years to Kim, a woman ten years his junior, but before they finally moved out from the "family" home nine months ago, they'd spent a year and a half in separate rooms, day and night. They would occasionally share some living space at mealtimes, or when they went through the sham of pretending to visitors that all was well.

However, they both knew that it was only a matter of time before they called it quits. And when that time eventually came, it hadn't ended well, with acrimonious recriminations on both sides and arguments over the financial details following the sale of the house.

He was just about getting used to being apart, if not actually coming to terms with it, when he received the email.

He read it again, trying to focus:

*Dear Mr. Meredith,*

*Unfortunately, your data, including complete credit card details, was leaked in the recent hacking of the 'Madison Avenue: Have an Affair' website.*

This was followed by his address and part of his credit card details, including the date of his 'last payment' to them.

Actually, this payment, for £15, had been taken by mistake from his account, and was later refunded to him as his initial 'introductory period' was part of a 'special offer'. He closed his 'account' soon after. Hardly the behaviour of someone who was a chronic sex addict or cheating philanderer, who was recklessly squandering his hard-earned cash on clandestine sex with married, or even unmarried, women. The truth was that he had never been unfaithful, well apart from the time when he and his estranged wife were 'on a break' – very Ross and Rachel, and very ironic, because he and his ex were most definitely no longer 'friends'.

The email continued:

*We also have access to your complete profile data, including your pictures, secret fantasies, conversations etc. . .*

*They certainly are secret,* he thought, *I don't even fucking know what they are!*

He read on:

*We also have access to your Facebook page, so if you would like to prevent me from sharing this dirt with all your friends, family and your spouse, then you need to send exactly 5 Bitcoins* . . . before providing him with an email address to send the money to.

*I'm not even on Facebook, and what in the name of god are Bitcoins?* wondered Sam, panicking now.

Until this point he had never heard of such a thing. But he was soon to learn that they were the blackmailers" favourite currency; one of the tools of their sleazy trade.

*Who are these people?* He thought, *these lowlife scum, with no morals or scruples, who prey upon people's vulnerabilities?*

The author of this grotesque communiqué then went on to explain that they were providing *'a chance to solve this case'* (now they were well meaning sleuths, for Christ's sake!).

*If you make a payment to the aforementioned address, we will not publish your data and we will not inform your contacts.*

The email then went on to advise where Bitcoins could be purchased – exchanges like Coinbase, Expresscoin, Local Bitcoins and various others – how bloody helpful of them!

Sam suddenly realised that he was actually shaking with anxiety and anger and fear; he decided that he needed to get out of the house and get some air to clear his head.

As he made his way along the street, he realised how dramatically his town and others locally had changed in recent years. Nowadays, most of the decent shops and restaurants were invariably located in retail parks, mostly situated some distance away from the town and residential areas, and for which you needed a car, or taxi, to access. He smiled an ironic smile at the ludicrous economics of that particular situation.

Sam recalled that when he was young there was even a department store in the town where he had lived, which had long since disappeared, along with tailors (several), restaurants, cinemas (several), travel agents, shoe shops, cafes, ironmongers, and electrical contractors. He remembered with some fondness how he, and probably millions of others, had crowded round Stepeks or Radio Rentals' windows on Saturday evenings to look at the football scores on the television screens as they came in on the video-printer, and on occasions had also watched the racing. It seemed like a different world – a million miles and years away. Nowadays, the main streets or shopping centres were mostly made up of discount or 'pound' shops of some description or other, along with charity shops, kebab shops, tanning salons and cash converters or other versions of modern-day pawnbrokers. And of course, ironically, amidst the 'for sale' signs and the other indicators of the economic downturn, there were the ever-present pubs and betting shops. And, for some reason, an abundance of hairdressers and nail bars.

*Aye we might be skint, but my hair and nails look great*, mused Sam. The situation depressed him so much he decided to head to the city centre for a change of scenery.

Sam took the bus into the city centre – when it eventually arrived. He could not recall just how long 'Missed Bus', as he liked to call the company who ran the service, had been in operation, but as far back as he could remember they had always been useless. They never seemed to arrive when they were supposed to, their schedule appearing to bear no resemblance whatsoever to the timetables displayed on the bus stops or the information on their website. In Sam's experience they often turned up two or three at a time or just not at all, and basically just seemed to please themselves.

Also, driver changeovers were frequent occurrences and took forever, resembling a ten to 15-minute tea break and involving leisurely conversation to the complete disregard of the passengers and any time constraints or appointments that they may have. Even more annoyingly, any concerns expressed in regard to this seemingly anarchic practice were invariably met with clear disbelief, resentment and often hostility, along the lines of "If you don't like it, there's the door". On one occasion he was even threatened with the police being called.

However, by far the most memorable reply he was offered, with no hint of humour or irony, was "How am I supposed to know? I'm only the driver."

The bus, when it arrived, was quite busy and he found himself sitting behind two racist pensioners, whose conversation it was impossible not to overhear:

"Honestly, Bella, I was just thinking the other day, y'know I honestly can't remember the last time I saw a

Big Issue seller who was from Glasgow. That cannae be right, can it?"

*Aye, you're right missus,* thought Sam. *What we need is more homeless Glaswegians!*

# CHAPTER 2

It was a typical winter's day in Glasgow (*if indeed there is such a thing*, thought Sam, *and if there is it's that it's totally unpredictable and impossible to typify*). He ruminated that you never really knew what to expect from the elements in Glasgow, as the Great British Summer had very much in common with the Great British Winter. He thought that if there was one song that defined the weather here it had to be 'Four Seasons in One Day' by Crowded House. *We don't really have multiple seasons like other countries*, he mused, *we have one, also known as "driech", and anything else is a bonus. And if the sun does come out, we're on the phone to friends and family* telling *them that the sun is out. And they're like, "Is it? Well, it's pissing down here! "And they only live three streets away!* As Billy Connolly once said, "If you don't like the weather, hang around for a few minutes."

Today was cold, crisp, and bleak, but not without its attraction and familiar seasonal characteristics. It had rained earlier, before the frost arrived, and the headlights of the cars blazed and glowed like neon in the shiny, wet day, reflecting in the road surface and creating a hazy, bright mosaic, complimenting the Yuletide feel. Sam liked the ambience you got at this time of year, which was different to any other time, even without snow. It was difficult to state what exactly created this alchemy, apart from the obvious icons, like Xmas trees and decorations.

Undoubtedly though, other factors blended harmoniously to contribute to this unique tapestry; the hustle and bustle of people wrapped up warm and snug against the elements; people out shopping, wandering into pubs and restaurants for some respite and sustenance. A feeling of general warmth and bonhomie existed, born of common purpose and routine, with the overcrowding and noise not causing any consternation but a feeling of familiarity and reassurance. He bought into it, and decided to go for a beer in the next pub he saw, which, as it happened, was on the next corner.

The place was absolutely jam-packed and throbbing with the syncopated, unintelligible cacophony of chat and laughter that creates a unique hubbub; the ever-present background in such places. A veritable Tower of Babel, it created the audio equivalent of staring into the middle distance, of not actually focusing on anything and ending up not actually seeing or hearing anything as a result. The addition of televisions broadcasting music channels at full blast didn't exactly make for a calm environment, either. Sam decided that it wasn't for him and went in search of somewhere more civilised.

The next place he decided upon was less hectic, but nevertheless certainly had its own charm and idiosyncratic atmosphere. There was a 'band' playing, whose 'musicians' must have had a combined age of several centuries, while overall the pub, like its clientele, had seen better days, and was sorely in need of a refurbishment.

However, the atmosphere seemed friendly enough, and he managed to manoeuvre himself to the bar and catch the attention of the barmaid.

"What can I get you, dear?" she asked.

"A glass of red wine, please", he replied. Her reply still made him smile and shake his head in disbelief. "I'm sorry dear, but the wine glass is out."

That's right, *the* wine glass! She pointed across the room to the person who was drinking from said glass. It was at that point that he decided to call it a day, as it definitely wasn't going to be his.

It was while he was leaving the pub, which was directly opposite a travel agent with a brightly lit window, that he came to the conclusion that what he needed was a holiday. He decided to look for inspiration inside.

# CHAPTER 3

She had been at home alone, having a few glasses of wine, trying on clothes, and putting on make-up in a quite relaxed and flighty mood; posing, pouting, and even kissing the mirror, leaving a bright lipstick stain there. However, after a few drinks she started to find more new wrinkles and grey showing through her frequently dyed and coiffured hair. This, combined with the wine, fuelled and confirmed her realisation that she was no longer vivacious, attractive and full of life, causing her to look at the same reflection again, this time with resentment and bitterness and with an overwhelming desire to smash it to smithereens.

As always, whenever she drank, she recalled and became distressed by the memory of the experience which had changed her life as she had known it; when her world had died.

It was over ten years ago, but she remembered as if it was yesterday. Her husband telling her that they had been conned out of a large sum of money by a business contact who had turned out to be a fraudster and a conman; a man who had told her husband that he had the opportunity to get involved with an excellent business and investment opportunity. Her husband had been convinced about it; the man had been adamant that this was a sure thing, and stupidly, he had believed and trusted him. He'd always maintained that he had done it for them, and that he believed that they were investing in something that would set them up for the rest of their life.

Afterwards, he had of course contacted the police, but told her there was nothing they could do. Unbelievably, he then decided that it was time to draw a veil over the situation, and declared that they simply had to move on. While she initially could not understand this very forgiving and reasonable attitude, she subsequently discovered the reasons for his complicity. But that was another matter. A completely different matter altogether, that caused her world to collapse and wither, destroying her life forever. As a wronged and scorned woman, she could not forgive as easily, and certainly not forget.

She needed retribution, and revenge.

# CHAPTER 4

Sam could not stop thinking about the implications of the email for himself and his family. His mother had passed away some years ago and his father, who was now in a nursing home, had dementia and therefore would hopefully be oblivious and unaffected. Kim's parents were also dead; she'd become particularly distant and difficult following her mother's death around three years ago and their relationship had never really improved significantly afterwards; they never regained any real closeness. Sam couldn't really care less what the rest of her family thought, but what about his own children; his son and daughter from his marriage to his late wife, his brother, and his family?

And then there was his late wife's family. What would they think if the threat was carried out? Would they believe him if he insisted that he had done nothing wrong?

He was so angry with himself; how did he end up

getting involved with such people? And what about his employment and work mates – how could he face them? And could he even go back, given the setting he worked in? It was impossible to avoid the irony that he could find himself on the receiving end of his colleagues' professional energy and interest. Would he lose his job, and if so, what else could he do? At 52 years of age, he wasn't exactly going to walk into another position, particularly with the stench of scandal like this blotting his copybook.

Sam reflected on his employment history, which, he considered to be particularly uninspiring. This attitude could probably be put down do how negative and vulnerable he was feeling, but nevertheless he just couldn't see his Curriculum Vitae getting prospective employers hot-footing it to his door.

When he left school, Sam had walked into a job in the Civil Service with The Department of Health and Social Security (DHSS), which he very quickly realised was not for him. It was too rigid, structured and disciplined. He was bored beyond belief, and, in retrospect, probably because of his youth and immaturity, he did not deal with this in a particularly responsible way. He was also expected to become involved with the Civil Service Sports Federation and Social Club and to socialise there with his colleagues, which he was not even remotely interested in doing.

Any extra-curricular activity was severely frowned

upon, so when his employers found out that he was moonlighting as a male model for the Scottish Knitwear Federation and also playing drums in a band, they nearly had a collective, corporate coronary. His behaviour was absolute anathema to them, and he was instantly regarded as a rebel and an insurgent influence.

However, in those days there were actually other jobs available, and consequently this probably led to him being quite cavalier in his attitude. Unfortunately, this did not go down well with his superiors, and led to several disciplinary incidents. From then on, his card was marked, and it was only a matter of time before he left through the door marked 'unsuitable for purpose'. He was most definitely a round peg in a place full of squares.

In the end he'd left of his own accord, taking undoubted delight and pleasure in telling his boss to stick his job where the sun didn't shine. However, he did resist the temptation some years later to punch the same little Hitler in the mouth, when he ran into him on a quick visit to one of his ex-colleagues in the office. The ex-boss was still, characteristically unable to avoid being a sad, officious prick, and escorted him off the premises.

After Sam left the DHSS, he applied to join the Fire Service, which seemed incredible to comprehend now. What on earth had he been thinking about? He had undergone the interview and physical test which involved running 100 yards with a hose. Him, who was one of the clumsiest people alive, a veritable bull in a china shop– a complete one-man disaster zone.

His clumsiness was effortless. Sometimes he only needed to walk past an aisle in the supermarket and stuff would fall as if mysteriously dislodged by a poltergeist. Unsurprisingly, he didn't make the grade, and god knows how many people were spared a horrible death.

Sam was still getting occasional work from the band at this stage, but it was becoming less regular as the other band members' work and family commitments militated against such frivolity. Also, he had gradually lost interest in modelling, due to stupidly feeling embarrassed about it – it must have been a Scottish male thing. The bottom line was, he needed employment. That was it, plain and simple. Any kind of gig would do; he had been out of regular work for over a year, during which time he had received absolutely zero offers of employment from the ironically named Employment Agency, or 'Burro', as it was known. So much for work being plentiful and available . . .

He remembered thinking at one point that he would never work again. Then, he got a phone call.

The phone call was from the Employment Agency, the first one ever, asking him if he would go for an interview with a local newspaper, which was looking for people to sell advertising. While it wasn't a job he had considered, he figured he had nothing to lose by going for it.

So he went along and had a meeting with the rather eccentric owner of the Mulvanney Newspaper group, which printed three eponymous publications, the *West End Weekly*, the *Northern News* which covered North Glasgow and parts of the East End, and also the *South Side Speaker*, which 'did what it said on the tin'. At the end of the interview, which he thought went quite well, Sam was asked to go home and write an essay explaining what qualities he thought he had to offer to the post. As he wasn't exactly brimming with self-confidence and conviction, he thought that was more or less that.

However, he somehow managed to cobble something together which he thought didn't look too bad, given his lack of experience. He wandered back along the next day with his offering, expecting nothing more than a polite refusal, and just hoping that they would let him down gently.

Surprisingly, however, he obviously did something right, and he couldn't believe it when inexplicably, they asked him to come back the next day to start work as an Advertisement Representative. That was almost 30 years ago, and he was now a highly paid Advertising Executive in charge of the advertising department of the *Cambusglen Chronicle*, having moved to a promoted post there some 25 years previously – a new start with a new employer.

Sam recalled that when he visited the Job Centre all those years ago to obtain information and discuss details of the job and interview with Mulvanney Media, the member of the Job Centre staff who dealt with him had not exactly filled him with optimism and positivity. This was primarily due to her issuing him with the memorable prediction, "I'll see you back here in a month," adding a warning that people were being hired and fired with alarming regularity by the owner of the newspaper group. All things considered, then, he had lasted well, particularly for him, given his track record. However, in subsequent years he had begun to see the writing on the wall. And he wasn't alone. Many of his colleagues shared his negativity and fatalistic outlook, due mainly to a chaotic, poisonous atmosphere which was becoming more prevalent, and the increasingly unreasonable and bizarre behaviour of the owner, which was driving many staff away into other posts and even professions.

Ultimately, these issues had resulted in increasing conflict and unrest amongst the staff, which unsurprisingly culminated in the collapse of Mulvanney Media following the owner stating his intention to sell up, with little regard for the existing workforce. Despite experiencing considerable anxiety regarding moving into a new work situation, Sam had settled in well to his new environment and position, and had gradually risen through the ranks to his current position, which he had worked very hard to achieve, and which he was very happy and content in. But if these threats were carried out, how much longer would he be here, and what were the prospects of anybody else employing him if he had to leave?

He suddenly realised, in a fit of panic, that he couldn't do anything else.

# CHAPTER 5

It was the year 2000; the year that Henrik Larsson (or as Sam's friend Billy, a Rangers supporter, called him, "That bastard Larsson"), scored **that** goal against Rangers, in Celtic's 6-2 demolition of their greatest rivals. It was one of the highlights of a welcome renaissance following domination by the 'enemy' for some time. The Schadenfreude was very welcome.

Sam still went to the games but no longer had a season ticket, having given it up due to the resentment and unrest it was causing in his relationship with Kim. For some reason she seemed to view his love of football, or "obsession", as she described it, as a threat.

Latterly, it had got to such a ridiculous stage that if they went to a pub showing football on a television in the bar, she made him sit with his back to the screen so he wasn't distracted and she had his undivided attention.

The grief that he got when he watched it at home,

meanwhile, was unreal. In fact, he didn't even need to be watching it. If there was football on TV, it was his fault, his sole responsibility; as though he was the programme controller for BBC, ITV, Sky and BT. She would accuse him, asking him questions like, "Why is there football on the TV tonight?"

Rightly or wrongly, he usually found that sarcasm was the best form of response, not because it helped in any way, but it just helped him deal with it better.

"It's an arrangement that they have between the TV companies and the football authorities. I don't know! Is this a trick question? Is there a prize if I get it right?"

Unfortunately, his sardonic approach fell on deaf ears and was followed up by a second rhetorical question.

"There was football on last night, wasn't there?"

"Really, I would write a letter if I was you. Look, it's not my fault there's football on the TV."

"No but if there's football on, you'll watch it."

"Well maybe, possibly, but look, why are you giving me all this grief? I don't give you a hard time when you watch all the soap operas, do I?"

"That's different!"

"Oh really, is it? Why is that?"

"Because if I don't keep watching them, I'll lose the plot."

He knew what he wanted to say but thought better of it – he was in enough trouble as it was. Not that it helped. Nothing would have helped at that stage.

The final nail in the coffin of that particular situation was well and truly hammered in when he took her car, which he had bought her, to a Champions League game and it was broken into and vandalised when he was at the match. Unbelievably, and to add insult to injury, not only was it a home match, but the car was parked directly across from London Road Police station at the time. To make matters worse, when he returned to the car a young boy was stood beside it, looking for money for "watching your car, mister."

Sam didn't know whether to laugh or scream.

# CHAPTER 6

The dawn of the new millennium was also the year in which Sam had watched someone trying to break into his flat through the spy hole in the door. He had been off work and was having a well-earned long lie after a reunion night out with the guys from the band, when he heard his and other tenants' door entry system buzzers being pressed, followed by a garbled adenoidal mumble asking something along the lines of, "Do you want any papers delivered?"

Sensing something was not right, he got up, put on a bathrobe, went to the door, and looked through the peephole, only to see a scrawny, plooky youth putting on a pair of gloves before first trying the door, then feeling inside the letter box for any key or other possible means of entry.

Sam's first thought and inclination was to open the door and stick one on the guy's chin, before common sense prevailed and he realised that in the event of his fist successfully connecting with the intended target, he could end up being the one charged with assault. Certainly, stranger things had happened, and in the absence of witnesses, he realised that it was a possibility.

While he was pondering this, he noticed his golf clubs sitting beside the door. *Well, it's my house*, he thought, *and if I'm inside it I can do anything I want.* So he selected a club, and when the would-be burglar put his hand through the letter box again, he rattled his fingers with it.

The response was instant. The gloved hand was retrieved, accompanied by a loud scream of pain and some industrial-strength language. Sam looked through the spyhole again to see him jumping up and down in pain, holding his hand and swearing loudly. In retrospect, he reckoned it was one of the best shots he ever played.

"Can I help you with anything, pal?" Sam asked, as he watched the youth curled up in pain. The guy looked startled and repeated his vague 'offer' of a newspaper delivery.

"No. I want you to get to fuck away from my house, is what I want," Sam replied, before adding, "or you can hang about till the police arrive, if you would prefer?"

At this, the guy turned and headed out, while Sam watched him walking away in front of the building, looking back at him as he went. Sam meanwhile was holding his mobile phone and pretending to speak into it, while staring straight into the eyes of the failed criminal, who still appeared to be in a state of shock.

There were no further incidents until a few years later, when someone did successfully manage to effect an illegal entry, in broad daylight. This time it was executed with the finesse of a cat burglar, with the criminal removing the whole window frame and leaving it lying complete and unbroken in the back garden. Unfortunately, the same could not be said for the rest of the flat, which was ransacked, emptied, and significantly damaged.

After considerable contemplation and consideration, and despite the couple's challenging relationship, he decided to sell up and buy a house with Kim in the area where she lived, prior to them then getting married. His flat had previously been rented out while he had been living with Kim at her flat, and the golf club incident had happened during one of their various separations, when he had moved back to his flat following it being vacated by the tenant.

He remembered that Kim had accused him of running back to the flat too readily, telling him that it seemed all too convenient for him to run away from their problems. He knew that she was right. He had been immature and selfish, walking out when he didn't want to and saying things he didn't mean. Some people don't really mean it when they say things like, "You'll be better off without me". They just need to go through the charade to see what will happen; to see if they will be rejected or made to feel wanted. Because they need the excitement of the risk of a split, while at the same time needing unconditional acceptance. "No matter how badly I behave, you will still want me," they hope. Unfortunately, those games can also backfire, and the other person thinks, *you know, maybe you're right. Maybe I don't need this shit any more.*

Unfortunately, after too many such episodes, that is exactly what happened to him. Ultimately, he had got what he deserved, which was nothing.

# CHAPTER 7

On one of the occasions on which Sam moved back to the flat, following another separation with Kim, a young professional couple had moved in next door. They seemed perfectly nice, and both worked full time, even on Saturdays. The trouble with that situation was that he didn't work full time, and neither did the couple's dog. It might have been one of the smallest dogs on God's earth, but it barked loudly and incessantly from the moment they left, which was usually around 7.30 a.m., so that put the kibosh on any chance of him having a long lie in. On one occasion he couldn't put up with it anymore, and decided to knock their door and tell it to shut up. Which it did for about five minutes, before resuming its mission to wake up everybody within a five-mile radius.

Unfortunately, the neighbours found out about this somehow, and one night, obviously after having a few drinks, the woman knocked at his door and proceeded to tell him what she thought of him.

Sam then proceeded to tell her what he thought of them leaving the dog, which obviously had abandonment issues, on its own for six days a week. He had actually considered contacting the SPCA at one stage, but decided against it, being of the view that the poor animal wasn't being deliberately mistreated. He also reasoned that it would probably be construed as mean, spiteful behaviour on his part, which would be likely to make things even worse. He needn't have worried. Things got worse anyway.

So he was glad when he moved out again to go back to live with Kim. As was his neighbour, who made it very clear that she was glad to be seeing the back of him when she was out walking the dog and saw him packing the van. The dog probably was too, but for once it was keeping schtum.

When Sam moved back to the flat again, just under a year later, following the last and final split between him and Kim, the couple and the dog had moved out, reportedly after having been burgled on several occasions. Clearly, the dog's bark was not worse than its bite, and being a watchdog was not its forte. This surprised Sam, given the noise it routinely made. Unfortunately, even if it did bark, nobody was likely to take any notice. Clearly it needed to read up on the job description.

# CHAPTER 8

The man had been blackmailed before, years ago. He recalled reading that email demand and being gripped by disbelief, fear, nausea, and desperate panic for what seemed an eternity, when time seemed to stand still. He snapped himself out of his reflections, and, when he was able to think more rationally and clearly, he realised that this time around, again, he had no choice. He had to pay the money, because the alternative was unthinkable.

The other thing that he needed to do was to work out how to raise the cash required, and then to explain it to his family. While he was considering this, his thoughts turned to the one person who he figured would want to do this to him. He had always been very concerned that he could not trust them to keep their word, or that having extorted him once, they wouldn't make further demands upon him for more money in the future.

Those fears appeared to have been proved right and were now being realised, as he was staring at an almost identical demand: £200,000 worth of Bitcoins, the same amount that he had paid out before. Only this time, he didn't have it.

He found himself staring in disbelief at the screen, and unable to believe that it was really happening to him again. The first demand related to something that had happened a lifetime ago, in a different time and place, to two different people.

\*\*\*

He had met her in a bar not far from where he lived; she worked there part time. She was as keen as he was to get together, despite him being married and considerably older. And she was a breath of fresh air; so young, and spontaneous. She wasn't asking anything from him, other than for them to be together for as long as it lasted.

As it was, it had lasted around three years, and they were three of the most exciting and enjoyable of his life. He wouldn't have missed the experience for the world, even with the unavoidable stress that came along with it. She had had her own place, but they would often spend time in hotels further afield, as he found it quite stressful going to her flat; he was constantly worried about bumping into someone there, as they both knew a lot of the same people in their local area, and it would have been very difficult to explain away.

He also worried constantly about what his family would think or do if they found out about the affair. But despite that, he didn't stop. They would text and call each other constantly throughout the day, in many ways they were like a couple of love-struck teenagers. He wasn't unduly concerned about his wife finding their messages, as he had bought a new mobile, which nobody else could access without a password. He had written her love letters, too, which he had been too embarrassed to post, and which he really needed to destroy.

He would "work late" a lot, and sometimes she would cook dinner, or they would get a takeaway and just spend time together talking about everything and nothing. His heart still skipped a beat when he thought of her.

But in the end she finished it, saying that she couldn't deal with the furtive, deceitful nature of it and having to share him with someone else, because she loved him.

And he had loved her, too. In fact, he probably still did. But at the time, there was no way that he was going to leave his wife.

Not that she'd asked him to. She just wanted more for herself. She certainly got that, and more. They both did, because of who she ended up marrying.

That situation was something he thought that he had dealt with and hoped had gone away, though, and he'd begun to hope he'd never have to think about it again. So why was he having to face the nightmare again now? The obvious answer was for financial gain on the part of the blackmailer. However, he knew that it was more than that. Much, much, more.

He read the email again, trying to make sense of it:

*If you would like to prevent me contacting your wife, family and friends and sharing the details of your deceitful and unfaithful behaviour with them, all you need to do is send £200,000 worth of Bitcoins to the email address below.*

He had limited knowledge of Bitcoins, other than the publicity in the press around their worth as an investment opportunity. However, after some research online, he discovered that they were the criminals" and specifically blackmailers" favoured currency, because they guaranteed anonymous and almost untraceable transactions and payments.

The email repeated the information he'd seen last time this had happened, explaining that if he made a payment to the address detailed, his secret would not be revealed to anyone, before advising where Bitcoins could be purchased and what they cost.

He started to shake and hyperventilate, as he allowed himself to think about the very real consequences of his actions for the people and family who mattered to him and who would suffer humiliation as a result of his actions. He also knew that it was a bit late to start feeling guilty, and that he should have thought about that before he entered into such a selfish course of action.

No, he really couldn't blame anyone else but himself for the unthinkable situation that he now found himself in. It was now almost three weeks since he had received the demand, and he had lost count of the number of times that he had read it.

This time there really was only one possible course of action. He realised this fact at the same time as he collapsed and fell to the floor from the searing, agonising pains in his chest.

# CHAPTER 9

As he had sat in the departure lounge at Prestwick Airport the previous day at 7:30am, with his first beer of the day in his hand, Sam had recalled with some amusement that whenever they went on holiday and had an early departure, Kim used to say to him, with disappointment and despair in her voice, "I don't know how you can drink at this time in the morning?" The answer to that was, of course, "Because I can." He had always regarded it as part of the ritual, occasion, and privilege of being on holiday. While he had always hated flying and the routine that went with it, he had always loved airports.

He remembered with some fondness a relationship he'd had when he was about 18 years old; the girl in question had a car, and to his parents' dismay, she used to pick him up in the early hours of the morning to drive down to Prestwick airport. They would just walk around the airport, maybe have a coffee, then buy some munchies and soft drinks before driving to the beach to watch the sunrise. They thought they were in love, and maybe they were, but it didn't really matter. It remained a beautiful unsullied memory, probably because they never blighted it by ever having sex, although they had developed foreplay into an art form.

Sam smiled, and shook his head in disbelief as he recalled how they had broken onto one of her friend's houses when the family were on holiday and spent the night there, after her father had thrown her out when she refused to stop seeing him. Apparently, he saw Sam as a bad influence . . .

While her family never found out about the breaking and entering, her staying out all night with him more or less finally put the kibosh on the relationship and, as people do at certain times in their lives, they just lost touch. When he saw her again several years later, she was married. However, they were able to talk easily and look back and laugh at that and all the other adventures they had shared. It all seemed a lifetime ago, but the memories were still very vivid, and had resulted in him thinking about airports in an unashamedly affectionate, romanticised way.

He still regarded them as unique entities, where normal demographics, social and fiscal rules didn't apply, having been granted the authority to function as an almost independent state whose citizens didn't have to pay any tax or duty on any purchases (within limits) and could consume alcohol at any time of day. However, the unfortunately and undeniable downside of this situation was the unfeasibly inflated prices charged for food and drink, which Sam still found very hard to swallow. Nevertheless, like everybody else, he behaved like he had just won the lottery because, hey, it was holiday time, and after all, the money wasn't real after all, (particularly when it came to Euros, which was practically Monopoly money).

Aside from the airport scenario, and the arrival in a new destination, Sam didn't really like travelling. He regarded it as a day taken out of his life; both the sitting about, waiting, and the actual flight itself, which he also hated for the claustrophobia it induced. He was an extremely anxious passenger, because he didn't really believe that humans should be up there in a huge lump of metal which had a habit of shaking and moving in a way that frequently terrified him. He recalled with some embarrassment, that whenever he and Kim were on holiday and they experienced turbulence, it was her that was holding *his* hand for reassurance, not the other way round. So much for him being the protector and comforter.

Sam also still retained an irrational fear of missing the flight, following one occasion on which he and Kim had missed the call for their flight, mainly due to Kim's insistence that they "had plenty of time" to go for a walk around the shops in the airport. He recalled with horror hearing their names being broadcast over the public address system, as the announcer basically grassed them up for being late. They endured the walk of shame as they boarded the plane and all the other passengers looked at them like criminals for holding up and basically blighting their planned idyllic holiday experience.

Of course, there was never any question of him having the pleasure and luxury of an 'I told you so' moment, either, if he wanted to get through the flight and the holiday without incident and rancour. No, discretion was very definitely the better part of valour, if things weren't to go even further south than the plane.

# CHAPTER 10

Sam had not taken any holiday for over six months because of the mess his life was in, so he had no problems in getting leave. However, it was still a source of great amusement and bewilderment to him that, following his visit to the travel agents, he had ended up in a place where he had never had any desire to go and which he had always regarded with derision and disdain. It was a panacea of bad taste, a place characterised and defined mostly by tales of drunken revelry and the nefarious 'talents' of one 'Sticky Vicky' – a legendary female 'performer' famous, or infamous, for nothing less than extracting a cornucopia of objects from her fandango to the delight of all and sundry on the Costa Blanca's most infamous resort.

And yet it was now a place which, in recent years, had been afforded something of a commercial renaissance, via an eponymous TV series which provided it with a degree of acceptability and renewed 'street cred'. It was also a place where he was now obliged to spend the next 14 days on his own. That's right – not just a week but a bloody fortnight!

"A special offer, and a particularly good deal," the travel agent had said, adding "you won't get a better price." What in the name of good God in Govan had he been thinking of?

Benidorm may have been a refuge for tourists caught in a time warp, but, strangely and surprisingly, he found that he quite enjoyed being a spectator at this social phenomenon of a mostly stereotyped (with very few exceptions), social sub-class of heavy drinking individuals with a shared tunnel vision and view of the world along with everything and everyone in it.

At least there was 'entertainment', and plenty of it. Apart from Vicky, there were singers, dancers, ventriloquists, and magicians. Plus, of course, the sexist, racist, bigoted, and plagiaristic "comedians'(one of whom actually made a point of telling the audience whose material he was stealing), who plied their trade nightly in the various prefabricated 'portacabins' posing as venues.

It was like taking a step back in time before the world grew up and developed values and a social conscience. But that, strangely, was what he found enjoyable about this 'Life on Mars' portal into a world unspoilt by the 'PC Brigade', where everybody had the same values and simple view of the world; where it was

OK to laugh at jokes which reflected a bygone generation's seemingly polarised values and views, viewed as archaic and unacceptable in a reputedly more enlightened age.

And yet, there was also much to admire and consider in the performers'' art and craft; they were mostly men in their late 50s and early 60s, chain smokers who were no longer in the best of health and who wore their cynicism like a uniform. But that was what defined them – they were old stagers who were from a bygone era, 'the good old days', when life wasn't so complicated and regulated. With very few, if any, exceptions, they had never produced any originally penned material and were never going to make the big time, earn big money or become a household name with regular TV appearances. That opportunity had long since passed them by. So now they had settled for a life more ordinary, a small fish in a small pond, earning enough to allow them to live in a nice climate, which they probably couldn't enjoy due to spending most days sleeping off hangovers and late nights.

Consequently, neither they nor any of the other staff in bars and restaurants, sported healthy tans or weather-beaten faces; rather, their pallor was wan and grey.

Sam suspected they probably lived in dreary, poky rooms, with very few possessions and very little quality of life, caught in a vicious circle, with one situation perpetuating the other. They, and the various other "artistes" had probably performed the same set every night for what seemed like an eternity. And yet, despite all that, there was a confidence and a professionalism which was admirable. They knew their craft, they knew their audience, and they knew how to give them what they wanted. It was effortless, relentlessly raw and abusive, with no excuses.

"Hello sir, what's your name? Any idea? Is this your wife sir? You must have money! How long have you been married? Are you still shagging? Does she like it? Is she good at it, yes, good for you? You ever wonder how she got that good?"

And so it went – an old, but reliable engine that would perform night after night until it ran out of steam or fuel, whichever came first.

"Is anybody sitting there, mate?"

The question roused Sam from his thoughts. He was sitting at the bar and there were two spare stools beside him, which the guy in front of him and his mate evidently had designs on.

""Is anybody sitting there, mate?", repeated the other man.

"No, no, help yourself", he heard himself saying to the younger of the two.

"I'm not sitting at table for that wanker to pick on me!"

Not realising that he was speaking to him, Sam

failed to reply initially, before eventually responding, "Sorry?"

"The comedian, he always picks on you if you sit at the tables. He's brutal." said the elder of the two men. Then, as if realising that he was the only one making conversation, he asked Sam directly, "You just arrived today?" He then made the question rhetorical by not waiting for an answer.

"We've been here for a week already. It's alright," he said, looking at his friend, who smiled and added "Cheap as chips an' all."

And that, Sam discovered, after he got chatting to both of them over a couple of beers, which he bought, appeared to be their mantra and main mission in life, to save money and find a bargain.

"How much did you pay to come here? We paid next to nothing, peanuts. This bottle of brandy that I carry around with me instead of buying drink at the bar, was only four euros – you can't beat it with a big stick. We come here every year. Stick with us and we'll show you around and where to go." According to the pair, this basically meant anywhere that didn't involve parting with money, whenever possible.

'Peanuts and Chips', as he decided to call them, then advised that they were going to see the latter's mate, who was a singer in one of the shows, because "He paid for me to come over," said Peanuts. *No surprise there*, thought Sam.

To be honest, he was surprised that they both breathed out! They were undoubtedly the most openly, unapologetic, tight-fisted couple of gits that he had ever met. And that was coming from a Scotsman! No stereotypes there, then.

They were both from Lancashire and a real odd couple; a 49 year-old man, near as damn it the same age as Sam, but who looked a lot older, which he readily acknowledged, profoundly proclaiming "Fuck, you look a lot younger than me!", and a 27 year-old man, who, despite his youth, sounded remarkably like Fred Dibnah, the late celebrity steeplejack, engineer and television presenter. Like Sam's first wife, Dibnah had died from cancer after a long illness, much like the chimneys which made him famous.

Against his better judgement, it has to be said, Sam went with the Lancastrians to the cabaret bar, where Chips' friend was performing. It was surprisingly busy for the time of year. There were various other 'artists and performers' on the bill, including page three girls posing as performers, but who were really just there to get their kit off and pose for photographs, at a price, with plenty of willing and receptive customers. The place was also full of what appeared to be females on holiday from some eastern European country, possibly Kosovo or Albania, or at least that's what he thought that they sounded like. They all looked like they had got dressed in the dark and bought their clothes over the telephone without the benefit of a photograph. But they were having the time of their lives, singing and dancing with each other, and oblivious to anybody else – apart from a small group who were unashamedly trying to chat up a group of Dutch men who'd been watching their team, Ajax, in the Champions League. The comical thing about this unbelievably hilarious tableau was that their attempts at drunken seduction consisted of monosyllabic conversation and stilted references to the only cultural and linguistic references that they had access to, i.e. Ajax, Amstel beer and, well, Amsterdam.

That was about it. Sam left them to it, thinking that if they managed to 'pull' on the basis of such a limited linguistic and cultural exchange, then they bloody well deserved it.

# CHAPTER 11

On rejoining his new-found companions, they advised Sam that it was their intention to head to one of the local 'nightclubs' or lap-dancing clubs, or, even more accurately– brothels. Sam smiled and grimaced in equal measure at a memory from his youth, when he and his teenage friends had climbed on to the roof of a Miners Welfare Club to watch the strippers through a skylight, despite the fact that, unbelievably, it was across from the local Police Station. God knows what they would've done if they had been caught, he thought, or even worse-fallen off the roof with a hard on!

Sam saw that his new 'friends' were well into their 'cheap as chips' routine with some poor unsuspecting and unfortunate people, and decided to leave them to it, wandering off to another bar-cum-club on his own, looking for God knows what.

That was when he saw her.

She was standing on her own next to the DJ booth,

and initially he thought she was with him or was maybe a 'groupie'. He figured she was probably in her late thirties, quite fresh-looking and naturally attractive rather than in a glamorous, showy kind of way. He was so lost in his thoughts he didn't even realise she was speaking to him until she'd come right up to where he was standing.

"Lost something?", she said, probably referring to his look of intense concentration.

Initially he was a bit thrown, and still not 100 per cent certain that she was indeed speaking to him. Nevertheless, he decided to take a chance and risk humiliation by responding.

"No, but I think I might have found something." He amazed himself, hearing those calm, confident words coming from his mouth.

"You looked deep in concentration," she said, in a very soft and kind way.

"Deep in something," Sam replied, which again surprised him, given how taken aback he was at her speaking to him. Even more surprisingly, she smiled at this. It was a nice smile and one that made him think that there was room for further endeavour.

"I'm going for a refill," he said, lifting his almost empty glass. "Care to join me?"

"I'll have a diet coke," she said, which made him think that she was making sure that she remained sober. It turned out she was on holiday with a group of women who were spread out all over different bars in differing stages of inebriation and merriment. However, her best friend, with whom she was sharing a room, had apparently capitulated early and headed back to the hotel and her bed.

She told him that her name was Heather, and after some polite and relaxed chat she also revealed that she was separated from her husband. However, she offered no further elaboration on the subject. It was just conversation, thought Sam. But it was also information.

Also, there was no suggestion that she was sad or upset about this, or in need of sympathy or counselling. On the contrary, she was particularly matter of fact about it, and consequently he felt no need to explore the subject further, choosing to simply enjoy the fact that she was there and, so far, happy to spend some time with him. In saying that, he did make her aware of his own marital position during the course of normal conversation, of course. But this, too, was information.

She also smelled fantastic, reminding him of a previous girlfriend, the first person he had lived with after his wife died. He told Heather how things had changed dramatically when that girlfriend first moved in with him, remembering that she had wanted to wash her hair but couldn't, because there was no conditioner and styling mousse!

That, he told Heather, was when he'd been

reminded after a long time on his own that women need to have special things, like ten different types of shampoo, in a variety of different and bizarre combinations like Crushed Garlic and Phlegm, Turmeric and Tripe, or Grapefruit and Grog. And that they also use Mousse, Oils and Gels, and that they wash their hair twice and three times before wrapping it in a towel. The idea of a man doing all of these things made him and Heather smile, particularly when they discussed how women use things like pumice stones and flannels, and that they have face wash as opposed to soap, and then they wash their face with a facial scrub until it glows in the dark. And how they top it all off by shaving their armpits and legs with their bloke's razor!

And these differences aren't the half of it, he continued, warming to this theme; the shower is really only the equivalent of a pre-wash, because despite the fact they've just had a shower women then wash themselves with – yep, you've guessed it – body scrub! He used to tease his then partner by telling her she might  as well clean the tiles, while she was at it. Unfortunately, he would then invariably take it too far, telling her she's missed the windows, or something.

He shared all of this with Heather, along with the observation that most men are like him, i.e. they get into the shower, wash themselves with soap and shampoo, blow their nose, fart, have a piss, fart again and smell it before drying themselves, leaving skid marks on the towel, which they use again the next day after they've stood on it and swirled it around the floor with their feet, which is where they leave it. He told her he couldn't fathom why women find that annoying.

Heather laughed and punched him playfully, before stroking his face and running her hands through his hair. He just smiled and responded by moving to kiss her on her cheek. To his surprise, she turned her head and kissed him on the mouth.

Sam reciprocated, but in a very gentle and measured, calm way. He found that he wasn't in any hurry, taking the view that it was unlikely and improbable that anything would come of it, given the circumstances. He was still thinking that when she asked, "Well, are you going to ask me to go to your hotel or not?"

He did, and she accepted his invitation. Despite his reservations (and presumably hers) about motives and sexual history, nature and lust took their course. It was wonderful – spontaneous, urgent, and exhilarating. She was enthusiastic, adventurous, and uninhibited, and he reciprocated accordingly.

"Love is all about chemistry, but sex is pure physics," he told her at one point. Well there definitely was chemistry and artistry and industry, not to mention sheer bloody ecstasy!

He was also amazed and reassured about how

comfortable it felt being with her after it and they chatted very easily. However, after they made love a second time, sleep took him, and there were no more words spoken. She wasn't there in the morning when he woke up, and he never saw her again. She was found dead the following day, having been murdered before she made it back to her hotel. This, unfortunately, most likely made him the last person to see her alive apart from her killer. He realised also, that if this were discovered, he would most certainly be the main suspect.

Once he'd realised exactly who she was, there were other issues to consider, too.

# CHAPTER 12

The Watcher knew everything about the Whore, had made it a priority, a mission, even, gaining information from a variety of sources and of course there was her own regular, dedicated vigil and almost obsessive surveillance. And of course there were also the Whore's regular posts on Facebook, where she very publicly lived out her life and regularly and brazenly flaunted pictures of herself and her relationships; out socialising; dining, or on holidays.

So when The Watcher learned that she was heading to the Costa Blanca on holiday with a group of female friends, they saw the ideal opportunity to seize the moment to finally get the justice that was long overdue; the revenge that so far had proved elusive and more difficult than originally anticipated.

Nevertheless, the Watcher remained convinced that all that was required was patience and the opportunity would come along eventually. It had not been difficult to organise a holiday away to Benidorm, and so far it was all coming together nicely. The Watcher knew what hotel the Whore was staying at, and had booked into somewhere relatively close, in order to be able to keep track of her.

The Watcher was not worried about bumping into her, as it was unlikely that they would have even polite dialogue, and there was no reason for her to be suspicious or concerned in any way. The Watcher simply maintained a respectable distance from where her movements could be monitored and tracked. So when the Whore and her friends left anywhere, the Watcher also left, on various pretexts, like a telephone call or needing some air.

On this particular night, the Whore and her friends had only gone as far as Sinatra's, which was just across the road and which could easily be observed from outside the Watcher's current pit stop. The Watcher was just about to go back inside when the Whore came out of the club along with a male, heading in the opposite direction from her own hotel and towards the main drag. The Watcher reckoned that she must be heading to the man's hotel and decided to follow them from a distance. Only a few minutes later they reached their destination, which, as suspected, was the hotel where he was staying. Well that was that for the night, thought the Watcher and headed back to the club to meet up with the others, who had moved on elsewhere.

The Watcher's absence was explained as a need for some air, advising that the plan now was for an early night.

However, the group proved persuasive, and instead they all moved on to another club, where they stayed for a couple more hours before finally calling it a night.

On leaving the others to walk back to the hotel alone, the Watcher, who was totally sober, couldn't believe their eyes – the Whore was also leaving the man's hotel on her own, heading back in the direction of her hotel. The Watcher quickly checked the surrounding area, and when it was clear that no one was watching, lifted an empty Coke bottle from the table and then very slowly and deliberately began to follow her.

# CHAPTER 13

As she made her way home to her hotel in the early hours, Heather shook her head and smiled as she reflected upon her desultory sexual encounter with a complete stranger– in a manner of speaking – and certainly in the biblical sense. She wondered about her motivation, and then about why she needed to explain or justify it to herself. It wasn't that he wasn't attractive, she actually regarded him as quite handsome and well presented for a middle-aged man. She hadn't asked him if he was married, although she found his assertion to the contrary to be quite endearing and amusing in equal measure. But that wasn't what had attracted her to him. No, it was more to do with how he had conducted himself and how he had made her feel about him, and, more importantly, herself.

It would be fair to say that she had not initially had a raging desire to jump into bed with him. Far from it, her libido was perfectly in check and of course she was a married woman. But that was another story, and if truth be told, not really a factor for a variety of reasons. As they spoke, which was also very easy and effortless, she found him to be funny and self-effacing, with no shortage of character and personality. He appeared happy just to have her company and not to have any expectations of anything else. More interestingly and crucially he also presented as very open and quite vulnerable, in a naive, honest kind of way. Also, he seemed genuinely interested in what she had to say. Consequently she had felt relaxed and had gradually become quite attracted to him. However, she was also all too conscious of her not too impressive track record and poor choices when it came to men and relationships.

She reflected, for the millionth time (no exaggeration) on her relationship with a much older, married man when she had been in her thirties. It had been a passionate, torrid affair, which had lasted around three years, and, of course it had ended in tears, for her more than him. However, she had been very reasonable and non-vindictive and had not resorted to the "hell hath no fury like a woman scorned" stereotype. Mainly because she was still in love with him and there was no point, reason or anything to be gained from it. Unfortunately, she would still see him around the local area on a regular basis, playing the part of respectable married family man, well regarded in his community, which she found very difficult.

Her subsequent relationship history had been a series of disappointing, unfulfilling encounters, where she had had sex for all the wrong reasons: pity, sympathy, a sense of duty etc, prior to her meeting her husband. While that had initially been quite a passionate and loving union, with her partner appearing kind, caring and dedicated to her, ultimately it had soured, due mainly to his subsequent cruel, domineering and selfish behaviour, which he had managed to keep under wraps until it was too late. She had also not previously been aware of his corrupt, illegal business interests and his involvement with some very suspect and undesirable individuals. But the real damage was done, when she foolishly made the ill-advised decision to confide in him with regard to her sexual indiscretion of earlier years.

This had subsequently eaten away at his male insecurity, particularly in times of disharmony and difficulty, resulting, on one particularly fraught occasion, in him threatening to go public with the details to both her and her ex-lover's families.

Their relationship had never been the same after that, particularly with regard to sex, with her latterly doing all she could to avoid being intimate with him, blaming everything from fatigue to depression. He had also ordered her to dress and behave in certain ways and to stop seeing her friends and forced her to perform humiliating sex acts. On the occasions that she did acquiesce, it was due to a number of factors, none of which included lust or passion.

No, it was usually as a result of her feeling guilty or mentally drained at the thought of the effort required to refuse or fear of the consequences.

Thankfully they had not had any children, mainly due to her being unable to conceive, because of gynaecological problems, which was also a source of great resentment and disappointment for her 'estranged' husband, who had never tired of telling her this. Also, although they had separated just over three years previously, they had never divorced.

He was also still in constant contact with her, calling her late at night when under the influence, asking her and often telling her what she had been doing that day and who with and often expressing his disapproval. He also frequently spread malicious gossip about her lifestyle and her relationships in the event of him perceiving that she was not co-operating with or resisting his attempts to control and manipulate her. She was also still required to provide him with sex on a regular basis under the same threat of him making her indiscretion of earlier years public.

When they had these encounters, he expected her to dress up for him, usually in some form of sexy underwear, but often in other kinkier outfits. He had also been putting pressure on her to take part in a threesome with another girl, but so far she had managed to resist that particular scenario. However, his continued controlling presence in her life also made it almost impossible to have meaningful relationships with anybody else, except for people that he allowed or coerced her into having sex with as a sweetener for his corrupt business deals. She despised him and regarded him as a narcissistic, sociopathic, abusive bully with no moral compass or concern for anything other than himself. He filled her with revulsion, and she regularly thought about simply telling him that she wasn't going to do it anymore, but couldn't cope with the possible consequences of doing so. He also possessed revealing photographs of her, and a sex tape, which she had misguidedly agreed to in happier times, which he constantly threatened to put online if she did not agree to his demands. Unfortunately she believed that he was capable of carrying through on all these threats and therefore she could not take the chance of calling his bluff, particularly, as he had already taken his "revenge" on her ex-lover in a particularly ruthless and callous way.

It was while she was contemplating the significance of all of this, that she heard the movement behind her.

# CHAPTER 14

After they had made love, Sam and Heather just lay together in a post-coital glow, and initially no words were spoken, which suited him fine. He was enjoying that unspoiled sense of fulfilment and satisfaction which comes – no pun intended – following an initial sexual liaison. It was while he was thinking this that she broke the spell by asking him the dreaded question, "What are you thinking about?"

Oh God, he hated that question. There was always an expectation that he should say something inspirational, romantic or profound, or something that involved the recently performed act, which granted had been very memorable.

However, he totally surprised himself when he heard himself say, quite spontaneously,

"This is just the best thing."

It was as though someone else had said it – like he had had no control. Had he really said it out loud? And he suddenly realised that he would have to explain what he meant so that he didn't come across as a shallow, one dimensional, self-satisfied prick.

"I mean, just lying here, together, enjoying the quiet and the intimacy," he added, which also surprised him, but on reflection felt like a good reply to have made.

She said nothing in reply, then she snuggled in close to him before replying, 'The actual sex wasn't bad, either."

He smiled, and relaxed, which led to some discussion about sex in general, and more specific discussion about their respective sex lives, or lack of it in his case. He joked that in the final, dying embers of his marriage, foreplay had consisted of three hours of begging.

Heather smiled and reciprocated by sharing details of an unhappy, tawdry marriage and an ongoing unsatisfactory and problematic relationship with her estranged husband, which he listened to in disbelief. For her part, she wasn't overly emotional while sharing this information with him, appearing to accept this as her lot.

Also, they both knew without any discussion, that this was going to be a one-off experience and decided independently to make the best of it by stopping talking and making love again, which was just as satisfying.

As is always the case with men after sex, he fell fast

asleep, while she took the opportunity to take her leave of him and disappeared into the night to her fate.

# CHAPTER 15

11 November 2017

*What a fucking mess!*, thought Sam. *My life is just one disaster after another. Why do these things always happen to me?*

Interestingly, the trauma, distress and initial panic that he had experienced as a result of the Bitcoin blackmail aberration had all but abated and subsided to the point that it was now a mere irritant. It paled into insignificance in comparison to his current predicament. Accordingly, he had subsequently decided to ignore it and place his trust in his faith that he had done nothing wrong. Besides he had something much more serious to worry about now – the very real prospect of him being charged with murder.

And murder of someone with connections of a less than desirable and respectable nature, no less; if he had known about these, he would have run a mile in the opposite direction. It was too late now, and of course there was no way he could have known, until she started to open up about her relationship and her life. He had only heard the rumours and the stories which had contributed to the reputations of both she and her husband. She had merely confirmed their identities, while obviously providing much more detail about his unsavoury character and violent reputation than her own.

Sam had never met Heather's husband, but he hailed from Calderhall, which was the same area as Kim and her family and where he had lived with her prior to their break-up. He was in no hurry to meet him anytime soon, particularly given the events of the previous last 48 hours; two days of trauma which had also served to distract him from another small matter that he had still not dealt with – his failed marriage.

Sam reluctantly acknowledged to himself that he was still having great difficulty in coming to terms with that particular situation and, more specifically, the thought of his ex doing all the things they did – and didn't do, with somebody else. He was aware that she was now seeing someone, whom he didn't know; he believed he had moved in with her (he had actually suspected that she was having an affair while they were still together), and he still couldn't cope with the image of her being intimate with someone else.

Kim would undoubtedly also inveigle her new man into undertaking all the jobs that he never got round todoing. He had good reasons for this, though – there was no point in him even attempting to do work around the house, as he was totally inept at DIY.

Sam blamed his father. He'd been a shit role model in that respect, as he had singularly failed to pass on the necessary basic, practical and useful skills required to be an old fashioned hunter, gatherer, protector figure, necessary to keep a woman feeling looked after and safe. Consequently, he had always hated having to suffer the indignity of having to pay tradesmen to come to his house and make him look useless and inept – real men, with an air of macho superiority, wearing steel-toed boots, checked shirts covered in sweat and paint stains, and belts with hammers and spanners in them.

What made it worse was that his dad had also been full of worldly-wise sayings like "I wish I knew then what I know now," to which he used to think, *but you still know fuck all. Either that, or you're keeping it to yourself.* The irony was that his father didn't even know who Sam was now when he visited him in the care home. He kept going anyway, as difficult as he found it emotionally, continually hoping for a window of lucidity that would allow his father to recognise him and have a conversation with him, if only for a brief time. He was a curmudgeonly old git, but he was his father and he loved him.

The other thing that really cut Sam up about Kim moving on was the thought of a total stranger walking his dog. Sometimes he was unsure what he missed the most, the relationship or the dog.

He'd loved that dog, Ziggy – his faithful, loveable Golden Labrador, who Kim frequently accused him of not walking enough. However, if he was honest, he could've been more pro-active in that department.

He would give anything to spend half an hour with him in the park now, including the picking up shit bit. And that, ironically, was what he was doing now after all, wasn't it?

Sam remembered with some fondness a particular day at the local park in late September, just before he and Kim split up, when, inexplicably, the sun was shining brightly and it was also, and unbelievably, searingly hot. Interestingly, and unusually, the place was practically empty apart from them, the odd jogger/power walker and other dog walkers, who seemed similarly bemused and in awe of the idyllic, if freakish conditions. He and Ziggy walked for what seemed like hours, man and dog in perfect harmony, and he felt seriously blessed to be there that day. It had felt positively spiritual, and he had experienced an uncharacteristic sense of wellbeing, in total contrast with the car crash that was his life. He suddenly felt very alone with a pronounced and renewed sense of helplessness, desperation and panic.

# CHAPTER 16

12 November 2017

Sam woke early but didn't feel like breakfast, so instead, he had a coffee on the balcony. He was joined by a pigeon who was in no hurry to leave, and not at all afraid to perch on the table, presumably hoping for some titbits. He tried to shoo it away, but it had attitude and just returned and came even closer, almost sitting on his knee at one point. He decided that he wasn't in the right frame of mind to get up close with vermin, so he left the pigeon to it and headed to a nearby cafe/bar, where he had a coffee and engaged in some people watching before ordering an early lunch as hunger caught up with him.

After he'd finished his lunch, Sam ordered a beer; as he sat sipping it, he started to read a copy of OK magazine which had been at the table when he arrived.

Or rather, he wasn't actually reading it, he was

looking at the pictures, having come to the conclusion that there was no actual reading material in it. It was just full of photos of celebrities famous for doing bugger all – 'Celebrities' who didn't have any talent or special skill, other than making a lot of money for doing 'hee- haw', which, he conceded, is undoubtedly a skill in itself. Theoretically, he supposed, you could argue that people like Jordan, or Katie Price as she now preferred to be known, the Kardashians, and their ilk, sell newspapers and magazines for a living – thousands of them, full of the same old self-obsessed drivel over and over. He read a headline – 'Jordan tells all' – for the millionth bloody time – *I mean, who gives a toss?*

Well, apparently the great British public did, realised Sam, because they bought the magazines in great quantities. It was sad but true, he reflected, that he lived in a nation of voyeurs, obsessed with the private lives of celebrities, royalty and, for whatever reason, footballers, along with their wives and girlfriends (WAGs) – a species of women who are content to both benefit from the social and financial status and bask in the reflected glory of their famous partners. And, who had, ironically in Sam's view, inflicted significant damage to so called "girl power" and female emancipation, by defining themselves, with very few exceptions, as no more than an extension of their famous partners' identities. *Hardly a desirable role model for a generation of young women,* he thought. He also mused that the readers of such publications, while having absolutely nothing in common with these 'celebrities', were nevertheless happy to exist in awe and reverence of them.

Sam couldn't help but think that if people stopped buying the magazines, then they – the talentless hordes – might have to get a proper bloody job.

Sam's memory took him back to an advert he had once seen in a newspaper in Toronto, while there on business some years ago, whose headline had simply read 'Make thousands without leaving your home – get in the game', which he felt sure had to have been a spelling mistake.

It was then that he realised that the *OK!* magazine had probably been provided by the cafe/bar, and that the establishment probably also provided copies of newspapers for customers to read. Sure enough, en route to the toilet, he spotted a Spanish newspaper. He picked it up, recognising the woman in the front page picture, before his hands started trembling as he read the whole story about the 'murdered woman' who'd shared his bed the night before.

The story also contained a picture of a man, whom he presumed to be her ex-husband. Despite his limited Spanish, Sam was able to determine that the police were also asking for anyone who had seen or spoken to her to come forward and contact them. *Well, I certainly tick those boxes and more*, he thought, but he wasn't of a mind to be contacting the police, the press, or anybody else for that matter. He could just imagine the conversation. "Hello, is that the police? Yes, I 'm phoning to tell you that I spoke to the woman who was murdered. In fact, I spent the night with her – well, some of it, but she left while I was asleep, so I had nothing to do with her murder."

"Bueno, y Muchas Gracias for calling senor and putting us right about that!"

Aye, right!

# CHAPTER 17

12 November 2017

Why is it, Sam wondered, that when you have a poor signal on a mobile phone call, the only phrase that you can hear people say clearly is "Can you hear me?", and nothing else? His phone had rung and he had answered it to find that it was Sandy, one of the reporters from work, who was contacting him to ask if he had any other information or local knowledge about the 'murdered woman' situation. Sam responded to this by assuring him that they would know as much if not more than he did. The fact that the signal was poor gave him an excuse to discontinue the call.

He had received a few more calls since, but had either ignored them or again claimed that the signal was poor; thankfully, they had not been followed up by texts.

Sam finished his lunch and walked to Levante

beach, then along the promenade all the way to Poniente Beach, passing the place where the doves gathered, which looked spectacular, as there seemed to be hundreds of them.

*I bet the mess they make is equally as spectacular,* he thought.

Sam recalled a time some years ago when he was walking through Queen's Park in Glasgow. He had wandered into a glade and found himself staring at what he reckoned was over 20 magpies. It was like a scene from Hitchcock's *The Birds* or a meeting of Magpies Anonymous.

Whenever he saw a magpie, or magpies, Sam, like thousands, if not millions, of people of a certain generation, would instinctively begin to think of the well-known rhyme associated with the distinctive bird, made popular by the eponymous children's magazine television series from the seventies, featuring one Susan Stranks, who, along with Sally James on *Tiswas* had accounted for and used up a fair bit of his teenage testosterone. From watching the program religiously, Sam knew the traditional children's nursery rhyme by heart:

*One for sorrow, two for joy*
*Three for a girl, four for a boy*
*Five for silver, six for gold*
*Seven for a secret never to be told*

*Eight for a Kiss, nine for a wish*
*And ten for a bird you must not miss*

It was therefore generally accepted that one Magpie is a sign of bad luck, and all numbers after that are predictions of good or bad fortune. Accordingly if you saw one, you immediately looked for and hoped to find another one nearby; they certainly tended to hang around in pairs – a kind of natural double act. Whenever the second part of the double act put in an appearance, you'd immediately heaved a hefty sigh of relief and felt a lot more positive about the day ahead, whatever it might hold. Unfortunately, this feeling of bonhomie and positivity could then lead to someone thinking that maybe they should take advantage of this sign of impending good fortune by maybe putting on a bet, or enter into all kinds of endeavours full of ill-advised, reckless abandon and optimism, in the expectation of a favourable outcome. This would be all good and well if it worked out that way, of course, but in the event of a negative response or disappointing result, the superstitious soul would invariably curse themselves for being so stupid, and their relationship with the accursed bird(s) would be soured forever. No more "Good Morning, General," followed by a cursory, friendly salute!

Sam kept walking until he found himself at a small square just off the main drag. He found a space at a small bar and ordered himself a beer. As he sat sipping his drink his attention was drawn to some people across the square – they looked like backpackers-young, healthy handsome, free and full of life and camaraderie, probably students making their way across Europe on a sabbatical of discovery.

God, he envied them, their youth, their vibrant enthusiasm, their companionship, their discovery and exploration of life and the time they had left to enjoy it; the magic of experiencing things for the first time with other special friends. It was a never to be repeated time of their lives.

Whenever Sam saw or encountered such young, healthy people, effortlessly exuding energy and glowing with happiness, he invariably felt a pang of sadness and regret that he had never taken the opportunity to have such an experience. Sure, he had been abroad both as a child and a teenager, with the school and on one occasion, with a friend from France.

He had shared a flat with the Frenchman, who had been in Scotland working at a school in Glasgow teaching French, around the time that Sam was working in his first newspaper job. After forming a friendship, Sam had gone with him to his family's home in Paris for a month on holiday.

While the experience was quite exciting at the time, he reflected that it was his friend who was the adventurous one – he had been in Scotland as part of an exchange program, whereas Sam, the safe one, was only too conscious that his ventures did not have the same sense of adventure that either Regis or the backpacking, bohemian experience entailed and afforded. Sam reflected further that as an adult, holidays had never been particularly positive experiences for him, for a variety of different reasons. He was actually a latecomer to holidays abroad, both with his mates and family. He hadn't done the lads" holidays as a young adult; missing that other rite of passage, of a crowd of guys off on their adventures. He firmly believed that this situation was directly related to and influenced by a significant event from his schooldays.

Sam recalled, with considerable sadness and disbelief, the occasion on which his primary school had arranged for his class to go on a trip to a 'camp school' in Peebles. Well, nearly all the class. There were 25 spaces on the trip, and 26 pupils in the class. So some soulless jobsworth had decided to exclude one pupil from a whole class of their peers for no reason other than that statistically that it was not possible to accommodate one more pupil, irrespective of the human and personal ramifications, of the consequences for the innocent and disbelieving victim of such an inhumane and reprehensible decision. The decision was taken that all the kids should draw straws; whoever got the short straw would be excluded. Sam still found difficulty believing that it had actually happened. But it had. And of course, he drew the short straw. The ignominious agony did not end there. They very kindly and magnanimously allowed him to go and visit them midweek in West Linton, Peebles, to see what a great time they were all having. And he did! What the fuck were they thinking about? It was positively barbaric.

On his first day at High School, Sam also remembered being the only boy who was wearing short trousers, leading to him being roundly abused and ridiculed as a consequence. Kids can be so cruel, as they say. Although their behaviour paled into insignificance in comparison with the incompetent, insensitive, despicable actions of the adult decision makers.

At least Sam wasn't the only person with traumatic school memories. He also recalled a discussion with a work colleague, who shared with him his own emotional tale of injustice and humiliation at the hands of authority. This sorry story involved him being asked to come up on the stage at an awards ceremony at the end of term. He naively and innocently believed that he was going to be presented with some mystery award, only to be loudly ridiculed and exposed in front of the whole school, as having not paid his 'dinner money' for a month. This was a pupil, a child – not an adult, not a wage earner, or the holder of the purse strings. A junior, a minor, dependent upon adults both parental and educational to look after his welfare. While there was probably a perfectly good and acceptable reason for his parents'' oversight, the powers that be chose not to discuss this with them in a confidential, respectful, adult way, instead choosing to both disrespect them and to publicly humiliate and victimise a child in front of his peers; the same officials who had been charged with the responsibility of his welfare while in their charge; the same adults who had no accountability for their unacceptable actions. *They should have gone into politics*, thought Sam, sardonically.

After some discussion and debate, he and his colleague had agreed that Sam's experience shaded it in terms of the scale and degree of the injustice and its long-term traumatic effect. Sam was certainly convinced that it had left him emotionally damaged, to the point where he believed that he did not deserve certain privileges or to be happy, like other people. He had even refused a kind offer from close family to take him on holiday as a child, when his own parents could not afford to do so, almost resenting their kindness and generosity.

Sam had also started to believe that there was some reason why that aberration was allowed to happen; some reason that no one was telling him about.

Looking back, he could not believe that his parents had allowed such a miscarriage of justice to be perpetrated against their child. He recalled that his dad had once thrown the parish priest out of their house following him trying to dictate, as they were wont to do in those days, what was the 'Catholic way'. And yet, this undoubtedly un-Christian and inhumane deed – man's inhumanity to man, or in this case, child – had been allowed to go ahead unchallenged and unpunished. Sam simply could not conceive of him ever having allowed such a thing to happen to his own children, or *them* ever allowing it to happen, come to that.

Sam was proud that both he and their mother had instilled in them an innate sense of what was right and wrong. So they wouldn't have needed him, or anybody else to tell them, as they were both perfectly capable of standing up for themselves and speaking their mind. So how come the powers that be couldn't make that basic differentiation? It was complete anathema and a disgraceful decision that he believed no human being could ever justify and explain to him, or to anybody else for that matter. But the fact that he would never know or understand what he did to deserve such a fate still bothered him.

What he did know and understand however was how it had affected him in his adult life; why he suffered from a lack of self-esteem, personal value and confidence. And why, when he failed at something and ended up with nothing, he believed that he did not deserve anything better.

Unfortunately, with this acceptance and resignation came an unresolved and misguided sense of injustice, resentment and anger. Often futile and pointless anger, which, on occasions, manifested itself in him railing against any perceived sense of injustice.

# CHAPTER 18

12 November 2017

Sam surveyed his immediate surroundings, noticing that the nearby tables were occupied by two middle-aged couples. The differences between them could not have been starker or pronounced; their demeanour, the way they were dressed and the way they interacted was very revealing. The seemingly elder of the two couples had clearly made an effort and given some thought to their outfits, while the other couple had clearly opted for the standard tee shirt and shorts – routine garb for the hotel pool. The younger pair also sat in silence and apparent abject misery for the entire duration, while consuming their respective meals.

The older couple, in contrast, had ordered a sharing platter, accompanied by either champagne or wine that was cooling nicely in an ice bucket; they never stopped talking or touching in an obviously tactile, affectionate and totally unselfconscious way.

It may have been his imagination, but it seemed to Sam that the male of the other couple, who seemed physically incapable of smiling, was only too aware of that fact, and it seemed to be making him look even more miserable, if that were possible.

Sam then suddenly realised, with some uncharacteristic insight, that he probably looked equally as miserable and felt a renewed sense of loneliness and despair. He knew that drink wasn't the answer, but at that moment he couldn't think of a better one.

# CHAPTER 19

12 November 2017

Sam made his way back to the hotel and after showering and changing, he embraced his decision to drink with considerable enthusiasm and vigour. However, for some reason the drink did not appear to be having the desired effect and after something of a fairly tame and half-hearted pub crawl, he decided to call it a night. As he was making his way back to his hotel, alone and a bit worse for wear, he heard a woman's voice. He looked up to see a hooker walking towards him, greeting him in familiar style.

"Hello, darling. You English? You want fuck, or I give you good blow job?"

Given the trauma Sam had experienced in regard to the blackmail nightmare and the resultant sense of self-loathing that came with it, this was the last thing he needed or wanted to hear. He made it clear that he wasn't interested, and thankfully she got the message and also uncharacteristically, didn't persist. However, he had only walked a few hundred yards further, along Calle Lepanto, when a male of apparently African origin appeared out of nowhere and greeted him loudly with, "Hola Amigo, you want good massage? We take good care of you."

Before Sam had the chance to decline this new service, the guy started manhandling him, grabbing his crotch and backside in a very sexually aggressive manner. While initially taken aback by this, he surprised himself by recovering his composure enough to make it clear that he wasn't pleased. "What the fuck do you think you're doing?" he protested.

Unfortunately the guy seemed to find this amusing and even something of a challenge, as he responded by doing the same thing again only more forcibly.

*Oh, fuck this*, thought Sam, and equally as forcibly said, "I told you not to do that again."

"Or what you do?" said the guy.

"Or I'll fucking do you," said Sam, as convincingly as he could, which the guy responded to by swinging a punch at him. Unfortunately, the action also caused him to lose his balance and gave Sam the opportunity to catch him on the way back up square on his nose, at which point he screamed out loud, shouting for help.

At this point, Sam decided that discretion might be the better part of valour and that it might be advisable to call it quits. His judgement proved sound as within seconds another male appeared and began to shout after him.

"Hey amigo, come back and we talk."

*Aye right, fuck this,* thought Sam, and then, noticing that he was outside a hotel, shouted back,

'this is my hotel, and I am going to call the police."

Fortunately, this appeared to do the trick, as they both disappeared instantly.

Sam went into the hotel lobby briefly, until he was sure that the coast was clear, then doubled back towards his actual hotel. He was silently congratulating himself at having managed to avoid any major incident or injury, when he heard a voice behind him.

"Hello, do you speak English?"

*Oh, fuck off,* he thought, *I don't need any more of this sleazy shit.* He was just about to give it both barrels, when he realised that it was not a foreign accent but a Scottish accent and a female voice. He turned round to find that it was indeed a woman, who looked to be in her mid-60's, smiling at him.

"Yes, I do. I'm Scottish too, in fact – from Glasgow."

"I'm not stalking you," she said, "but I thought if you were going my way we could walk together, if you don't mind?"

"No, not at all," he heard himself say, and he introduced himself, glad to have the company of someone who wasn't trying to harm or exploit him.

"I'm Trish," she said, before adding, "Are you OK? You seem a bit. . . I don't know, nervous?"

So, he told her all about his recent escapade, which she listened to in apparent disbelief; the story definitely broke the ice, though, and they walked and talked until they realised that they were at her hotel, the Venus, on Avenida Filipine, which, as it happened was very close to his own hotel, the Pueblo, on Calle Ibiza.

"Well this is me here," she said with a smile. "Thank you so much for seeing me home safe." She reached over, pecked him on the cheek, and turned to walk away, and then turned back and added, "Can I buy you lunch?"

"What?" he asked, sounding every bit as surprised as he felt.

"Let me buy you lunch, tomorrow, as my way of saying thanks. If you're not doing anything else, that is?"

He wasn't quite sure why, but he hesitated, before saying, "No, I mean yes, no, I mean no I'm not doing anything else, so yes, that would be nice." They arranged to meet at a nearby beach bar the next day.

# CHAPTER 20

13 November 2017

Sam had another restless, disturbed sleep and awoke at 7:00 am, when the events of the previous night gradually began to filter through to his consciousness. As he recalled them, a horrible thought occurred to him. With a sinking feeling, he jumped out of bed and reached for his trouser pocket and the money that ought to have been in it, only to find it was gone.

"Bastard!" He exclaimed, involuntarily, realising that he had been mugged. He remonstrated with himself for being so stupid not to have realised sooner – not that it would have made a difference.

He also mentally admonished himself for his habit of always carrying unnecessarily large amounts of cash with him, instead of keeping the majority of it in the safe.

He was always telling himself off for this, and finally

his failure to address the failing had yielded a perhaps inevitable outcome. He cursed himself again, "You fucking idiot. When will you ever learn?"

He contemplated the implications of his predicament, immediately checking how much money he had in the safe, hoping, rather than believing, it would be enough. After checking, however, he doubted that it would suffice, unless he only ate once a day, at breakfast, and helped himself to as much fruit and as many pastries as he could from the breakfast buffet to have as lunch later.

On the positive side, his health would benefit. He was likely to be sober for the rest of the holiday, if it could still be called that.

He went out to the balcony for some fresh air, and to check the weather. It was another hot and sunny day, and there were already people at the pool. The pigeon was back again, too. Only today it had brought its pals along. He wondered what the collective noun for a group of pigeons was. He then found himself wondering if they had arrived randomly or if it was an organised meet; a Pigeon AGM, if you like.

Sam realised that he felt hungry for the first time in days and despite the fact that he had arranged to go for lunch with Trish, decided that he would head down to breakfast. Hopefully, when he came back the maid would have been in and changed the sheets, thereby removing any evidence of anyone else having slept in the bed. He deliberately spilled some red wine on them to be sure. He went to breakfast, but when he came back the maid had still not been in. He decided to arrange the sheets so that the wine stains were more obvious. As he moved the sheets he heard something falling on the tiled floor. Initially he couldn't see or find anything but on looking under the bed he saw that it was an earring. Heather's earring!

# CHAPTER 21

13 November 2017

Sam didn't know what to do with the earring, so he decided to put it in the safe in his room along with all his other valuable property, or what was left of it, until he had a better idea. He had just locked it in the safe when the maid arrived. He made it obvious that he was leaving to let her get on with it, while also making an issue of apologising for the wine stains on the sheet.

"No hay una problema, Senor."

As he made his way down to the pool, Sam began to think about the fact that he had not worn any protection when they had sex. Heather had not challenged him about it, which he had thought strange and a bit remiss of them both in terms of the possible implications.

However, he had told her that he was sterilised and she didn't need to worry about becoming pregnant, which seemed to offer sufficient reassurance. After that, their passion had taken over.

Sam thought back to his Vasectomy op. He and Kim had decided some years ago that as he was older, he should have the 'snip" rather than her, in case she changed her mind in the future should they not work out and split up. Not exactly a positive outlook and prediction, but, as it turned out, an accurate one, nevertheless. He wondered if they had known something even then and had unknowingly cast the death knell on their relationship. Nevertheless, the decision about the vasectomy was made quite amicably with no animosity or discontent.

On the day of the actual event they had a massive argument, which would have given him an out, should he have wanted it. But he didn't, so he decided to be grown up about it and do the decent thing, even although that meant him going on his own for the procedure.

He arrived early, feeling quite nervous and he certainly didn't need any more time to dwell on it, but that's exactly what he got, because they kept him waiting for 45 minutes, during which time he wrestled with and reconsidered his decision several times over. He was actually on the verge of leaving the premises when he eventually got the shout that it was his turn. Although by this point he was an absolute basket case.

\*\*\*

The Doctor was very apologetic, in fact, he couldn't have been nicer. "I'm very sorry to have kept you waiting; you deserve to have a very straightforward, painless vasectomy."

Sam remembered thinking at the time that this implied that there were different kinds – "Now, this week we have on offer the Extremely Painful, the Unbelievable Agony or the Relatively Pain Free procedure. Which would you like?"

*Have a wild and crazy guess, Sherlock!* He remembered thinking. *Thank god they kept me waiting, otherwise I could've been in real trouble.*

While they might have said he deserved to have a pain-free vasectomy, it was a pity they didn't manage to deliver it. He'd believed the doctor when he said it, but the bastard was obviously an accomplished, bona fide liar and a fraud.

Sam nearly jumped off the table at one point; the doctor hit something he shouldn't have, and Sam wanted to hit him back. It was clearly all very straightforward to the medics, because while they were cutting, tying or burning the tubes they were talking to him all the time and having casual, meaningless conversation. "We'll just do the other side now," they informed him at one point, as though he was at the barbers. Except you don't leave the barbers with blood dripping from your nether regions and walk funny for a month after it.

# CHAPTER 22

13 November 2017

Sam walked to the nearest supermarket and bought a British newspaper, which carried the murder as its headline story, unsurprisingly, as it was the only story in town. It reported that a post-mortem, or 'autopsia' was due to be carried out the following day.

Sam knew from his own experience that the most common type of autopsy was a coroner's post-mortem, which was usually carried out to find out why someone had died when the cause was not known, or perhaps because the death was sudden or suspicious.

The consent of the family is not required for a coroner's post-mortem, but the coroner's office will usually work closely with relatives to make sure they understand what's happening and when the funeral can take place.

Sam recalled a story that had been covered by his newspaper, which involved a body that had remained lying in the morgue for an interminable period of time, due to the only relative of the deceased not having the necessary funds to pay for a funeral and not meeting the criteria for financial assistance, which stipulated that appropriate funeral arrangements had to be in place before support could be given. It was a classic 'Catch 22' situation, which, sadly, had dragged on with no apparent prospect of resolution.

He didn't know exactly how the system worked in Spain, but Sam imagined that given the circumstances, the consent of the family would not be required. Having said that, he expected that family members would nevertheless most likely be making their way to Benidorm, if for no other reason than to allow formal identification of the body and of course to take possession of Heather's personal effects once the police had completed their forensic examination. Unless, that is, they were required for evidence.

Sam wondered what details the family would be given about the circumstances of Heather's death, and whether that would include the fact that she had been intimate with someone prior to her death. For the first time, the thought occurred to him that she may possibly have been raped and abused by her attacker, which caused him considerable stress and generated even more complex and conflicting emotions, out of respect for Heather and concern for himself. He hoped desperately that this was not the case and that he was overreacting, due to anxiety and panic. Certainly, no such information had been released to the press by the police at this stage.

Sam knew that in the UK, post-mortems are usually carried out within a day or two of death, so they rarely affect the timing of funerals. Pathologists will usually prioritise post-mortems for members of religions that hold funerals quickly after death, or if there is another reason why a delay is to be avoided. Coroners' officers, who are familiar with these circumstances, will do what they can to expedite the process.

He felt it would be sensible to understand more about the whole procedure in Spain, so went online on his phone, where he discovered that in the event of a death occurring in suspicious circumstances in Spain and it requiring investigation, anyone with knowledge of the death was eligible to register it; it would normally be done by a member of family, or a friend or neighbour of the deceased. The death would also need to be registered with the Civil Registry office of the area where it occurred, and the certificate of death would need to state the cause of death in order for this to happen. Burial or cremation would normally take place within 24 to 48 hours.

In Heather's case, if her next of kin, who might well still be her estranged husband, requested that the body be repatriated to the country of origin, this would need to be arranged with the attending doctor when the death certificate was being completed. If insurance was in place the appropriate travel agency or insurance firm would then take over arrangements.

Sam reasoned that, given that Benidorm was primarily full of thousands of people who were only there for a limited period of time, there would be an urgency to obtain as much information as possible; not only to help figure out what to do with Heather's remains, but also to help determine not only the cause of death, but, if possible, who the perpetrator was, preferably while they were still on the island.

His stomach knotted at the thought that the post-mortem would reveal that Heather had had sex prior to death, with the semen providing the police with his DNA, but fortunately, he wasn't on any database, due to never having been arrested or charged with any offence, so he would be OK as long as no one had seen her arrive or leave.

The only pictures that had been published by the newspapers were of Heather's passport photo, and a photo of her ex-husband, accompanied by very brief unflattering background information, which stopped just short of calling him corrupt, and in possession of some very dodgy connections. No doubt more pieces would follow as the reporters started to dig deeper.

No reference was made to any CCTV coverage of the incident. However, Sam knew that this didn't necessarily mean that there wasn't any available. It was possibly just a case of the police being very careful and selective about what information they made known to the public and press at this stage.

There had not been any police activity at Sam's hotel and nobody at his own hotel had asked to speak to him. He honestly couldn't remember if anybody had seen them arrive together on that fateful night. He also reasoned that if there was CCTV footage, it would clearly show that Heather had left the hotel alive, before meeting her fate at the hands of someone else, who might or might not be identifiable by the same technology. Should he just sit tight and wait for this to all play out? So far, that was what he was planning to do, mainly because nothing like this had ever happened to him before, and he was at a loss about what else to do.

The only other person that Sam had ever known who had been murdered was a woman, Alice Muldoon, who was killed in the Queens Park area of Glasgow some ten years previously. The fact that the murder took place in such an ostensibly respectable area of Glasgow caused consternation and disbelief at the time, although what the general populace might not have realised was that statistically, the leafy and ostensibly respectable and desirable suburb was second only to the city centre for violent crime at the time. This had not been the first murder committed in the area in recent years.

Alice's death occurred a few weeks after the shocking and infamous murder of a local woman, Moira Jones, who was murdered very close to her home in the idyllic setting of a park that was used by thousands of people every year. The case had sent shockwaves through the city. People were appalled at the brutal and callous nature of the apparently motiveless attack, while the police were unable to offer any rational explanation or justification. Not that there could ever be any.

Strathclyde Police launched a murder investigation, and the park was sealed off while forensic experts carried out painstaking searches of the undergrowth. In the days that followed an almost unprecedented questioning of nearly 2000 people in the area was carried out, including 700 motorists, 80 taxi drivers and 405 pedestrians. CCTV footage was released, and Moira Jones' family made an emotional appeal for information, which ultimately lead to the conviction of an itinerant Slovakian, Marek Harcar, who was later sentenced to 25 years.

Sam was back living in the flat in Queens Park at the time, and had got to know Alice Muldoon when she had come back to his for a drink with a few other people, after a night out at Samuel Dow's pub in nearby Strathbungo. She worked there part time, and Sam's band had been playing. He found her to be a very warm and intelligent person, who was also very personable and pleasant company. She also had taste, and like Sam, enjoyed a glass of red wine – when he asked her to pick a bottle from his collection, she selected the best and most expensive bottle that he had.

She spent a few hours easily and happily chatting about her life and plans for the future before heading home to her own flat nearby. Yet, as had been the case with Heather, after Alice left his flat, he never saw her again. She was murdered less than a month later, while making her way home along Battlefield Road. It transpired she was forced into the park by a Lanarkshire man named Alexander Anderson, who'd been living in a nearby homeless hostel for people with drug related issues – he raped and killed her there, and was later captured on CCTV.

Alice's body was found the following morning by a dog walker, in a secluded woodland area under a cluster of branches. Interestingly, her murder had not received the same level of coverage and publicity as the earlier Moira Jones killing, despite being equally as shocking in nature and Alice, at 42, being only two years older.

Also, while Sam had fully expected to be interviewed, given his recent contact with the unfortunate woman, the knock on his door by the police never materialised. He remembered feeling a sense of relief about that, as although he had nothing to hide or be concerned about, he also believed that he had nothing to say or tell the police that would be helpful. Also, the thought of being questioned made him nervous for reasons that he couldn't understand. The difference now was that he had good reason to be nervous and very concerned – again, not because he had done anything wrong, but because of the fact that he was literally an innocent abroad. He had heard many stories of travesties of justice being perpetrated in foreign countries against British people on holiday, possibly for just being in the wrong place at the wrong time.

*Lucky white heather*, he thought. Although, given current circumstances, that probably wasn't appropriate.

# CHAPTER 23

11 November 2017

On hearing the noise behind her, Heather was initially startled. She turned around to find the person she was face to face with, and couldn't say that she was surprised at what she saw. If she was honest, she had probably both dreaded and expected this moment in equal measure, while accepting that it was destined to happen at some point in her life. And strangely, now that it was here, she felt a sense of relief, while also realising it might just provide an opportunity to exorcise some of her demons and perhaps, at the same time, express and accept both shame and regret for her actions.

Or so she thought. Unfortunately, the other person had also waited for this moment, and they saw it as serving a very different purpose with only one outcome.

The assailant made clear that she had no interest in

entertaining or listening to Heather, who was not going to be given any time or opportunity to confess any guilt for her sins, and certainly would not be granted any kind of forgiveness or absolution.

"Well, there's no point in me being apologetic then, is there?" said Heather. So instead, she decided to reveal some "home truths" about her accuser's husband, while she had the opportunity.

"I was in love. *We* were in love . . .", she pleaded. "But I finished it, not him, for reasons you won't understand or believe. It was a long time ago, and I've moved on. There were others before and after me, too, he wasn't an innocent. But I was truly sorry about what happened to him."

Unfortunately for Heather, the other woman clearly was not prepared to accept any explanations, excuses or accusations.

"He died because your husband blackmailed and terrorised him to the point that his health deteriorated and eventually failed him," she retorted, her anger overtaking her.

"He brought my husband to his death."

"I don't think you can say that for certain," said Heather. "But I know what he did, and I'm sorry, really."

"I don't want your pity or an apology," came the reply. "I just want you to know that I think that you and your husband . . ."

"Ex-husband," interrupted Heather, while realising that strictly, and legally speaking, this was not the case.

"Don't make me laugh," said her accuser. "You're both as thick as thieves still, everybody knows that. You deserve each other."

"Nothing could be further from the truth," said Heather, while realising that anything she was saying was falling on deaf ears. Nevertheless, she needed to have her say.

"We still have some shared business interests, that's all, but not for much longer. I need to be free from him for good. He's made my life a misery for years."

The woman stared at Heather with nothing but hatred in her eyes and spat, "You probably deserved it! I just want you to know that I think that you and your husband are scum. And I hope you both rot in hell." At that, she turned on her heels and walked away.

*I probably did deserve that*, thought Heather, then realised that she was trembling, and not because she was cold. She started to cry but managed to stop herself, determined not to give into how she was feeling or to draw any attention to herself.

She realised that the road she was on was totally deserted, and she was alone. However, as she was gathering herself together and regaining her composure, she heard another noise behind her. Before she could turn round, something hard hit her forcefully on the head, and she felt herself blacking out.

She didn't know how long she was out cold for but as she felt herself coming round she realised that there was something in her mouth stopping her from breathing, and pressure was being applied to her throat and the back of her head. The last words she heard before she lost consciousness again were simply "Kim Meredith."

# CHAPTER 24

14 November 2017

As he sat at the beach bar awaiting Trish's arrival, Sam thought to himself, *What in the name of good God am I doing here? Considering all the shit that I'm dealing with at the moment, why did I agree to meet up with a complete stranger who I know absolutely nothing about?*

He was also wondering if he would recognise her, given he'd been in a semi-inebriated, disorientated state and it was dark when they met. However, he looked up and saw her at the entrance, looking around, trying to locate him in the busy space.

He stood up and gestured towards her, attracting her attention then watching her as she approached. She gave the impression of probably having been a relatively stylish, if not particularly attractive woman in her younger years.

The intervening years had not been kind, though, and every one, and then some, of what must have been her sixty-something years were clear to see. She had the sort of nicotine-stained skin that seemed to radiate from the inside out. She appeared tired and worn down by whatever had happened to her in her life, and a lot had happened to her, as he was about to discover.

Trish immediately insisted that lunch would be on her, while she also enquired if he needed any money, given his misfortune from the previous evening. He assured her that he was solvent but thanked her for her generosity.

However, the truth was that he might well have difficulty in raising cash, as he had attempted to withdraw some money from the cash machine the previous day and it had retained his credit card. *Nothing like kicking a man when he's down*, he'd thought.

"Yes, that's me – Mrs Generous-and-stupid-and-gullible," she said when he'd mentioned her kindness. Then, seeing his confused expression, she added, 'sorry, just ignore me, it's nothing."

It clearly wasn't nothing, though, so he gave her an understanding, sympathetic look that said, "It's OK if you want to talk." And talk she did.

Sam listened unbelievingly as Trish related, in a very matter of fact way, the incredible details of the trauma and misfortune that had befallen her and her family some years before, culminating in her husband's untimely death, aged 65. In her mind, her husband's death was directly related to the stress brought about by them being extorted of over £250,000 by a fraudster, under the pretext of a business investment and opportunity.

She insisted that the conman had been extremely plausible and convincing; apparently, he'd claimed to have opened an offshore bank account in Bruges in the couple's name into which he had put £50,000 – he'd even provided them with details of what seemed like a genuine high street bank account as proof.

On the strength of this, they then sold a flat they'd owned in Costa Blanca, and gave him the £30,000 profit.

Even more unbelievably, in the months that followed, they gave him further sums amounting to over £200,000. Shortly after this, their 'business partner' advised them that the investment had failed; all the money had been lost, and there was nothing anybody could do about it. She told him they had consulted a lawyer, the police and then a solicitor, all of whom confirmed that there was nothing that they could do. They subsequently discovered that the fraudster had bought a flat in Finestrat, near the Old Town in Benidorm, presumably from the money he had conned them out of.

While Sam expressed his sympathy and support following Trish's revelations, he felt slightly uncomfortable at her confiding in him, a relative stranger, to such an extent and with such personal information. He told himself that that she just needed to talk to someone about the situation, although it seemed a little odd – she was on holiday with her friends of many years, whom, he presumed, might have been more obvious confidants. He made no comment or observation, though, and put it down as Trish simply being inappropriately familiar.

It was a beautiful sunny day and they enjoyed the rest of their lunch together, sharing stories of previous holidays in a variety of different places. Soon enough the conversation turned, inevitably, to the subject matter of the murdered woman.

Following the news of the death, the resort was awash with rumours; the talk was that she had previously worked as an escort and had a reputation as a professional "honeytrap" who had orchestrated cons and blackmail schemes with her husband. According to these reports, he was a corrupt businessman, who was also believed to be involved in drug dealing and various other illegal practices.

Heather's version of events had been significantly, and understandably, different. Trish, meanwhile, had further inside knowledge – she told Sam that a British tabloid newspaper had intended to print a story about the couple's illegal lifestyle but had decided against it for fear of litigation. Sam had wondered how she could know this, but didn't pursue the matter further. However, he made a mental note to make a call to a friend at one of the tabloids to check the story out.

They finished their drinks and Sam again thanked Trish for her generosity, while she reiterated her offer of financial support. She also asked him if he was planning to watch the Fiesta the next day; he told her he planned to wander out at some stage.

"Well, maybe I'll see you there, then," she said, before giving him a peck on the cheek and heading off along Avenida de Fillipinas in the direction of her hotel.

As he watched Trish leave, Sam realised that, despite her seemingly pleasant demeanour and generosity, there was something about her that was troubling him. He just couldn't quite put his finger on it.

# CHAPTER 25

14 November 2017

Sam bought a newspaper and headed back to the hotel, where he intended to spend a couple of hours at the pool before the sun departed. Although it wasn't hot enough to actually sunbathe, it was pleasant and sunny enough to simply take the air and enjoy a bit of relaxation. However, he found after reading his newspaper, which had nothing new or of any note regarding Heather's murder, that he wasn't able to concentrate and focus sufficiently to enjoy his book – a murder mystery, no less, by his favourite Scottish author, which he had previously found quite gripping.

He was also pleasantly distracted by a very attractive and glamorous looking woman, sitting by the pool, who was also reading a book, at least, she was when she wasn't returning his own glances. However, when the temperature began to cool in the late afternoon she took her leave, at which point Sam also decided to call it a day and headed back to his room.

After enjoying a beer on the balcony, where there was no sign of the pigeon or his pals, Sam showered and changed before heading out for some food. He decided that he would visit the Old Town to eat for a change, and asked the receptionist to call him a taxi. He was given a recommendation by the taxi driver, who dropped him off at a very quaint and rustic taverna, up a side street and just off the beaten track.

After enjoying some lovely Tapas food, Sam made his way through the winding cobbled streets until he found a bar which was fairly quiet. It was showing football on Sky, and Sam remembered that the Republic of Ireland (ROI) were playing in a World Cup qualifying match against Denmark. He asked the barman if he could put it on instead of the lower league Spanish game currently being shown, and as no one else in the bar appeared to be interested in that match, including the barman himself, he was only too happy to oblige.

While the ROI went into an early lead, they were 2-1 down by half time. Nevertheless, hope springs eternal, as they say, and Sam had his fingers crossed that the Republic would stage a comeback in the second half; he ordered another beer as the game kicked off again.

However, a few minutes into the second half, some

Spanish people entered the bar, and the barman inexplicably changed the channel to a friendly match between Russia and Spain. While Sam expressed his surprise and annoyance at what he regarded as poor public relations at best, and disgracefully disrespectful behaviour at worst, the barman just shrugged his shoulders, more or less indicating that his fellow countrymen's wishes took precedence, despite Sam's protestations that he had already been drinking and watching the ROI game. Sam subsequently expressed his disgust with what the barman's unreasonably partisan behaviour by pushing the relatively untouched beer in his direction and vacating the premises.

He decided that that he didn't want any more to drink and headed back to the hotel; starting out on foot, but hailing a taxi when he realised that he felt very tired and in need of an early night. The next day he learned that the publican may have done him a favour; the Republic of Ireland ended up losing 5-1.

# CHAPTER 26

15 November 2017

Spanish holidaymakers, many of whom have apartments in Benidorm's Old Town, far outnumber the Brits on holiday in the resort in summer, to the extent that it is possible to walk the length of the Poniente beach without hearing a single British voice. In the evenings, the streets of the old town that separate the two beaches and the promenade that runs behind the length of Levante beach are filled with Spanish families taking their 'paseo', or constitutional. By contrast, during the month of November, when Benidorm celebrates a fiesta for its patron saints, the Virgin of the Suffrage and St James the Apostle, there is a clear British presence and participation.

The fiesta takes place over seven days, when the town virtually shuts down and takes part in celebrations which last all day and night, every day, and include processions, live music, dancing in the street and sporting events. The parades take place on 14 November, with a spectacular firework display that marks the official end of the Benidorm Fiestas.

A British fancy dress party is always held on 15 November, with a parade in the early afternoon, starting on Avenida del Derramador before continuing along Calle Gerona, past the British Square, then onto Calle Ibiza and Cuenca streets and finishing at the Avenue Philippines. The tradition started over 20 years ago and the event gets more and more popular each year, with thousands of attendees, most of whom celebrate in fancy dress.

Initially, the Watcher had planned to use the crowds and the general confusion surrounding the festival and the parades to provide cover and camouflage for the scenario they'd planned. However, the unexpectedly fortuitous events of four days ago had proved too advantageous and tempting to resist.

# CHAPTER 27

15 November 2017

Sam made his way along the West Side of the Rincon De Loix area, or Nausea Corner, as it is also affectionately known, arriving on Calle Gerona, which was usually part of the parade route. However, he noticed that it had been re- routed to avoid the area cordoned off near the scene of the crime, which lent a quite surreal, macabre feel to the festivities. He was watching the various colourful and impressive floats going past when he felt a tap on his shoulder and turned round to see Trish, dressed in an impressive pixie costume.

"Hello, stranger, I see you made an effort," she said, smiling.

He realised that she was being mischievous and sarcastic, referring to the fact that he had not bothered to dress up for the Fiesta.

"Wasn't in the mood," he heard himself say, and realised that he really meant it.

"Let me buy you a drink to cheer you up, then," said Trish, smiling.

He was about to respond by offering to pay, before he remembered his dire financial predicament, which meant that he would be lucky to last the rest of the week unless he managed to find some way of accessing cash. So instead, he accepted her offer, and they walked to a nearby bar that was a bit quieter than most of the others. She asked him to try and get a seat while she went to the bar, returning with two drinks.

"You always seem to be the one buying," he said, while taking the opportunity to advise her that this was not likely to change in the immediate future due to his unfortunate financial predicament.

"I told you I'd be quite happy to help you out with that," she said.

"No, you're OK," he said, unconvincingly. "I'll figure something out."

"Well you know where to find me if you don't. I'm here until the end of next week, so just go to the hotel and ask them to phone room 47, and if I'm in I'll be happy to oblige. Just ask them to leave me a message if I'm out. Anyway, we'll probably run into one another again."

*Yes, we probably will*, he thought.

"We certainly seem to keep doing that," he said.

"Must be fate. Or are you saying that I'm stalking you?" asked Trish, smiling.

"No no, not all," said Sam, "don't be silly," although he couldn't help remembering that this was what she had said to him the night that they had first met.

He also suddenly realised what it was that had been troubling him. For some reason however, he stopped himself from impulsively asking her about it. Instead, he asked:

"Where did you get the information about the tabloid not printing the story about the murdered woman?"

Trish seemed taken aback by the question. Sam repeated it.

"What? It, eh, it was just something I heard, or maybe I read it in one of the other papers, I can't really remember. Why?"

"I just wondered, because I work in the press, and I hadn't heard any information like that from anyone," said Sam, which was true, because he hadn't spoken to anybody. This was mainly due to him still feeling quite vulnerable and worrying about the questions that he would get asked.

"Why are you interested?"

"Just professional curiosity," he lied, hoping that he sounded convincing and not too keen to find out more.

"So, are the stories or rumours true?" he asked.

"What stories?" said Trish, which he thought was strange given that she had previously referred to them freely and unsolicited.

"The ones you said the paper was afraid to print."

"How would I know?" said Trish, quite defensively.

"I don't know; just because of what you said before, that was all," Sam replied, curious to hear her response.

"I only know what I've heard from people over the years. Most of it was about him, because of his alleged criminal connections and shady business deals. But the talk was that she'd had a chequered past before she met him, and that she was happy to do whatever he asked her, as long as he looked after her."

"Looked after her?" said Sam, curious.

"You know, kept her sweet and in the style she was accustomed to," replied Trish.

"No, I don't know," said Sam, suddenly conscious that he was sounding defensive himself. He decided to change tack. "Did you know her?"

"Not personally. I just knew of her, and him. Most people do from that area. They're quite a well-known couple, and 'business partnership'. The last phrase was delivered mockingly.

"But she told me that she and her husband had split up," blurted Sam, instantly cursing himself for being so stupid.

"You *knew* her?" said Trish, disbelievingly, conscious that she had used the past tense.

"I, eh , I spoke to her briefly in the nightclub, the night that she was, eh, I mean before she was found, you know," stuttered Sam, hoping that he didn't sound too anxious or for that matter, guilty.

Trish looked at him, weighing up what he had just said, before asking:

"Do the police know? Have you spoken to them? I imagine they'll want to question anybody who saw or spoke to her."

"No, I only spoke to her briefly and don't know anything that would be of any use," he said, feeling his heart pounding and realising that he was having difficulty maintaining eye contact with Trish, who was now looking at him in quite a different way.

He needed time to think, so after some more relatively inoffensive and awkward small talk, he thanked her again for the drink, promised to return the favour soon and excused himself, informing her that he was tired and needed to take a nap, which was true. He hadn't had a good night's sleep in days and he was beginning to feel the effects of it. He also wondered if it was affecting his ability to think straight.

Sam headed back to his hotel and went straight to bed. He was exhausted but every time he nearly fell over, something else would pop into his head and keep him awake. It reminded him of being in hospital, a place where you are supposed to go for rest and recuperation. Aye, right! He had never been able to sleep in a hospital and he doubted that anybody else had, either. As soon as you nodded off they'd wake you up to ask you a hundred and one questions, one of which was invariably, "Do you have any trouble sleeping?"

"Not normally. Only since I came into this shithole."

If it wasn't the noise of other patients moaning or shouting "Nurse!" every five minutes, it was the nurses wanting to take your blood pressure, change your drip or ask you the same questions all over again another hundred times, or to really annoy you by asking you if you wanted something to eat or drink.

*Only if you're going to shove it up my arse, because it clearly says Nil by Mouth above the bed if you'd bothered* your *arse to look!* He actually remembered an occasion when a nurse had woken him up to give him something to help him sleep! He could do with a little of what they'd given him then, now.

# CHAPTER 28

15 November 2017

After punching the pillow for nearly two hours and sleep refusing to come, Sam decided that he would wander down to the bar as it wasn't warm enough to sit at the pool. However, to his horror the place was full of pensioners having a tea dance, so he gave up and thought that in the absence of any medication he would try another tack. He needed something to take his mind off the situation for at least a few hours, and he also needed cheering up.

What was it people said? Laughter is the Best Medicine.

He decided to test out the theory, and see if Benidorm's resident jokers could provide the cure.

After a shower and some food, Sam decided to opt for the comedian/ventriloquist guy with the monkey that his 'cheap as chips' acquaintances had told him about. He recalled that they had said that he was on at the Stardust Club, not far from his hotel, and headed out there, hoping that the 'entertainment', in conjunction with some alcohol, would both lift his spirits and relax his mind.

On entering the club, which was almost full, he saw that it wasn't the guy with the monkey that was on but another comic, apparently a 'cockney', decked out in a Union Jack suit, who was ritually abusing the rather quiet and reserved crowd.

"Good evening Ladies and Gentlemen! What a bunch of sad looking bastards. Have you all been at the same funeral?"

This only elicited a quite nervous snigger and Sam wondered if the background of the girl's murder had contributed to the sombre mood in some way. However, the guy was clearly a seasoned pro and wasn't deterred in any way, carrying on regardless.

"Are you having a good time, madam?" On receiving a polite yes and a reserved nod from his target, he responded with the tried and tested, "Well, tell your face, then," which elicited a slightly more enthusiastic response.

"So you *do* know how to laugh? Thank fuck for that, I was beginning to think you were all on the same medication."

*Sod this for a game of soldiers*, thought Sam, and was on his way out the club when the guy said,

"But you know what they say: laughter is the best medicine."

Given his earlier ruminations, it gave Sam pause for thought and he, mistakenly or otherwise, took it as something of a sign or omen and decided to stick around for a while longer.

"What a load of old bollocks that is, eh?" pronounced the comedian. "I think you'll find that medication, preferably prescribed, is the best medicine. Otherwise, you would have people going to see their GP and having the following conversation:

'I've not been feeling that great, doctor. I think I'm a bit run down. I wonder if you could give me something?'

'There you go, that should do the trick.'

'What is it, doctor, a prescription for Prozac?'

'No, it's actually two tickets for Live at the Apollo. The missus and I can't go.'

"What a load of shit! I mean, what's next?" he continued, "Humour for a Tumour? I can just hear the conversation with my agent:

'Right, I've got a gig for you, it's at the hospital, in Intensive Care. Yes, look, don't worry, it'll be fine, you'll be great, you're perfect for it, you'll kill them – sorry, figure of speech obviously – you know what I mean. But, you know what? I think there might be something in this hospital gig thing.'

"Honestly, hospital gigs would be good, but hospice

gigs would be even better, ideal really, because you could probably do it every other month without worrying about doing the same material or playing to the same audience."

He wrapped up, with a "Too far?" Apparently not. If anything, he seemed to have finally found his audience's level.

As Sam headed towards the bar to get a drink, he thought he recognised some people standing there and then realised it was his long lost amigos, Chips and Peanuts, the two guys he had met on the first night.

*Well they're going to have to buy their own drinks this time,* he thought, given his rapidly worsening financial situation and ever decreasing resources. However, he noticed that there was someone else with them and he wondered if they had found a new and unsuspecting benefactor.

"Hey mate, mate, over here!" he heard someone shout, and then realised that one of them had spotted him and was trying to attract his attention. He acknowledged their efforts with a wave and made his way towards them, after he had bought a drink for himself. They greeted him like a long lost friend, all smiles, hugs, and handshakes, and they even offered to buy him a drink. Well, they actually asked their new friend to buy him a drink. They introduced him as Mikey, who was also from Lancashire.

"He's on his own, like you, just arrived yesterday, so

we've been showing him around the place," said Peanuts.

*I'll bet you have*, thought Sam, and wondered how much it had cost him. Mikey, for his part, just smiled benignly, seemingly oblivious to his predicament.

"Where did you get to that night?" asked Chips. "You just disappeared. Did you hear about the girl that was murdered? We were sure we saw her in the club we left you in. Did you see her? Davey said he saw you talking to her." (So *that* was his name.) "You didn't pull her, did you?"

"Or murder her even?" added Peanuts, before laughing. "Don't worry your secret's safe with us – but it'll cost you a drink."

Chips continued, "She was quite a girl, according to the papers and what people have been saying."

Sam wanted to defend Heather, but thought better of it. "You don't want to believe everything you read, or hear," he said, before changing the subject. "I thought you said the guy with the monkey was on here?"

"He was supposed to be, but we don't know if he's still to come on or if we've missed him. Mikey says he heard somebody saying it's his night off and the other guy is on in his place. We were going to head off somewhere else if that's the case, because he's shit. You want to come with us?"

Sam was trying to think of an excuse not to when

he felt this arm being tugged from behind, and looked round to see another familiar face.

"I thought I recognised that voice. Are you sure you're not stalking *me* now?" said Trish.

Sam wasn't sure whether Trish was a preferable option, but rather than get into introductions he offered to buy her a drink "for a change" and made his excuses to his 'chums' who smiled knowingly.

"Bit old for you, is she not?" said Peanuts. "Catch you later, mate."

Sam bade them farewell, then turned to Trish to ask her what she wanted to drink.

"Actually, let's go somewhere else a bit quieter, where we can talk. It's too noisy in here, you can't hear yourself think. And the comedian is rotten."

Sam didn't argue.

# CHAPTER 29

15 November 2017

They found a relatively quiet bar tucked away behind a café a short distance away and Sam brought two drinks from the bar to the table that Trish had chosen at the back of the bar. There was music playing but it wasn't loud, and if anything Sam got the impression that the guy had been looking to shut up for the night when they arrived. There was only a few other people at another table, who had followed suit and ordered another round of drinks too.

"So, how have you been since I saw you last?" asked Trish.

"Aye, OK, same old, same old, nothing new to report," replied Sam.

"Well that's not strictly true," said Trish. "You're buying the drinks, so that's new for a start." She saw Sam's pained expression and responded with a placatory smile, squeezing his hand gently. "I'm just teasing," she said.

"So, have you come into money then?" she added, playfully.

"I wish," said Sam, before adding, "but I'm not totally skint yet and I just thought that I should buy you a drink for a change."

"Well that was very nice, and it's appreciated, but I told you not to worry about it, and if you need any money it's not a problem."

"No you're alright, I'll manage," he heard himself saying, while at the same time wondering if he would. But he also didn't feel right about accepting her offer of financial assistance, particularly given that this was a woman who had reportedly been scammed out of a large amount of money by a conman. Yet here she was offering money to a relative stranger.

"I think you must be the one who's come into money," he said.

"What? No, not at all" replied Trish, before adding:

"Well, I got some money when Frank, my husband died a few years back, but that's nearly all gone now.

"But I wouldn't see someone stuck, particularly on holiday and especially after what happened with you being mugged and all, unless you're making it all up and trying to con me?"

That was when Sam remembered again what it was that had been bugging him; this time he decided to confront her about it.

"How did you know that I had been mugged?" said Sam,

"What?" said Trish, sounding perplexed and a bit flustered.

"How did you know that I had been mugged?" repeated Sam,

"You told me," said Trish, managing to make it sound more of a question than a statement.

"No I never," said Sam, "because I didn't realise it until the next day, and I never told you then, either."

Trish stared at Sam, appearing startled and unsettled, before stammering, "I . . . I suppose I must've just assumed that's what happened," before adding, "I mean, what other reason could there be?"

"I suppose so," said Sam, before adding, "Sorry, I just needed to ask. I hope you don't mind?"

"No, not at all. As long as you don't mind me asking something I need to know," said Trisha.

"Oh, what's that?" said Sam, quizzically.

"Did you murder that woman?"

"What?" said Sam, aghast and nearly choking on his drink.

"The woman who was killed, did you murder her?"

"No, of course not, are you serious? Why would you even ask me that?"

"Because of the way you reacted when we spoke previously. You seemed anxious and unsettled, and you obviously knew more than you were saying."

"I don't know anything, I only met her that night" pleaded Sam.

"And you didn't spend the night with her?" asked Trish.

"No, well, yes, part of it, but she left my hotel and I didn't kill her. Why are you asking me if I spent the night with her, what difference does it make?"

"To see if you were going to be honest this time, because you lied when we spoke previously," replied Trish.

"Yes, I suppose I did," said Sam, adding, because I was worried what you would think. I was worried about what everybody would think. Who wouldn't be?"

"And you should have gone to the police," said Trish.

"Well, I didn't for the same reason" said Sam, becoming quite irritated now.

"Well if you don't, I will," said Trish.

"What? Why? And say what? I don't know anything. I told you, she was killed after she left me."

"Well, you would say that, obviously. Look, if you are innocent you have nothing to worry about."

"It's easy for you to say that," Sam blasted back. "This is a foreign country and they will just be looking for someone to put the blame on. I could end up in prison. You don't seriously think I did it, do you?"

"I don't know what to think," said Trish.

"I'd rather you didn't go to the police," said Sam.

"Only if you agree to do so, because any information would be helpful," said Trisha. "You can think about it tonight and we can speak tomorrow again. Now," she went on, casually, "would you like another drink?"

# CHAPTER 30

15 November 2017

After he left Trish, having refused the offer of another drink, Sam's mind was full of questions with very few answers. He had no idea where he was going, and just started walking, almost on automatic pilot, along the still relatively busy streets parallel to Levante beach. Soon, he realised that he had taken an unintentional detour somewhere along the line and that he had no idea where he was. *How can you take a detour if you don't know where you're going?* he thought to himself.

He also realised that he was going to have to ask somebody for directions to get him back on the straight and narrow, when another ridiculous thought came into his mind.

*Is it easier for a man to ask directions if he is walking rather than driving?*

He smiled as he thought what a sexist and

ridiculously stereotypical and discriminative piece of nonsense that is – that all male  drivers are incapable of asking for directions and that therefore, by implication women, apparently, don't have a problem with it.

*Well, maybe,* he thought, but asking and taking directions are two totally different things; certainly from his experience with women to date, and in particular Kim, they didn't readily accept the latter very readily, no matter how well-intentioned the offer of them was.

Sam wondered if it would be different if the information was being provided by a complete stranger rather than their well-meaning, supportive nearest and dearest. It seemed to him that it was like admitting defeat. And, consequently, it was doomed to end in failure and argument, no matter how sincere and genuine your intentions were, and no matter how you approached it. You could ask the most reasonable of questions . . .

"OK, where are you going?
And it would snowball from there . . .

"I don't know where I'm going, do I? That's why I'm asking directions! I got lost last time, didn't I?"

"I'm only trying to help."

"Directions would be helpful."

"Rrright, OK, so, where do you know?"

"I know the road that I went last time."

"But you got lost last time."

"I know, but that's because I took a wrong turn."

"OK, where?"

"If I knew that I wouldn't have got lost and ended up going all around the houses."

"Houses, what houses? There aren't any houses."

"It's a figure of speech, y'know what I mean, I went all the way round the one way system."

"It'd be hard not to, that's what you're supposed to do on a one way system?"

"Oh is that right, Columbus? OK, you tell me where I went wrong."

"You didn't read the sign."

"No and neither did you, smart arse!"

"What?"

"Never mind – what sign?"

"The sign at the exit, you can't miss it."

"Well obviously I did."

"OK, look I'll draw you a map."

So you'd draw them a map – a perfectly good map, easy to follow, very clear – CRYSTAL, in fact – then show it to them, mark out the route they were taking and explain it to them very patiently and methodically bit by bit, to make sure they'd understand it all . You'd know they did, because they'd tell you they did. And then what did they always do? They'd say, "Oh, never mind, it's OK, I'll just go the way I know . . ." !

With Kim, this routine had been the same with any

kind of discussion which for some reason ended up involving some sense of competitiveness; this seemed to be the case for most of their conversations. Latterly, any attempt at serious discussion or conversation also invariably ended in disagreement, at best and at worst a serious, inexplicable argument. Whatever the reason, he had just seemed to be able to annoy her effortlessly.

*Why is it*, he wondered, *that when you are having a disagreement, or a heated exchange of views with someone and making good points, they respond by resorting to the predictably contrived and desperate tactic of "Don't shout at me," which even although you haven't raised your voice one single decibel at that point, unfortunately elicits the desired response of "I'm not shouting," usually in a very loud and angry voice? Mission accomplished. Argument lost.*

*Just like me,* thought Sam as he hailed a taxi.

# CHAPTER 31

16 November 2017

Unsurprisingly, Sam hadn't slept again, his mind running wild with the potential implications and consequences of his and possibly Trish's actions. So he had risen around 6.00 a.m. and gone out to the balcony to clear his head and to think things through again. He couldn't make sense of why Trish was so concerned with his situation. Did she really think he could murder someone? And was she right to tell him to go to the police and tell them what he knew? And where was the bloody pigeon when you needed someone to talk to? Maybe the pigeon thought he was a murderer, too!

He also began to think that he was behaving like someone who had something to hide, when in fact he had done nothing wrong. Was this why Trish was beginning to doubt his innocence? Or was she causing him to behave like he had because of her veiled accusation and insistence that he contact the police, threatening to do so herself if he didn't? He began to think that maybe if he stopped acting as if he was guilty of something she would stop thinking he was – but this was easier said than done.

Trish had also insisted that they swap phone numbers, asking him to call her the next day to arrange a time to meet to discuss the situation further. Sam knew that if he didn't call her, she would call him. And now something else was bothering him, nagging away at him, something that didn't feel quite right. He just hadn't worked out what it was yet.

But he would worry about that later, because there was still another matter he had to attend to, namely that of his quickly deteriorating financial situation and the circumstances surrounding it.

# CHAPTER 32

16 November 2017

While Trish had offered to help Sam financially, he didn't feel right about it before, even less so now. He had decided that he needed to do something about it by himself, by seeking out the little bastard who had robbed him. It wouldn't be too hard to find him, because he knew where to look. And Sam reckoned that with the element of surprise and the added benefit of being sober this time, he would be able to get the better of his assailant, to the extent that he could intimidate or frighten him into coming across with the money. And in the event of him not having the money, then he could always just take it out on his face. He was still angry enough to want to beat the shit out of him.

After further deliberation, Sam decided to do a daytime 'recce' of the area to check out the street layout and vantage points in order to develop the best strategy and point of approach.

As he made his way along the road from the hotel to the main drag, he saw a stray dog sniffing its away along the other side of the road, no doubt looking for food. It occurred to him that it was a sight that you very rarely saw back home anymore. In his neck of the woods, dogs were rescued or picked up by the relevant authorities and taken to shelters to be reclaimed or rescued by owners and members of the public, respectively.

He also realised, however, that he had never actually witnessed a stray dog being picked up by the authorities, and started to think of them as some kind of secret, almost phantom service, who very quietly and stealthily scoured the streets looking for strays, in some kind of twilight zone. Whatever process was in place, Sam was very grateful for it, as it had enabled him and Kim to acquire Ziggy, who had been found wandering the streets near to where they lived. This situation initially appeared likely to militate against the likelihood of the authorities releasing him to their care, as, apparently, there's a reluctance to allow dogs to be re-located in the area where they are found, in order to minimise the likelihood of them coming into contact with their previous owners and the complications that this could cause.

Thankfully, however, they were prepared to relax their regulations, and Ziggy was theirs to take home and he'd lived happy ever after, even if they hadn't.

It was while he was pondering the image of the mythical 'Dog Rescue Service' and their shadowy pursuit of their quarry that an image came into his mind. It was an image that both intrigued and troubled him, while also possibly offering some insight into how recent events had unfolded. Initially he was reluctant to give it any credence, attributing it to his fertile and sometimes over-active imagination. However, the more he thought about it, the more possible and reasonable it seemed. He just couldn't work out why.

# CHAPTER 33

16 November 2017

Sam made his way back to his hotel, and on entering his room he saw that the chambermaid had been in. She had folded the towels into the shape of an animal again. Yesterday it had been a dog, the day before a swan. Today it was an elephant. So there was quite literally, and ironically, an elephant in the room. As he unfolded one of the towels, he realised that it was quite a complex process; the skill involved really was quite impressive.

It made him wonder how she had ended up as a cleaner, before concluding that clearly there was more money in cleaning than in towel origami, or whatever it was called, which didn't say much, or maybe said a lot, depending on your viewpoint.

Perhaps, he mused, it was part of the job description nowadays; he wondered if they were required to go on a course or asked to select skill or career options.

"The options available are balcony brushing, lavvy scrubbing or towel origami," the hotel manager might declare. No contest. Maybe that was what made the rest of the job bearable, and therefore it was accepted as a necessary and valued facet of their duties. Or maybe it was more of a tolerated extra – "As long as you get your work done, you can make as many towel animals as you like." He began to speculate whether they were assessed on and rewarded for their efforts, like some kind of performance bonus. He decided that he would be sure to leave her a decent tip to show his appreciation and approval of her craft.

On a more serious note, he had always considered a chambermaid's job to be really hard work, particularly when it came to stripping and changing the bed linen. Certainly, it remained a chore that he always dreaded and which he also found quite physically taxing. And that was only him changing his own bed. God knows how many rooms they were cleaning a day. Then, as if emerging from some kind of a dream, he thought to himself, *why the fuck am I thinking about all this shit?* And then he realised that, as with the chambermaids, it was probably serving as a diversion from the reality of the other shit he was dealing with. It would take a very special cleaner indeed to clean that lot up.

# CHAPTER 34

16 November 2017

Sam went to a nearby café bar and made himself eat something; he reckoned he would need both strength and energy for the task in hand later that night.

When he returned to his room, the pigeon was on the balcony with a pal, who was equally as bold and belligerent. He informed both of them that they had an empty, left them some tidbits, and told them that they should feel free to bring their companions round for a catch up, on the condition that they cleaned up after themselves. He wasn't optimistic that they were listening.

He spent the majority of the day by the pool, heading to the room around four-ish, in the hope that he might fall asleep and catch up some of what he had lost. However, he only dozed fitfully and didn't really feel rested, so he decided to get up, then showered, dressed and went for dinner around 6.30pm, at a nearby bar and restaurant.

Sam had decided that he would wait until Trish phoned him and speak to her then, although he had still not come to a clear decision about going to the police. He had still not heard anything from Trish by about 8.30 p.m., so headed out to the main drag just before 9.00, and positioned himself at a bar nearby to the place where he had been accosted to wait for any sight of the thug who had mugged him.

He was stone cold sober and sat just inside the entrance, sipping water. He was confident that in the shade and darkness of the evening, he would not be spotted. He had also muted his phone to prevent it from going off accidentally and inadvertently drawing attention to him.

By around 9.30 p.m. he was beginning to doubt both the wisdom and probable success of his venture, when he saw the guy he'd been looking for emerge from a lane off the main drag. After pacing up and down furtively, he attempted to engage some males in conversation. However, Sam noticed that they weren't subjected to the same level of personal attention that had been paid to him, nor the same amount of persistence, as he soon wandered off again. Sam watched him prowl in and around the lane for around ten minutes, until he stopped to light a cigarette.

Sam cautiously and carefully moved out of the bar

while his intended adversary's attention was momentarily distracted, and slowly made his way behind the lane to plan his approach. He knew that he had to be quick, and that his first contact had to disable his target reasonably quietly in order not to alert him, his colleagues or any passers-by, although the chances were that most people would likely ignore any fracas and just keep walking. That was certainly what had happened the night he had been accosted. He'd also scanned the area for CCTV cameras, and positioned himself out of sight of where they might possibly be. He moved slowly and quietly until he was only a short distance away from his quarry and until he was facing the other way. He also checked that there were no other people in the immediate vicinity, then quickly and deliberately headed straight towards him.

His heart was thumping in his chest as he waited for the point of contact, which came when his target turned round to face Sam, at the point when he was practically upon him. This also served to startle the thug , which worked in Sam's favour and allowed him to plant a well-placed 'Glasgow Kiss' on the bridge of his nose, and his knee in his groin, causing him to double up and fall in a heap towards him. Sam grabbed him by the throat, both to silence him and to push him backwards in one motion into the cover of the lane. While he was still trying to process what was happening, Sam grabbed him from behind, and positioned his arms and hands behind his neck and throat – the guy could hardly breathe, never mind speak.

It was this point that he again began to doubt the sanity of what he was doing.

He was in a foreign country, after all, and God knows what could happen to him if it all went tits up. Also, this guy was clearly connected, at some level, to some seriously corrupt and dangerous individuals.

*Fuck it,* he thought, *I'm already up to my arse in alligators, it can't get much worse, so in for a peseta in for a pound, or euro, or whatever.*

"Hello, Amigo," said Sam sarcastically. "Remember me from the other night? My name is Sam, and we're going to play a game called 'Sam Says', which means that you do whatever I tell you to do. Comprende, Amigo?" He repeated it, and the guy tried to nod his assent, while clearly struggling to move.

"This is the second time we have been up close and personal, only this time it's my turn to ask the questions. And you'd better have some fucking answers. And, some fucking money, because you owe me about two hundred and fifty euros, plus interest."

The guy was gasping for breath, while also trying to get a look at Sam's face.

"Just fucking calm down, and I'll let you breathe and speak, unless you try to be a hero, in which case your air supply gets cut off again," said Sam, trying to sound as tough and nasty as he could.

"So how much money have you got, my man? And don't fucking lie to me or I'll take it out of your face and bite your fucking ear off."

This seemed to do the trick, as the guy gestured to his jacket pocket, for Sam to check, which he did. Sam reckoned the guy had about 500 Euros in the first pocket he looked in, and around the same in his next pocket.

Sam removed 300 Euros and put them in his denims , advising the guy that was them quits, unless he wanted to make any more of it. Initially, he thought about only taking the 250 but thought that seemed far too little and too reasonable an approach, which was not the image he was intending to convey.
The guy nodded his assent, and Sam warned him against making any noise or shouting for help when he let him go, although he didn't think he would have the energy. Indeed, when he removed the pressure from his throat, the guy let out a gasp and fell like a rag doll to the ground. Sam warned him against mugging or accosting anybody else, to which the guy rasped back, "I never do it again, I promise. I never do it before!"

"What, you expect me to believe that?" said Sam, incredulously. "You made an exception just for me? Aye, right, my fucking arse! Why me, then?"

"The lady, she pay me to do it, just for a joke, you know, a laugh."

"A laugh? What are you talking about? What lady? Talk sense, you idiot!"

"The lady from the Hotel. Trish, I think is her name."

*What the fuck?* thought Sam. *What hotel? This makes no sense.* His head was reeling, but somehow he knew that the guy was telling the truth. There was no reason for him to lie.

Within minutes, the guy had told him everything. His name was Akmal and he had recently arrived in the country from Algeria; as well as being involved with pimping prostitutes, he also worked in the hotel Trish was staying at, the Venus, as a barman, odd job man and general dogsbody.

Akmal claimed that Trisha had persuaded him to mug and 'gently rough up' Sam on his way home the next night, paying him 500 Euros for doing so. On hearing this, Sam wished he had taken the whole 500 when he had the chance.

The guy claimed that he thought it was for a joke, but in reality he'd not been given a reason. Sam was actually beginning to almost feel sorry for the guy. He told him that under no circumstances was he to tell Trish about their 'meeting', and that if he did, or if anything else happened to him, he would contact the police and the hotel to advise that he had murdered the woman tourist.

"But that is lie!" said Akmal, horrified and

panicking. "You don't say that, because it is lies. You can't prove this!"

"I don't need to prove it, Sparky," said Sam, growing more confident by the second and continuing to smile. "That's a job for the authorities.

"But I imagine that you don't need the aggro or the attention, given your situation, if you know what I mean.

"Everything all straightforward and above board in terms of visas and work permits, eh, Sparky?" said Sam, quietly speculating that the regulations and procedures were possibly not as strictly observed in Spain as they were back in Britain. However, Akmal said nothing and continued to look worried.

"Didn't think so," said Sam, adding that he had better make sure that that was the end of it. However, he was conscious that he had made the same threat to call the police the night he had been mugged, and clearly had not carried it out. "I didn't call the police before, because I wanted this little opportunity to meet up with you again.

"And I wouldn't have missed it for the world," he finished, smiling and trying to sound as menacing as he could.

"OK, I say nothing," said the guy, looking and sounding defeated.

"Oh, I know you won't," said Sam, at which point another guy appeared at the end of the lane, obviously looking to see where and how Akmal was.

"Hola, senor, buenas noches," said Sam, as he passed him without looking back.

# CHAPTER 35

16 November 2017

Sam was making his way back to his hotel when he realised that his whole body was still shaking following his altercation with the Algerian; he subsequently decided that he needed a drink and a distraction to help him calm down and take stock of this dramatic and unexpected turn of events. He then turned around and made his way back towards the main drag, where he shortly found himself back in the same club he had been in the previous night, having walked there on automatic pilot. The guy with the monkey was still not on, and the place was relatively quiet as whatever that night's entertainment was appeared to be on a break.

Sam ordered a drink at the bar, trying to gather his thoughts and attempting to make some sense of what Akmal had told him. However, at that point the next act made their entrance; this time it was a woman, or rather a man in drag, who was even more near the knuckle and risqué than the 'cockney' guy, even if it was tired and predictable stuff.

"Thanks for that lovely warm welcome – I like nothing better than a warm hand on my entrance!" He should have been paying Julian Clary royalties for that one!

He carried on. "I was watching a programme the other night, called *Sex– How to do Everything*. Did anybody here see it? I promise you if you did, you would remember. I mean, it's not every night you turn your TV on to see some crazy bint with her finger up a naked man's arse.

"I normally don't need to turn the telly on for that to be honest! Anyway, she's talking away, in a quite matter of fact manner, giving it, 'How's that for you?' like she'd just cut his hair! And he's like, 'Alright, I've had worse days'! And then, I shit you not – no pun intended – she says, 'Could you orgasm?' and he says, 'No, but I could re-decorate that wall'! OK, he didn't, but he should've, it would have been more entertaining."

*I know what you mean*, thought Sam. *It must be in the delivery.*

The guy was on a roll now.

"And then, she then she went on to list all the things you shouldn't put up there. Seriously, like we need her to tell us the blindingly obvious; things like lightbulbs, screwdrivers – because it's an easy mistake to make– deodorant cans, and torches.

"I can just hear them explaining that at Accident and Emergency:

'We were looking for something and I tripped and fell and the torch just ended up embedded in her bum.'

"And courgettes! Actually, that's about all they're good for- and mobile phones! To be honest, I wouldn't have thought there was any chance of you getting a signal up there!"

*No, but there's more chance of that than you getting a laugh up there,* thought Sam, and headed out somewhere else less busy and quieter to think, which wasn't easy, as the place was still very busy. After walking a relatively short distance, he found somewhere that offered sanctuary, sustenance and relative calm.

After considerable deliberation, Sam decided that he believed the Algerian's story. However, he could not for the life of him figure out why Trish would ask someone to do what he did to him. But he needed to try to find out. He just wasn't sure about how to go about it, particularly given their previous conversation and with the threat of her going to the police hanging over him. If nothing else it explained how she knew he had been mugged before he'd told her.

His mind was racing.

What the fuck was she playing at? And were the situations linked in any way? Did she really believe that he had killed Heather? And was the attack and mugging in response to that? But they hadn't even met at that point, so how could she link them together?

As if in response to his question, his phone rang. And, of course, it was Trish.

"I thought that we agreed that you were going to call me?" she said, somewhat indignantly.

"I had some business to attend to," said Sam, firmly and unapologetically.

"More important than the business we discussed?" asked Trish.

"Just as important, if not more," said Sam, deliberately testing her resolve and determination.

"Oh really, well I think we need to meet and discuss the situation further. I've been thinking, and I have a proposition for you to consider."

"Oh, aye, what kind of a proposition?" said Sam, although what he really wanted to say was, "What's your fucking game?" He held his true feelings close, as he was intrigued to hear what the proposition was.

"Well we can discuss that tomorrow, but there's not much time left to sort this," she said.

Sam thought that it sounded like some kind of a veiled threat, almost like the blackmail email that he had received. However, he agreed to meet her again at the same beach bar as before, at around mid-day.

# CHAPTER 36

17 November 2017

When Sam awoke around 7.00 the next morning, after finally falling off to sleep around four, he was greeted by a warm  if not particularly bright day. The sun was struggling to emerge from the large, puffy clouds which seemed to be chasing and catching it with effortless regularity as it tried, unsuccessfully, to escape from their relentless pursuit.

The pool area was deserted and the pigeon and his pals appeared to have followed suit. After showering, Sam went to breakfast and then headed to the local mini market to buy a newspaper to check if there were any new developments or information about what was most definitely the only story in town.

However, it was mostly the same details regurgitated; quotes from the police that "enquiries were continuing" and appeals for the family to be shown respect and sensitivity at such a traumatic and emotional time. Further appeals were also made for anybody who might have seen or noticed anything to come forward.

Sam headed back to his room, made himself a coffee, and spent some time reflecting on the events to date, which still seemed to make little or no sense. Maybe he would get some answers from Trish today. Maybe he would just ask her what the hell her game was. Or maybe he wouldn't. He was still very reluctant to confront her, for fear of what she would do. He just wasn't sure what her reasons were for anything, and why she appeared to have targeted him.

Sam simply wasn't convinced that her threat to go to the police was borne of a sense of righteous decency or a particular moral code. He also couldn't escape the thought that he was missing something obvious, which made him feel very vulnerable and anxious about what the next development was going to be.

Trish was already at the beach bar waiting for him when he arrived. He couldn't say that he was pleased to see her.

"Good afternoon – I've ordered you a beer," she said, handing him a food menu. "Lunch is on me."

"I'm not hungry," said Sam, making it clear that he was not in the mood for casual and false small talk.

"Somebody got out of the bed on the wrong side," said Trish, frowning.

"You said that you had a proposition for me?" said Sam. His mind was racing, and he was desperate to know what lay behind all this intrigue.

"Well, it's really more of a solution to our situation," said Trish.

"Our situation?" said Sam, both intrigued and excited, hoping that her reply would finally reveal the motivation and truth behind her behaviour. He managed to remain calm, adding, "I didn't think that *we* had a situation."

"Well *you* certainly do, and I think I can help you with it," countered Trish.

"And what situation would that be?" said Sam, with as much poise and firmness as he could manage.

"You have a very short memory," said Trish, calmly, but with a trace of impatience.

"And so have you," said Sam. "I told you, I haven't done anything."

"Yes, I know what you said, but really, I thought we agreed that it doesn't look good, and I don't know that I believe you. Quite frankly, I'm not sure that the police would either."

"So what are you saying?" Sam asked.

"I'm saying that I need a good reason not to go to the police, and so far I haven't got one," Trish replied. "So far, you've lied to me about spending the night with the dead woman, and why would you do that if you had nothing to hide?"

"How did you know that I had lied about spending the night with her?" Asked Sam , as he suddenly realised what it was that had been annoying him when they last met.

"Because you admitted it the last time we met."

"Yes, but only after you accused me of lying about it," said Sam. "So, how did you know? Were you following me?"

"No of course not," said Trish. "Why would I want to follow you? I didn't even know you."

*You didn't know me the night I was mugged either, but you were following me then, weren't you?* thought Sam. *Was it to check on me? To see how I was after my tussle with your hired muscle?*

He suddenly realised the reasoning behind her behaviour.

*No, of course it wasn't; it was clearly in order to get the opportunity to talk to me, to ingratiate yourself and then arrange to meet up with me. And then regale me with all the personal details of the traumatic experiences you have allegedly had to deal with in your tragic life. But why did you want to tell me your stories, and were they even true?*

His impatience grew, and he lashed out. "No you didn't know me. And you still don't," he barked, instantly regretting it as he didn't want to piss her off to the extent that she would decide to go to the police.

He suddenly felt very hot and sweaty, and took a large swig of the beer that Trish had bought him; it was very cold, very refreshing, and very welcome.

He wanted to tell Trish that he knew all about her deal with her little Algerian friend, but decided to keep it to himself for the time being until he had more time to think. And she still hadn't answered his question. Instead, he said, "You also said that you didn't know the woman who died, either, but you seem to know an awful lot about her."

Trish looked visibly annoyed by Sam's retort, but seemed to control her irritation sufficiently to remain reasonably calm.

"Most people knew the same information that I knew about both her and her husband, but nobody was prepared to say anything. So, I imagine the tabloids were nervous about printing any of it for the same reasons, because of his reputation and connections. And, he had previously successfully sued someone for defamation of character.

"There was also a bit of an outcry some years ago when it was made public that he was given a grant by a company which was, and still is, funded by taxpayers' money, to set up an internet based investment company, which later folded. I think she was also a partner in it. He was banned from being a director for five years after he failed to pay hundreds of thousands of pounds in tax and National Insurance. And as if that wasn't enough, he was also granted thousands in legal aid to fund an appeal against the judgment, because he claimed to be separated from his wife, when everybody knew they were still together.

"Anyway, he lost the appeal but then subsequently opened up a series of nail bars in the Glasgow/Lanarkshire area, which I think he still has, along with his brother Terry, who's even more corrupt than he is."

"As I said, that's a lot of information to have about someone you say you don't know," said Sam. "So what's the proposition you have for me?"

"It'll keep," she said, before adding, "I need to give some thought to whether I trust you."

"Trust me with what?"

"A matter of life and death," she replied and then got up and left, shouting over her shoulder at him as she went.

"I'll be in touch. Don't leave the country!"

# CHAPTER 37

17 November 2017

It was still early, but Sam wasn't in the mood for any kind of company or socialising, so he decided to head back to the hotel by himself. He knew he wouldn't sleep because his head was too full of information and nagging, spurious questions with no answers.

For the first time in a few days, he began to think about Heather again, the person whom he had known all too briefly and who was now gone, dead, and lost to her family and friends forever. But now he needed to know why. Had it been anything to do with him? He failed to see how it could be – they had never met previously and their time together was fleeting.

Also, while their liaison had been a highly enjoyable and sensual experience at the time, the subsequent tragic events had tainted and blighted his memory of it forever, and made it impossible for him to think of it in any positive or affectionate way.

Sam began to think that if he knew more about Heather's life he could maybe understand more about why someone would want to kill her, and perhaps even work out who was responsible. He thought back to that night, and recalled what Heather had told him about how controlling her ex-husband was; ordering her to wear fewer close-fitting clothes and telling her to cover herself up with frumpy jumpers or a fleece when at work. He had even visited her at her workplace to check that she had done as she was told, and would be abusive towards her if she hadn't complied. And this from the man who demanded that she wore sexy underwear and outfits for him on a regular basis.

Sam also remembered that Heather had told him that even after she had left him he had continued to stalk her and to inundate her with abusive and threatening phone calls and texts, whist making it known that he knew where she had been and who with. When Heather had tried to block his calls, he had changed the settings on his phone. He would also turn up at her house uninvited and would then refuse to leave until she threatened to call the police, which often made him worse, threatening her and on occasion resorting to violence. He had subjected her to a persistent regime of terror, to the extent that she was constantly in a state of fear; too terrified to do anything.

Was her murder a way of getting back at him for things he had done to others, wondered Sam? Or , was her husband involved in some way?

Sam had heard that victims are usually murdered by people they know, but as far as he was aware, Heather's estranged husband had been back in Scotland at the time of her death, although according to the newspapers he could be arriving in Benidorm soon. Could he have arranged for her to be killed through his reported criminal connections? Or was that just too far-fetched and dramatic? He realised that there was absolutely no evidence to that effect, and this was just wild speculation on his part. On the other hand, he realised there most likely *was* evidence that Heather had gone to his hotel and spent most of the night there.

He knew it was really only a matter of time before this information became known. And he knew how that would look. He wondered what the police, Heather's family and her estranged husband would do once it became public.

He needed to stop worrying about that now, though, and think instead about Heather and her life and if, or how, their encounter had led to her death.

Sam recalled the details of the affair that Heather confessed to, noting that affairs, like murders, are also normally carried out by people that the adulterers know, with familiarity often breeding consent. This was the scenario that Heather had described, after all.

That certainly appeared to have been the case as far as Heather's abusive husband was concerned, even although the affair in question had been over for years before they met and married. But then he was not a reasonable man, if what Heather had told him was true.

While Sam would normally have regarded the phrase 'hell hath no fury' as being associated with women, he also understood that men who feel betrayed or sinned against are more likely to pursue and exact violent revenge against their partner. His journalistic background afforded him both privileged exposure and advantageous access to research relating to such investigations and relevant findings.

He was aware that men are also more likely to perpetrate and practice the modern, reprehensible and despicable trend of 'revenge sex' or 'revenge porn', posting pictures or sex videos, which their ex-partner foolishly allowed them to take. They are also more likely to resort to vengeance of all sorts, in fact. Heather's estranged husband certainly ticked all those boxes, too.

Sam reflected on his own feelings when he'd thought that Kim was having an affair. While he still wasn't sure if she had or not, he recalled the terrible sense of betrayal he had felt and the feelings of vulnerability, hurt and worthlessness that he had experienced. Not to mention the anger.

For the first time, Sam realised that there was

another victim in Heather's situation; the sinned against wife, who may, or may not have found out about the affair. But it had all happened a long time ago, as Heather had said, and he didn't even know if the woman was still alive. However, he was sure that if the wife had discovered the deception, she would have questioned everything and everybody and eventually also started to wonder how she hadn't known herself, and whether anyone else had.

With any loss, once the anger and denial subsides, people then begin to question themselves, and perhaps also blame themselves. The injured party begins to wonder if they were guilty of taking their loved one for granted, or if they were so wrapped up in their own little world that they pushed them aside. Sometimes the situation becomes too painful for them to cope with, and they resort to suicide. But sometimes, they resort to attributing sole and total blame on either their errant partner or the other man or woman. Unfortunately for Heather, thought Sam, her estranged husband had chosen the latter option.

Sam suddenly realised that he was back at his hotel, but was absolutely no further forward in terms of understanding or making any sense of what was becoming an increasingly complex and troubling situation.

# CHAPTER 38

17 November 2017

Sam had initially contemplated buying a bottle of wine, taking it to his room and drinking it on the balcony but then had a notion to have a drink in the hotel bar instead, reasoning it would normally be quiet at that time of night. In the end he decided to go for both options, with the former as a contingency plan in order to help him sleep, or in the event of the hotel bar being either busy or undesirable.

He purchased a bottle of Rioja from the supermarket next to his hotel and deposited it in the room before heading down to the bar, which was indeed relatively quiet, with only a handful of people at the tables. The clientele were mainly older couples, listening to a guy playing Spanish guitar, plus a few individuals perched at the bar.

He ordered a beer, and consumed half of it in one

thirsty and swift gulp, before almost draining it completely with a second substantial draft. After covering his mouth and stifling a belch, he decided to order another.

"You look as if you needed that," he heard someone say in a Scottish accent. He looked up and saw an attractive, middle-aged woman smiling at him from the other end of the bar; it was the woman he had seen at the pool a few days before.

*Yes, you're probably right – more than I realised,* he thought.

"Aye, I, eh, didn't realise how thirsty I was."
The barman arrived with his second drink. He looked at his new acquaintance, pointed to his drink and politely enquired "Can I get you one? Sorry, I don't know your name."

"Audrey. Audrey McPherson," she replied, before adding, "Well, that's very kind of you to offer." She looked back at him enquiringly.

Eventually realising that she was expecting a reciprocal response, Sam said, "Sorry, I'm Sam," consciously not offering his surname, but not entirely sure why he was holding back.

"Well, Sam, I'll have a gin and slimline tonic, if that's OK."

"No problem," he said, and nodded to the barman.

"You here on your own?" asked Sam of his new found companion, before adding, "I'm sorry, that's a bit forward, I didn't mean to be rude."

"No, it's perfectly OK, I didn't think you were being rude. Yes, I'm staying here on my own but I've friends who are staying here elsewhere. We booked separately for two weeks. but unfortunately I couldn't get a room at the same hotel."

"I see," said Sam. "Are you heading out to meet up with them?"

"Well, yes, that was the plan, to go and see a show. Apparently there's a ventriloquist guy with a monkey, who's supposed to be very funny – the guy, not the monkey – well you know what I mean."

"Yes," said Sam, smiling at the ironic coincidence, before adding, "Unfortunately I'm not entirely sure that either of them is that reliable."

Seeing Audrey's puzzled expression, he recounted his own failed attempts to date to be entertained by the evasive, errant double act.

"Oh, right, I see," said Audrey, evidently not entirely sure that she did. "Well, anyway, unfortunately some of my friends had a wee bit too much to drink earlier in the day and are obviously still sleeping it off, because I haven't had a call from anyone so far. So I decided to have a drink and consider my options."

Before waiting on a response from Sam, she continued. "So, why aren't you out enjoying the festivities?"

"Oh," said Sam, not really expecting the question,

"I've been out most of the day and I just fancied a quiet night. I saw the bar was quiet and thought I would have a drink before I headed up to the room."

"Well I'm glad you did," she said smiling warmly at him, before adding, "You look remarkably sober for having been out all day – are you here on your own?"

"Yes, I, eh . . . was taking it easy, didn't feel like getting wrecked early on and missing the rest of the day," realising that he had just contradicted himself by saying that he was now having an early night. Luckily for him, she didn't seem to pick up on this.

"But you're making up for it now, eh?"

"What? Oh, the beer. No, I'll probably knock it on the head soon,"

"Is my company that bad?" she said, feigning annoyance.

"What? No, don't be silly, that's not what I meant at all."

"It's OK, I know, I'm only teasing," said Audrey, smiling.

*Yes, you certainly are,* thought Sam. And, more pertinently, *I don't believe it, where is this going?*

*Do I really need another situation?*

He began to wonder if he was being set up. *No, you're just paranoid. But with good reason,* he told himself. However, his thoughts were interrupted by the noise of some revellers nearby, followed by what sounded like the sirens from a couple of emergency vehicles.

He hoped it wasn't the indication of another homicide. After all, he thought, the perpetrator was still at large.

As if reading his mind and reacting to the noise outside, Audrey said "To be honest, I was also a bit unsure about heading out and walking the streets on my own after that poor woman was found murdered. Just terrible – she was still so young."

"I know, you're right and of course it's perfectly understandable you should feel like that, it was a terrible thing that happened," said Sam. Inwardly he was thinking, *Jesus, that's the last thing I want to be talking about.* He was also thinking about how he could change the subject, when she managed it for him.

"So, were you meeting friends today ?"

"Eh, yes, just some people I met on my first day," he lied.

Audrey looked at him for what seemed like an age, before leaning in closer to him. "I hope you don't mind me talking to you, but I've seen you around the hotel and at the pool, and find myself very attracted to you."

There was a further pause, before she added, "So, I thought I would grab the bull by the horns and speak to you in the hope that you found me attractive as well.

"To be honest, I had been sitting in my room, contemplating a night on my own rather than another one out with the girls, because I'm still feeling a bit tender after yesterday. Or rather after last night – I over did the drink a bit. However, I started to think that it was silly to stay in on holiday, and I also realised that a night in front of the TV with a bottle of Rioja Blanco wasn't going to cut it."

"Nice bottle of wine, that," said Sam, probably because he thought that he should say something. He also wondered if she was referring to his own decision to call it a night.

"Oh, don't get me wrong," said Audrey. "I love Rioja Blanco, but the thought of finishing it on my own didn't do it for me. I realised that I needed more stimulation. But then I'm a bit like that. And I am a doer not a thinker.

"When I know what I want, I do what needs to be done to get it."

*Christ, I don't bloody believe this,* thought Sam. *Why, all of a sudden, have I become so attractive and interesting?*

He then began scanning the room to see if anybody was watching them. However, all of the other patrons appeared remarkably disinterested and unconcerned with both of them.

"Well you're certainly very direct," he said.

"Well, as I said, I'm a doer! When I want something, I don't see the point in beating about the bush. Do you find that intimidating or threatening?"

"No, not at all," said Sam. And he didn't. Truth be told, he quite liked sexually confident and forward women. In fact he found it quite a turn on. But he wasn't about to tell Audrey that. Not because he thought that it would cause her any concern or that she wouldn't be able to handle it. He just didn't think he would feel right about saying something so forward himself, given how the situation was making him feel about himself, which was uncertain, tense and totally lacking in confidence.

He wasn't sure how tonight was going to end up but he decided to switch off his phone in case Trish decided to call him. But before he could do so, a mobile phone rang, and he nearly jumped out of his skin. Then he realised that it was Audrey's phone.

As it happened, the phone call was from one of Audrey's friends, calling to tell her that they were all meeting up at the Talk of the Town nightclub, where the guy with the with the monkey was performing.

"They hope!" said Sam, when she told him.

"I think I should probably go" said Audrey, "Would you like to come along?"

Sam didn't really know what to say. Although he was enjoying her company, he wasn't sure if he wanted to go public and be seen in the company of another woman at this time, for reasons he couldn't quite understand or explain to himself.

However, given Audrey's anxiety about walking the streets on her own, he made her an offer.

"Don't worry about me, you go and have your night with your friends. But I'll walk there with you if you like, just so I know you're safe. Hopefully a couple of your friends who are in the same hotel can see you back here safe and sound."

"Oh that's very nice of you, Sam. I'm sure I'll be fine really. I've actually been to classes and I have a self-defence certificate, believe it or not," she said, flexing her muscles theatrically and smiling. "But I would still like you to walk there with me. Are you sure you won't come to the show? You'll be missed."

"That's nice of you to say, but I think I'll just have that early night I planned to have originally if that's OK?"

"I suppose it'll just have to be," said Audrey, finishing her drink and making to leave, linking arms with Sam as she did so. The nightclub wasn't far, and they were there in no time at all.

"Sure you won't change your mind?" asked Audrey, feigning a petted lip, and opening the door to the club.

Sam didn't hear or see her, as he was preoccupied with something else. Something totally unexpected.

"Sam, are you alright?" said Audrey, concerned now. "You've gone a funny colour."

"What? Eh, no, no, I'm fine, I just remembered something that I forgot to do earlier, but it's OK. Nothing serious, it'll keep."

"So, are you coming in? I'm sure I can see a man with a monkey on the stage," said Audrey, waving at a group of women standing at the bar inside. She turned back to look at Sam, who had stepped back away from the door and was now walking backwards away from her.

"No, I'm fine but you enjoy your night and we'll catch up another day," he said smiling almost apologetically.

"OK, I'd like that," said Audrey, as she made her way inside to her friends and a man with a monkey.

# CHAPTER 39

17 November 2017

*Why the fuck did I react like that?* thought Sam, as he made his way back to his hotel. Certainly he had not expected to see Trish in the club, but why did he panic?

He knew fine well why. It was because he was with Audrey.

But why was that such a big deal? Was he worried about how Trish would react and what she would do? Why did she affect him like this? He had to remind himself again that he hadn't done anything wrong, but she always managed to make him feel as if he had, effortlessly.

Or was it because he didn't want Audrey to know that he knew Trish, however brief and recent their acquaintanceship might have been, and for her to start asking questions as to how and all that that entailed?

Another thought occurred to him. Did Audrey

know Trish? And had Trish paid her to keep tabs on him, maybe even rob him again, just like she did with Akmal? No, no, that didn't make sense, otherwise she wouldn't have asked him if he wanted to go to the club where Trish was, if they were indeed connected.

Sam was almost certain that Trish had been amongst the crowd of women that Audrey had waved at in the club. However, he couldn't say for sure, because he had been so concerned that Trish shouldn't see him that he hadn't felt able to linger to check for any length of time in case she did.

But had she seen him? Sam really wasn't sure if she had or not.

He was certain about one thing, though: this situation could not go on any longer, as it was now becoming intolerable and causing him indescribable stress and anxiety.

*Maybe I should go to the police before Trish does*, he thought, *and just tell them the truth and trust in their ability to make sense of it all.*

Then he began to wonder if it might be better if he were to grab the bull by the horns and confront Trish about the whole situation, including her reasons for paying Akmal to assault and mug him.

His head hurt.

# CHAPTER 40

18 November 2017

The next day Sam woke around 8.00 a.m. and went out on to the balcony. It was a particularly beautiful and unseasonably hot day and there were already people at the pool, with a few pigeons also evident around the fringes.

Assuming that he'd been dumped by his feathered friend in favour of better pickings, he headed down to breakfast, leaving his towel on a bed by the pool en route. His intention was to spend some time relaxing by the pool this morning, or at least to try to. So, after a very light breakfast of cereal, fruit juice and some cheese and cold meats, he made his way to the pool, settled down on a sunbed, and began to reflect on the events of the previous evening – specifically his meeting with Audrey.

However, his thoughts began to drift towards the

conversation he had had with Trish the previous day, and the information she had given him about Heather's estranged husband and his business interests.

Sam was aware from recent press and media investigations and coverage in his own publications, that nail bars or salons were one of the fastest growing business on the High Street, with more of them being opened than any other business in the last year. He went online on his smartphone to research the situation further, and confirmed that there were an estimated 30,000 nail bars or salons in the UK. In a sinister twist, it seemed that many of the staff were smuggled into Britain illegally by organised gangs of human traffickers, with several hundred having been prosecuted to date that year alone.

On arrival, the women were reportedly treated as slaves and made to work as prostitutes and drug farmers. Many young females interviewed by police had described how they were illegally trafficked to Britain from Vietnam, with the promise of a job in a beauty salon or as a model. They were also reportedly led to believe that the British authorities dealt with illegal immigrants more leniently than authorities in other countries.

Research had also revealed that Vietnamese drug gangs used nail bars as a convenient legal cover for their activities, while male workers were also trafficked with the promise of highly paid jobs, then made to work long hours in menial hard jobs like car washes for a pittance. Police raids had found there to be illegal workers in Glasgow, Clydebank and many areas of Lanarkshire.

Some workers would arrive and simply claim asylum, giving them the legal right to stay in the UK while awaiting a decision on their application, a process which could take months, even years. While they waited, they'd often be put to work in a salon, paid in only food and accommodation in unhygienic and overcrowded, cramped conditions or living in the salon itself.

So, this was one of the businesses that Rab Lindsay was into, thought Sam. Well, according to Trish it was, and she seemed to know a lot, while claiming she didn't.

What was she up to, he wondered? And why had she been following him since he arrived? He had to assume she'd been doing this, as it was the only explanation for her knowing that he and Heather had gone to his hotel.

He also now knew that it was no accident that she had bumped into him that fateful night after she had paid Akmal to mug him. But again, why had she done this? He still couldn't figure it out. Was it related to Heather's death in any way? And did she really believe that he had caused it?

Surely if she thought he was a murderer she wouldn't be happy to meet up with him on his own in isolated locations late at night? Particularly if she believed that he regarded her as a threat to him and wanted to stop her going to the police.

And would she really go to the police, given her own illicit involvement in inciting and paying someone to commit a criminal act? An act perpetrated against someone she didn't know from Adam less than a week ago, but who she was now threatening to expose as a criminal, too. Not just a criminal, either – a murderer. A murderer of a woman that she also claimed not to know but again seemed to know a lot about.

He needed to try and make sense of all the information that was running around chaotically and amorphously in his head. However, his ability to concentrate was being hampered by a large crowd of people from Northern Ireland who had arrived at the pool and were being particularly and irritatingly raucous. Two of them, whom he took to be a mother and daughter, had decided to sit very close to him; they'd taken the art of banal and mind numbingly boring conversation to another dimension, having been discussing milk and bread for what seemed like an eternity.

He had just decided that enough was enough, and was about to call it a day, for his sanity if nothing else, when Audrey appeared beside him, looking particularly attractive and glamorous. She was wearing a black and gold patterned bikini, covered by a sheer black chiffon-type wrap, while her hair was wrapped in a matching scarf. The outfit was rounded off by a pair of black and gold roman-style sandals.

"Good Morning, Mr Sam, how are we on this lovely day?" she asked, smiling at him.

"I'm very well," lied Sam, adding; "I was actually just thinking about heading off elsewhere for some lunch – it's a little bit too noisy and busy this morning for me." At this, the young woman from 'Norn Iron' and her 'mammy' threw a withering look in his direction.

"Sounds like a plan," said Audrey. "Would you mind if I joined you? I never made breakfast and I'm feeling quite hungry."

Sam wasn't really sure how he felt about this, given the events of the previous evening, but found himself responding, "Sure, if you like, that would be nice," before adding, "I just assumed that you would be meeting your friends."

"Maybe later. I haven't made any arrangements so far and anyway I can catch them anytime. And it's nice to have a bit of male company for a change."

"You mean I didn't put you off by boring you to death last night, then?" said Sam.

"Not at all! Hopefully the feeling is mutual?" Audrey asked.

"Absolutely," said Sam. Surprisingly, he actually sounded as if he meant it, and then realised that he did, as he had indeed enjoyed her company. He also couldn't deny that he felt attracted to her.

"OK, in that case I need to go and change into something more suitable," said Audrey, adding, "Don't worry, I won't be long. I'm not one of those women who take ages to get ready."

"I wasn't worried," said Sam, I was just thinking that you looked lovely as you are."

"Flattery will get you everywhere," she replied, smiling, before heading off to change.

After some thought, and recalling the two couples that he had seen at the beach bar earlier in the week, Sam thought that he should probably change out of his swim shorts and tee shirt if he wasn't to look out of place beside Audrey. So he called to tell her that he would meet her in the lobby in five minutes, and after changing into dress shorts and a casual shirt, he was there in ten. Audrey arrived five minutes later.

While he was waiting for Audrey, her comment about not being "one of those women who take ages to get ready" reminded him of the wife of one of his friends from years ago, who had always been late for everything. The issue was so bad that if they were going out together or with other couples they had to tell her that they were meeting at least an hour earlier in order that they weren't kept really late, particularly if they'd booked a meal or a show.

Even more annoyingly, she had a habit of then spending half the evening in the bathroom once they were out, doing god knows what. He remembered commenting to his wife and his other friends, both male and female, who had agreed with him, that she never looked dramatically different on her return. Sam actually regarded it as quite ignorant, disrespectful and selfish, and never understood how his friend put up with her, as it would have driven him mad. If truth be told, he found it hard to hide his annoyance and consequently they had never got on.

It was all the more unbelievable, then, that in later years, after she and his friend had separated, she had contacted him out of the blue and then subsequently turned up at a couple of his gigs with the band. She actually managed to get there on time, too! In later years, Kim, who had always been the exact opposite – punctual and conscientious – accused him of similar tardiness, and if he was honest, she had had a point. For whatever reason, he had gradually become increasingly more laid back and lethargic whist also being less considerate and attentive towards her and his responsibilities in general. He wondered if it was because he knew that it didn't matter anyway, as nothing he ever did appeared to make any difference to their relationship, which to all effects and purposes was over by then.

His thoughts were interrupted by Audrey, who arrived looking even lovelier than before. She certainly had an effortless style and poise about her, to the extent that he regarded her as totally out of his league, which then made him wonder again about her apparent and inexplicable interest in him. However, he had decided that he would proceed cautiously and hope that eventually everything would be revealed and make sense. At least she was still alive, which had to be regarded as a positive for both of them, given his track record so far.

*What would she think if I told her everything?* he wondered. *Would she also insist that I go to the police and then, like Trish, threaten to do so, if I didn't?*

*Would her attitude towards me change dramatically because of being afraid of what might happen to her? And if so, who could blame her?*

His head still hurt.

# CHAPTER 41

Trish hadn't really expected or anticipated recent developments. However, whist it didn't really make a great deal of difference to the overall situation, she was slightly concerned that there was a danger that the introduction of a rogue element could affect the decision-making process. Nevertheless, she still believed that it wasn't anything that couldn't be overcome, and that hopefully, with the right influence, inducement and leverage, it might actually work out in her favour. The intended outcome – justice for the innocent and the dead – could still be achieved. After all, there was still a trump card to be played.

# CHAPTER 42

18 November 2017

Sam and Audrey walked towards Levante Beach, then walked the length of the promenade to the Placa de Castell, or Castilla Mirador, as it is also known, a beautiful promontory situated on top of the rock separating the Levante and Poniente beaches.

The rock was actually the base of the fortress built to defend the people of the region from Algerian pirate raids during the fourteenth, fifteenth and sixteenth centuries. With its stunning blue and white marbled balustrades and immaculate tiling, which arguably look more Greek than Spanish, this whitewashed and decorated Belvidere effortlessly highlighted this part of the landscape, while providing a sensational viewpoint of both beaches and out to sea.

They found a very pleasant café bar and ordered lunch and a bottle of Rioja Blanco to share. It was all very pleasant, providing welcome respite from the ongoing trauma and inner turmoil that Sam was experiencing. However, he found that his mind began to drift towards thoughts of whether he should tell Audrey all about his predicament and Trish's part in it. He hoped that he would then be able to press her for more information about Trish and the nature and extent of her relationship with Heather, if indeed she had one. However, Audrey again managed to distract him from his thoughts by raising her glass towards him, clinking it with his and proposing a toast.

"To the guy and his monkey, Cheers."

Sam realised that he hadn't even asked about how her night was and if she had enjoyed the act and apologised accordingly for this omission.

"So, how was the 'guy with the monkey'?" he asked.

"I don't know," said Audrey, "he was just finishing as we arrived. I don't think we are meant to see this act."

"At least you actually saw him. I was beginning to doubt he actually existed. So, did you just stay there, or go somewhere else?" asked Sam, more out of conversation than curiosity.

"No, we just stayed and watched the next act, a Beatles tribute act. They were very good. But there was a drag act on after them and she, I mean he, was rubbish."

Sam smiled. "I know, unfortunately!"

Audrey surprised him by saying, "Anyway enough about monkeys and drag acts, tell me about you, Sam." He was not expecting such a direct question and consequently he was initially quite taken aback.

However, he was able to recover his composure sufficiently to appear unfazed, and proceeded to tell her some pretty basic stuff about his life, which was mainly what he thought she wanted to hear – that he was still married, but that it was over and they had been separated for some time. However, he did not go into any detail about his marriage or the reasons for it ending. Nor did he attribute any blame for this to either himself or his estranged wife, instead sticking to some fairly routine stuff about this holiday being a much needed break from the pressures of work and other stresses. He also didn't make any mention of or reference to the blackmail threat.

Audrey shared some equally basic and safe details of her own life and current circumstances; she was also married, but had been separated from her ex for some time, although they had never got round to formally divorcing. However, she was adamant that this wasn't due to any lingering affection for her estranged husband, informing Sam that they hadn't spoken for years despite having a daughter, who was in her thirties, who lived with her partner in Madrid. She worked there, teaching English, and the two of them saw each other about four times a year, taking turns to visit each other.

She took her mobile phone from her bag and began showing him some photos of her daughter, who was very attractive, like her mother.

"She has her mother's looks," said Sam.

"There's that flattery again," Audrey said, smiling and adding, "It's nice, I like it. Do you mind if I take a selfie of us?"

She got her phone ready, again not waiting for an answer.

"I'm flattered that you want to have your picture taken with me, but to be honest I'm not that keen on getting my photo taken," said Sam. "I'm not very photogenic." In truth he didn't know how he felt about being photographed with anyone under the circumstances.

"Oh, behave" said Audrey, and took several photos of them, which she then looked at to check before sharing them with him.

"Do you want me to send them to you?" she asked, adding "You'll need to give me your number." At the same time, she began flicking through the photos on her phone.

"Would you like to see some of the photos that I took last night in the club with the crowd? Look, we actually got one with the guy with the monkey."

And indeed she had. There she was with all her friends and the guy with the monkey. And in amongst them, at the back of the crowd, was Trish. Just there, and no more, but she was there, looking equally as ill at ease as he felt about being photographed.

As Sam wasn't that taken aback to see Trish in the photograph, he didn't react in the obviously dramatic and unsettled fashion as he had the previous night, which thankfully Audrey hadn't mentioned again.

However, it was now clear that Trish and Audrey were acquainted, but to what extent? Was she just part of the crowd or were they close friends? And if so, was Trish aware of his recent liaisons with Audrey? Or perhaps even involved in them in some way? While he was ruminating over all the different options and permutations of the situation, the waiter approached and asked if there was anything else he could get them.

"Just the bill," said Sam, looking at Audrey, hoping for her agreement as he didn't want any more to drink.

Also, as much as he was enjoying her company, he also felt that he needed to have the time on his own that so far he had not been able to manage, to try and come to some conclusions and hopefully, decisions. Audrey nodded her assent and went into her purse, saying, "This is on me."

"Not at all. I invited you, so it's my treat," replied Sam, feeling flush with his new found solvency.

"I think you'll find, if you remember, that I invited myself."

Sam knew that she had indeed invited herself, but

decided that discretion was the better part of valour in his instance and insisted. "It's been my pleasure; you can return the compliment some other time if you want."

"Well I do want," said Trish. "How about tonight? Dinner on me. I know a great restaurant called El Ducado, which does the most delicious Mediterranean food. Or if you don't fancy that idea there's a really nice Chinese restaurant near the main drag we could go to."

"You choose; I'm happy with either, but I can't help thinking I've ended up getting the better deal," said Sam, now completely abandoning all his previous reservations and caution.

"Not at all, it's worth it for the company alone," said Audrey, stroking his arm affectionately and looking meaningfully into his eyes.

Sam was thinking that all of a sudden the situation seemed to be moving along at something of a pace, while also questioning its legitimacy. But this was not reflected in his response.

"What time do you want to meet up?"

So much for taking a cautious approach!

"Why don't we meet up at 7.00 p.m. in the hotel bar?" answered Audrey.

"Sounds like a plan," said Sam, finishing his wine, paying the bill and leaving a tip before they headed off back to the hotel.

# CHAPTER 43

18 November 2017

When they arrived back at the hotel, Audrey thanked Sam for a lovely day and kissed him on the cheek, while adding that she was looking forward to more of the same later. On arriving at his room, Sam lay down on the bed, with the intention of going over all the events of the last few days again and hopefully making some sense of it all. However, probably because of the effect of the food and wine, he drifted off after just a few minutes and awoke feeling quite groggy and disorientated about two and a half hours later, roused by the noise of his phone ringing. He didn't even need to look to know it would be Trish.

"Good evening, how have you been today?"

"Busy," he said, dispassionately.

"Oh really, doing what?" she asked.

"Enjoying my holiday," replied Sam, trying not to

sound too disagreeable and dismissive, for fear of aggravating her unnecessarily.

"You don't sound like you're relaxed and enjoying your holiday. Are you sure you're OK?"

"I've been better, but at least the weather's been nice," he answered.

"Yes, it has, and it's quite mild tonight. Fancy a walk and a talk ?"

"I can't tonight," said Sam. "I . . . I'm meeting someone."

"Oh, that sounds interesting," said Trish. "Anybody I know?"

"What? No, no," said Sam, momentarily startled and unable to think of anything else to say. Fortunately Trish filled the silence.

"Well how about lunch tomorrow, then?"

Sam wondered if she knew that he'd been seeing Audrey, but realised there was nothing to be gained by being difficult and dragging the situation out. Besides, he was intrigued to find out what she wanted to talk about and what her 'proposition' was.

"OK, where shall we go?" he asked.

"How about we meet outside the same beach bar on the Levante promenade? We can walk along to the Balcon del Mar and have some lunch."

"Where is that?" said Sam. When she explained further, he realised it was the same place that he had gone with Audrey the previous day; she'd just been using a different name for it.

*What the fuck is going on?* he thought. *Why is she suggesting the same place I had lunch with Audrey? Am I reading too much into this and is it just a coincidence? Or does she know that we were there yesterday and deliberately messing with my head?*

Despite his reservations, he heard himself saying, "OK – sounds like a plan. What time?"

*So much for rest and contemplation,* he thought as he ended the call, having agreed to meet Trish at 12.00 p.m. the following day. *I'm beginning to think that there are forces at work, deliberately trying to stop me from making sense of this whole fucking mess.*

Reality intruded, and he remembered that he needed to get showered and changed to meet Audrey in the bar in less than an hour. "No rest for the wicked," he muttered to himself, then instantly reproached himself for doing so. If he didn't believe that he was the good guy, nobody else would.

# CHAPTER 44

18 November 2017

Sam arrived at the hotel bar at 7.00 p.m. exactly. It was relatively quiet. He sat at the bar and proceeded to assess his surroundings and the people inside, which had now become something that he did routinely, a commonplace occurrence as a consequence of recent events. He got the impression that the people in the bar appeared to have already dined and were now enjoying a post-meal drink. Sam ordered himself a drink, not feeling the need to sink it in a couple of gulps this time.

There was no sign of Audrey, and ten minutes later she still hadn't appeared. However, she arrived a few minutes later, looking stunning and turning a few heads in the bar, not all of them male, either. The woman certainly knew how to dress and make an entrance, he thought.

"Sorry I'm late," she said.

"A woman's prerogative," replied Sam, adding, " . . . And when you look like that, it's worth the wait."

"You really are quite gifted in the flattery department," said Audrey. "A girl could get used to it, given the opportunity."

Sam didn't respond, instead asking Audrey what she wanted to drink and then ordering.

"Shall we get a seat?" said Sam rhetorically, slipping off his bar stool and handing Audrey her gin and tonic. As they sat down at a nearby table, Audrey said, "I didn't book anything. I thought we would just see what place had availability and take it from there."

"That's fine with me," said Sam. "I'm sure it'll be lovely wherever we go."

"Well if the company is anything to go by, we're off to a good start," said Audrey, smiling and raising her glass.

"I'll drink to that," said Sam, "Cheers."

# CHAPTER 45

18 November 2017

Sam and Audrey were lucky and managed to get a table at El Ducado, where they enjoyed lovely food and drink, although Sam found himself being quite restrained in his consumption of the latter, while not being entirely sure why.

As they ate and drank, they talked about anything and everything, but nothing really significant, revealing or meaningful. As they finished their meal, Audrey looked at Sam and said, "I really enjoy being with you, Sam, you're very good company."

Sam, surprised again at such praise, said in response, "Who's the flatterer now?"

"I've been taking lessons from a master," said Audrey. "And besides I thought it was time I returned the compliment."

"Well thanks, I'm very flattered," said Sam, "And

the feeling is mutual."

Audrey smiled, looked at Sam lingeringly, then touched his hand before saying; "I'm glad, and so happy that you walked into the hotel bar yesterday."

"Me too," said Sam. Because he couldn't think of anything else to say, he added, "So, what do you want to do now? Do you want to go to a show?"

"What, to look for the disappearing double act?" said Audrey. "Doesn't seem much point from what you've said."

"I suppose so, we'd probably just be disappointed again."

"And neither of us would want that, would we, Mr Sam?"

Sam wondered if she was referring to the fact that he still hadn't told her his surname, but he decided to ignore it.

"No, we certainly wouldn't."

Audrey smiled. "I was thinking more along the lines of a quiet night in; maybe you could help me finish that bottle of Rioja Blanco?"

Sam couldn't think of anything that he wanted to do more, but alarm bells were ringing loudly in his head. What was he doing? Was he out of his fucking mind? Could he really go ahead with this? At the same time, it felt completely right, completely natural. At least, that's what he told himself.

*It's not like she's going to have to leave in the middle of the night to go anywhere*, he reasoned, assuming that they would be going to her room.

So, instead of being cautious, trusting his instincts and thinking with his brain instead of his bollocks, he again heard himself saying "sounds like a plan", while realising that this was in danger of becoming something of a catchphrase.

He drained the last of his beer from his glass, as he said it. Audrey finished her gin and tonic, then slowly got up from her seat and headed towards the door.

Sam reciprocated by following her.

# CHAPTER 46

18 November 2017

Audrey's room was a small suite, with a separate lounge area; it was bigger and nicer than Sam's, if a bit untidy. However, she didn't seem particularly bothered or embarrassed by this and simply moved the clothes and any other stuff from the area where the two sofas were in order that they could sit down, which Sam did. She poured them both a glass of the Rioja Blanco, and sat on the opposite sofa rather than beside him, raising her glass in a toast, while maintaining eye contact with him and smiling seductively.

"Very nice," said Sam, after taking a drink of his wine.

"I'm glad you like it," said Audrey, standing up and moving towards him. She leaned down and kissed him full on the mouth, running her hands through his hair. Sam stood up and returned the kiss, while also pulling her towards him and feeling himself becoming aroused.

"I need to powder my nose," she said, walking towards the bathroom, leaving Sam sipping his wine and shaking his head almost in disbelief, as he thought about the events of the last week and where he was now.

Audrey emerged from the bathroom wearing the chiffon wrap that she had worn at the pool earlier in the day. Only this time she wasn't wearing a bikini under it. In fact she wasn't wearing anything else at all. She again sat down on the sofa opposite Sam and asked if he liked her 'jammies'.

"Very much," said Sam, "And also what's inside." He marvelled at his own confident, calm demeanour; inside he was feeling quite uncertain and nervous, while at the same time being very excited.

"You could run courses in flattery," she said.

"It's all about the quality of the material you're working with," he replied, "And I'm not talking about the 'jammies'."

*Christ, where is this coming from?* he wondered to himself, but grateful that it was coming from somewhere.

"Would you like to see more?" Audrey asked.

"That's the best rhetorical question that I have ever heard, bar none," said Sam. He was on a roll, now.

"I'll take that as a yes, then," said Audrey, getting up

from the sofa and opening the curtains and blinds before turning off the lights. "I prefer the moonlight," she said.

She then returned to the sofa opposite Sam and began to touch herself all over. "I'm very wet," she moaned, softly.

"And I'm very hard," said Sam, touching the all too obvious bulge in his denims.

"Maybe we could help each other out with our respective issues, then," said Audrey, getting up and moving towards the bed.

"You read my mind," said Sam, desperately trying to sound and remain calm and in control.

Audrey lay down on the bed and continued to fondle herself more sensuously and urgently. "Oh god, I want you so much," she gasped.

Sam began to remove his clothes, moving towards Audrey on the bed as he did so. When he was beside her, she reached out and grabbed his erect manhood and began to fondle and play with it. Sam reciprocated by finding her sex with his hand; it was very moist, and receptive to his touch. Audrey began moaning very loudly, and pushed Sam's head down between her legs, which she then proceeded to wrap around his shoulders.

When he found her sex with his mouth and tongue she let out a groan of pleasure that made him even harder. She began to shake uncontrollably, rising up off the bed till only her hands and feet were touching it, and letting a guttural, high-pitched, almost silent scream and a stream of obscenities, before collapsing back down on the bed with a soft moan.

When she had recovered her equilibrium, she said, "I need to feel you inside me, but I want to taste you first." She began to touch and fondle his erection until it was so hard it was almost painful, before moving down the bed and taking him in her mouth, looking up at him and holding eye contact the whole time.

Sam was in so much ecstasy that he began to worry about being able to control his urges in order to fulfil Audrey's need to have him inside her. So he reached down and gently lifted her head.

"If I don't get inside you now, there won't be any point," he said.

"I want you to come," said Audrey,

"And I will," said Sam, "but I want it for both of us."

"So unselfish," said Audrey, and moved herself up till she was on top of him, feeling him filling her effortlessly. She began slowly moving up and down, moaning and sighing loudly. Gradually, however, she began to move faster and more urgently, to the point where she seemed to be losing control and heading towards another climax. Suddenly, she stopped and rolled off on to her back, pulling him on top of her. Sam felt as if he could have climaxed there and then, however he wanted to savour the experience, which he was finding increasingly erotic, and to enjoy being inside Audrey a little bit longer.

He tried to hold off his orgasm by slowing down, but not for long, as Audrey began screaming dramatically, as she again approached another fulfilment. Sam lost control, giving in to his own carnal urges and then felt the inevitable spasmodic, blissful and ecstatic feelings envelop him as he juddered to a sensational climax.

"That was delicious," said Audrey, after she had recovered her breath and bearings.

Sam didn't think he would be able to say anything coherent, so decided to say nothing. They lay together on the bed, bathed in sweat, with shafts of moonlight piercing impudently through the gaps in the blinds. Slowly and gently they both reached out and found each other with their hands and mouths, barely touching and kissing each other, in a very soft and sensual way.

Sam found himself simply looking at Audrey lying naked beside him; he began tracing his fingers slowly and sensuously over the length of her body.

She was in sensational shape for her age, and her skin was surprisingly soft and firm, as were her breasts – so much so that he wondered if she had had surgery to have them lifted or enhanced. Either way, he found himself becoming aroused again and had to shift his position on the bed to accommodate his increasingly expanding appendage.

Audrey, noticing his predicament and discomfiture, reached down and began teasing and tormenting his now swollen, erect member, whist kissing him ravenously on the mouth. Sam responded by first squeezing and then kissing her breasts, which elicited mellifluous moans and sighs of pleasure from Audrey.

"I want you to take me on the balcony," she said, grabbing his arms and pulling him off the bed towards the window.

While initially a bit taken aback by Audrey's unexpected and seemingly spontaneous request, Sam realised that he was also in the full throes of rampant, unbridled, joyous sex, which he was not about to pass up. *In for a penny*, he decided again. He had mistakenly assumed that she wanted to have sex lying down on the balcony, where they would be hidden from the rooms that overlooked them. However, this was clearly not the case, as she stood leaning on the wall facing the hotel opposite, with her legs apart and her bottom positioned so that he could enter her from behind. While initially feeling a bit reticent and apprehensive about the exhibitionistic nature of the situation, Sam also realised that he was finding the whole experience extremely erotic and intoxicating and complied accordingly, with considerable gusto and abandon.

Sam could feel the gentle touch and caress of a

slight breeze on his torso; along with the danger of being seen or heard, he found it to be a real turn on. He felt Audrey's muscles tighten as she made a slow, sensuous moaning sound before telling him breathlessly that she was about to come again. This heightened his own arousal, and ultimately brought him to another shattering orgasm.

They both came together and collapsed in a heap simultaneously, lying spent on the floor of the balcony for some time, before either of them was able to move. Sam's legs felt as if he had borrowed them from someone else, they were so weak. After several minutes of relative silence, Audrey rolled over towards Sam and curled up beside him. She kissed his neck, looked at him and said, "I knew I was right about you."

"Meaning what?" he replied.

"You don't disappoint," she said, smiling lasciviously.

"Ditto," said Sam.

# CHAPTER 47

18 November 2017

Sam and Audrey lay on the bed with just a sheet over them, drinking wine and reflecting on their recent intimacy and the events that had taken place since their initial meeting.

"It seems we've known each other a lot longer than a couple of days," said Sam.

"Probably because we have managed to squeeze a lot in," said Audrey.

Sam nearly spilled his wine. "More flattery!" he laughed.

Audrey, realising what she had just said, also burst out laughing too. "This is lovely, Sam," she said. "I'm very happy, and very satisfied."

"Me, too," said Sam, who was just happy that, unlike Heather, Audrey hadn't asked the "What are you thinking about?" question. Not because he didn't want to answer it, which he didn't, but because he knew if he thought about it, it would affect his mood. And, he was right, because as soon as he began to think about it, he realised that he couldn't possibly begin to feel really happy or content until the threats hanging over him were dealt with.

It was also in danger of ruining the special moment they were sharing together. Audrey seemed to sense this. "Oh that wasn't very convincing," she said, and on receiving no response or reassurance, she sat up and looked at him.

"What's wrong?"

Sam was still contemplating telling Audrey about the shit storm he found himself in and also about his initial and subsequent meetings with Trish, particularly as there was every chance that they would run into her again while together. However, clearly this was now a different proposition, given their apparent relationship, whatever the extent of that was.

And, even if she and Trish weren't particularly close, he realised that the prospect of taking Audrey into his confidence still filled him with dread. Mainly because of the worry and the fear that she would not believe that he had had nothing to do with Heather's murder and judge him like Trish had done. He decided to continue to play things close to his chest for the time being, and placated Audrey by telling her that it was nothing to worry about, hoping that she didn't push it any further. Thankfully, for him, whether it was the way he said it or the look on his face, she didn't ask why and after cuddling up together they both drifted into sleep, wrapped in each other's arms.

# CHAPTER 48

19 November 2017

It was another glorious day when Sam awoke, not least because he was still in Audrey's bed. He had dreamt about Heather, but the dream was one of those that involved him being aware, while he was dreaming, that it was just a dream and nothing was real. However, a further surreal element was that this also included anything that had happened since he arrived in Benidorm, including his meetings with Trish and Audrey. So when he woke up he half expected to find himself back home in Glasgow.

Not surprisingly, on discovering that it was all still very real, he found that he had mixed emotions; while on one hand he wished that the situation with Heather hadn't happened, he also found himself feeling relieved and glad that Audrey was real and still lying beside him. Unfortunately, reality again intruded into his world as he remembered that he had arranged to meet Trish at the beach bar at midday.

Sam felt bad about not telling Audrey that he was meeting up with Trish, but he just felt that he wasn't yet ready to try and explain everything that had happened yet. Christ, he could hardly believe and make sense of it himself. No, he would go and hear what Trish had to say and make decisions accordingly, assuming that she was going to say something.

He also reminded himself mentally to remember to turn his phone off so that if Audrey decided to call him later, it didn't become awkward.

Audrey told Sam that she didn't feel like breakfast when he woke her to ask her, so he told her that he was going on his own and he would catch her later at some point. If truth be told, Sam didn't really feel that hungry either, but he was glad of the opportunity to make his escape without any need for explanations. However, he subsequently also decided that he might as well have breakfast as he had no desire to go through the charade of lunch with Trish, even if she was buying.

Sam showered in his own room and then went to breakfast, after which he went back to his own balcony and sat there, pondering his imminent meeting with Trish, and wondering what it would bring. There were already people at the pool but no sign of the pigeon or any of his pals at the pool or on the balcony.

At that point Sam's mind drifted back to the very

passionate encounter on Audrey's balcony the previous evening. The memory caused him to feel aroused all over again, and he had to stop thinking about it in order to remain focused on the more pressing matter at hand. However, he also had to smile at the memory of a conversation initiated by some women at his workplace some years previously.

One of them had mischievously asked who had had "done the business" on a balcony on holiday, while citing it as an almost obligatory rite of passage for couples going on holiday together – much like the unwritten law stating that couples are expected to have sex the night before one of them goes off on holiday on their own or with friends.

He remembered that the subject had generated much light-hearted banter and debate, finally descending into farce and hilarity as the main point of contention ended up being what the difference was between a balcony and a veranda. *Oh, if only such trivia was all he had to worry about now*, he thought.

# CHAPTER 49

19 November 2017

Trish was at the beach bar when Sam arrived, rising from her seat to greet him and give him a peck on the cheek. However, Sam was in no mood for false pleasantries and slowly moved his head back and away from her. Trish reacted to this by looking offended.

"Nice to see you, too! Can I get you a drink, or will we walk to the Balcon?"

"I don't want a drink," said Sam. He had absolutely no desire to sully the memory of the enjoyable day he had spent with Audrey the previous day by spending time there with Trish, either.

"Well, this is a good start" said Trish. "Do you want to walk, or sit here and talk?"

"That depends on what else you have to say," said Sam, curtly.

"Well that very much depends upon what *you* have

to say to *me*," Trish retorted.

"In regard to what?" said Sam, being deliberately obtuse, but at the same time sitting down at the seat opposite.

"In regard to what we spoke about before," Trish replied, with incredulity in her voice. "I can't believe that you have to ask; have you really forgotten?"

"Oh no, I remember fine," said Sam, boldly. "You're referring to how you tried to blame me for something I didn't do and to make me feel guilty about it."

"Maybe you feel guilty because you *did* do something," said Trish, reactively.

"Look, I admitted that I spent part of the night with the woman, but she was killed after she left me. I didn't murder her!"

"Yes, I know that's what you keep saying, but if you didn't do it, why are you so reluctant to go to the police?"

"I already told you why," said Sam, "Why don't you believe me?"

"Why should I believe you? If anything, it just makes you look even more guilty, that and you begging me not to go to the police."

"You can't seriously think that I killed her?" said Sam, "What possible reason could I have? I liked her. We had a lovely night together."

This elicited a fairly disgusted and scornful look

from Trish.

"Spare me the details of your sordid little liaison. I've only got your word that you had a 'lovely night', anyway.

"For all I know it could've been the exact opposite," she added, inverting her little finger in an exaggerated drooping gesture, "Resulting in a disappointment or a rejection. And maybe you couldn't handle it. Maybe she left after you had an argument, or you felt humiliated and followed her to get even, to take your revenge."

"Where are you getting this nonsense from?" said Sam. "I mean really, honestly? In the time we have spent together do I seem the kind of person who would do something like that?"

As soon as he had said it Sam realised how incongruous it was with the reality of the situation, given what he now knew about Trish's actions and specifically her involvement with Akmal. When he first met her he would never have believed that she could've been responsible for sanctioning and commissioning such an act against him. However, he still didn't think it was the time and place to be up front with her about this. He wasn't altogether sure why but, for whatever reason, he believed that this might yet prove to be more valuable and helpful to him in the days to come, as few as they were. So, he decided to keep it to himself for the time being.

"Oh come on, we still don't really know one another, do we? It hasn't even been a week," Trish said, reading his mind.

*It seems like longer*, thought Sam. Then, reflecting upon his conversation with Audrey the previous evening and her comment about squeezing a lot in, he actually found himself trying to suppress a smile.

Trish looked at him. "I'm glad you find this all so amusing. For all I know, you already knew her and had planned this whole thing."

"What?" said Sam, totally taken aback by this ridiculous accusation. "You're the one who knew her!" he said, instinctively and defensively, and cursing himself for saying it.

He hadn't planned on revealing or discussing the information divulged by Audrey about Trish and Heather's history just yet, again for reasons that he didn't fully understand.

"What do you mean by that?" said Trish.

"You admitted to knowing her and her husband when we spoke previously," said Sam, hoping that he sounded calm and convincing.

"I said I knew *of* them," replied Trish, reactively and aggressively, and looking at him with what seemed suspicion in her eyes. "As did a lot of people, remember?"

"Well, you knew more about her – them – than I did. I hadn't even heard about her – them – before I met her. And now I wish I hadn't met her at all."

"I thought you had a nice time together?" said Trish, sarcastically.

"You know what I mean."

Trish didn't respond, while continuing to look at him accusingly. At least, that's how she made him feel. So much so that he felt the need to respond.

"Look, if I had left my hotel and followed her it would probably have been picked up by CCTV, and that didn't happen," he said, calmly.

"Only because it's a CCTV blind spot," said Trish, before adding, "according to the papers."

"I don't recall reading anything in the press about CCTV location information," said Sam, eying her warily.

"Maybe I heard it on the TV, or from someone in the bar the other night, I can't remember," said Trish, in a fairly casual and throwaway manner.

*Well I can always check that out with Audrey,* thought Sam, *and ask her if she knows anything about the CCTV.*

Trish interrupted his thoughts. "So, have you decided if you are going to go the police or not?"

"What will you do if I don't?"

"Remember the proposition we talked about?" said Trish.

"WE never talked about anything. YOU mentioned it then said it would keep," Sam reminded her. "So what's it all about?"

"Maybe we can do each other a favour," said Trish.

"What kind of a favour?" said Sam, intrigued and hopeful that he would finally get some information that would help explain the whole mess he found himself in.

"It'll keep," said Trish, before getting up to go and then looking back over her shoulder and adding, "but not for much longer. I'll be in touch."

# CHAPTER 50

19 November 2017

After Trish left, Sam ordered himself a beer and sat looking out to sea, wondering how this situation was going to pan out. He began to wonder again if he should just go to the police; hopefully that would get Trish off his back, and everything out into the open. But then he realised that that would probably result in him having a whole other set of problems to deal with, starting with him having to prove his whereabouts at the relevant time on the night in question, if he was to establish his innocence.

The police would no doubt want to know why he hadn't come forward earlier, and with all of this happening in a foreign country, he might also be required to remain in Spain for a considerably longer period of time. He hesitated to contemplate it, but he could even end up in prison, and a Spanish prison at that; apart from being unthinkable, this obviously had implications for his job and life in general. *But what life do I have?* he reflected, ruefully. *I don't have a life. I was an accident waiting to happen, and that has finally happened. And I might not need to worry about that for much longer if I can't prove that I didn't murder Heather.*

Sam's head was really hurting now; the horrible shaky feeling in his stomach persisted, and was showing no signs of quitting anytime soon. He finished his drink, no clearer or further forward in terms of making a decision.

As he was making his way back to the hotel, his phone rang – he'd forgotten to turn it off after all. He saw that it was Audrey and was immediately relieved she hadn't phoned while he was with Trish. He realised that once again he was behaving like he was guilty of something. This also finally made him decide that he was going to have to tell Audrey everything that had happened, and just take the chance that she would react in a reasonable and sympathetic way, even if Trish was her friend. He needed to know if that was the case, and if there was anything she could, or would, tell him about Trish. It was a chance he was going to have to take. And he wouldn't need to wait long.

"Hello stranger, you left in a hurry. Where are you?" asked Audrey, when Sam picked up the call.

"Just on my way back to the hotel," said Sam. "I went for a walk after breakfast. Where are you?"

"I'm just having some lunch at the pool bar," said Audrey. "Want to join me? I brought my book but I can't seem to concentrate. I wonder why?"

Sam's mind was so preoccupied that he totally missed the reference to the previous night's events. "Why?" he asked.

"Why do you think, lover? I was paying you a compliment!" said Audrey. "Are you ok?"

"Oh right, yes, sorry," said Sam, feeling awkward. "Look, I think we need to talk, Audrey, but probably not at the pool. Can you come to my room after you've had your lunch?" he asked, as he approached the entrance to their hotel. There was a short silence on the other end of the phone, which seemed like an age, before Audrey answered.

"Sounds serious, but yes, of course. Let me know when you're back."

"I'll text you in a few minutes," said Sam, who had gone straight to his room and was thinking that he would need a drink to get him through it. He poured himself a large glass of red wine and after taking a gulp, he sat down and wondered where he could start to explain the almost unexplainable. But explain he did, with the aid of another glass of red, to a very shocked and disbelieving Audrey, who had arrived looking very serious and concerned and who had also needed a drink to get her through it. After the initial shock had stunned her into silence, she'd eventually found her voice and had gradually begun to ask some questions as he went along. It was clear that she wanted to know all about the events of the previous few days, from his intimate liaison with Heather to the tragic events that followed and his subsequent encounter with Trish.

Sam proceeded to recount their various meetings and conversations, culminating in telling Audrey about Trish threatening him with the police and offering him a mystery 'proposition'. He deliberately left out his subsequent encounters with Akmal, and the latter's claim about Trish engaging his services, though. Neither did he go into any detail about the information that both Trish and Heather had given him about their respective past lives, as he wanted to know what Audrey knew and could tell him.

After almost two hours and nearly another bottle of Rioja Blanco, with both of them talking and listening and asking questions, a picture emerged which affirmed much of the information that Trish had previously provided about her past but with much more detail added.

Audrey knew Trish, but she maintained that she wasn't that friendly with her, despite the pair living near to each other. She claimed that Trish was "just part of the group," if a bit of a loner. She also confirmed much of the information that Trish had told Sam about Heather and her estranged husband, Rab, reiterating a lot of the rumours and allegations about the much talked-about couple.

Audrey also informed Sam that Trish knew Heather better than anyone, while also indicating that no love was lost between the two women without offering any particular reasons why. Sam was too focused on getting basic information to push it any further at that point.

At the end of it all, Sam found himself feeling relieved, if somewhat surprised, that Audrey appeared to accept and believe his version of events after her initial shock. Unlike Trish, she hadn't made him feel like a murderer or threatened to go to the police. Unfortunately, she wasn't able to offer any possible reason or explanation for Trish's behaviour, though, or her apparent obsessive interest in Sam and his situation, unless she really believed that he was guilty of murdering Heather. Like Sam, Audrey wondered why Trish had not just gone to the police. And she agreed that it all seemed very strange. Interestingly, Audrey also advised that she knew nothing about any closed circuit TV blind spot, when asked about it by Sam.

The combined effect of the cumulative emotional highs and lows of the last few days and the wine they'd been drinking had made both Sam and Audrey feel very tired, and they agreed that they needed to sleep, even if only for a short while. Audrey's demeanour and body language indicated that she probably needed some time to come to terms with all the information that she had just been given, and that she felt she needed to be alone. Sam accordingly did not push it by inviting her to stay, believing that discretion was the better part of valour.

Nevertheless, she very politely thanked Sam for the drink, his company and his honesty and then pecked him on the cheek as she left to return to her room, while indicating that she would be in touch. He hoped that she would. And then unfortunately he realised that Trish would be, too, and probably much sooner.

# CHAPTER 51

19 November 2017

While the Watcher realised that the current situation couldn't really have been predicted or anticipated, the main thing was that, via some careful planning and cunning, things were now perfectly in position to ensure that all went according to plan.

The Watcher's extensive, dedicated research, vigil and surveillance had proved beneficial. It had yielded valuable information not only about the Whore but others who were also crucially important to the final outcome.

As far as the Watcher was concerned, it was really only a matter of time before the objective was achieved.

And as far as the Watcher was concerned, it didn't matter what it took, how it was achieved, or at what individual cost, just as long as it was done, preferably without any comeback or risk of discovery. So far, fate and circumstances had converged favourably to allow that to happen. So that in itself was surely a sign that it was meant to be, wasn't it?

Yes, as far as the Watcher was concerned there was no doubt. The intended goal was so close to being fully realised that nothing or anybody could be allowed to get in the way of what was now clearly destiny.

# CHAPTER 52

20 November 2017

As it turned out, Sam didn't hear from Audrey again that night, and nor had he really expected to. Also, despite his tiredness and semi-inebriated state, his mind was still active and restless. Consequently, he slept fitfully, before exhaustion caught up with him and he finally found himself in the arms of Morpheus sometime around 4.00 a.m. However, Trish was as good as her promise to be in touch soon and Sam was awakened by her calling him the next morning at 7.30, telling him – not asking – that they needed to meet as soon as possible.

"I'll come to your hotel," said Sam and arranged to meet her there at 1.00 p.m.

He went to breakfast but hardly ate anything, other than cereal and toast, while drinking copious amounts of fruit juice, coffee and tea.

It was a particularly grey, driech day, which reminded Sam of Glasgow. He almost wished he was back there, with this whole nightmare behind him, or even better, having never happened.

After breakfast, he bought a newspaper and went back to the room to check for any update on the situation. However, there was nothing significant other than confirmation that the local police were continuing their investigations by carrying out visits to nearby hotels.

The newspaper also stated that the authorities had secured the co-operation of a Scottish police officer who was reportedly familiar with the murdered woman's history and situation.

*Be interesting to find out if that includes her estranged husband's illegal business activities and his controlling and abusive treatment of his wife,* thought Sam, but if he was being honest, he wasn't really that hopeful given the way things had turned out so far.

Even the Pigeon appeared to be considering his options, possibly having been made a better offer.

# CHAPTER 53

20 November 2017

As he headed towards Trish's hotel, Sam toyed with calling Audrey to tell her where he was going, but decided against it, feeling that the next contact really needed to come from her. Instead he made up his mind to turn his phone off, deciding that whatever was going to happen, he did not wish to be interrupted. As he was about to do so he received a text from Trish telling him her room number again and saying that she hoped he was on his way.

Sam was experiencing considerable stress and anxiety about the situation he found himself confronted with. However, he was determined to be calm, firm and positive in his response to any demands or threats from Trish; hopefully this would bring things to a head and result in some kind of resolution.

When Sam arrived at Trish's hotel, the police

presence was clearly apparent; initially he assumed that it was related to the murder investigation. He was suddenly gripped by panic, though. Jesus, had Trish gone to the police? Was this a trap? Surely she wouldn't do that, for fear of drawing attention to herself?

He realised that it was probably just part of the police operation; perhaps they were simply making routine enquiries at all hotels in the area. As he made his way through the hotel no one paid him any attention, so he continued his journey unhindered.

He found Trish's room on the second floor of the hotel and knocked on the door softly but firmly. She opened it almost instantly. She welcomed him in and gestured towards the sofa in the small lounge area of her room, which was split level, with a mezzanine. She asked Sam if he wanted something to drink.

"Just some water, if you have any," said Sam, as he felt his mouth starting to dry up.

"So, how have you been?" she asked, as she handed him his drink.

"Better," said Sam, very drily, deliberately making Trish aware that he was not happy about his current predicament and her role in it.

"So, what conclusions have you come to, if any?"

"Sorry?" said Sam, trying to sound as assertive and confident as he could, while also recalling his resolve to be firm and positive.

"In regard to our previous discussion." she

responded, with a look of impatience that indicated that she expected a response from Sam.

"You said something about a proposition and us doing each other a favour," he said, trying to seem as calm and in control as he could, but not entirely certain he was managing it. Why did she make him feel so anxious and guilty, when he had done nothing wrong? Maybe if he kept telling himself that he would start to believe it.

"All in good time," said Trish. "But you haven't answered my question, particularly in regard to whether you have decided to go to the police or not. And if you're not going to go to the police, I have to assume that you're guilty and that you did murder that woman."

"Why? That's nonsense. Are you saying that you're going to the police?"

"If I tell you that I intend to go to the police with that information, will you kill me too?"

"What? No! Don't be ridiculous. I never killed anybody, and I couldn't," said Sam.

"Not even to protect yourself?"

"From what?" I keep telling you I haven't done anything wrong."

"That's not your call to make. It's for the police to decide, based upon the available information."

"Why are you so intent on telling the police?" asked Sam.

"I'm not," Trish replied, "I just need to know what you're prepared to do to prevent me from doing it."

"What? What does that mean?" said Sam. Not getting a response from Trish, he added, "I'm not going to kill you, if that's what you mean. I told you I couldn't kill anyone."

"Not even for money?"

"What kind of question is that? No, of course not, and what's money got to do with it?"

"Just something to sweeten the deal."

"Deal? What deal?"

"You remember the proposition we spoke about?"

"There you go with that WE stuff again," exploded Sam. "You mean the proposition YOU spoke about? And keep speaking about, without actually saying what it is." His mind was racing. Where was she going with this?

"I said that we could do each other a favour," said Trish.

"Yes, but you didn't say what," Sam replied, hoping that she was finally about to reveal what it was she wanted.

"I won't go to the police, if you do something for me."

"What?" asked Sam.

"I want you to kill someone."

# CHAPTER 54

20 November 2017

Initially, Sam wasn't sure if he had heard Trish properly. But then he realised that he had heard her perfectly well and that it was all very real. His initial thought was that she was clearly mad. Or was she just testing him to see what he would say?

Without waiting on an answer Trish continued.

"I'll keep quiet about your little secret if you agree to do this one thing for me. I'll also pay you £30,000 to show my gratitude and appreciation."

Sam just stared at her disbelievingly for a moment.

"Are you fucking serious? You think I could do that? This isn't a fucking movie, this is real life. This is *someone's* life, we are talking about."

*Or death,* he thought.

He remembered that this was the woman who had paid someone money to rough him up for reasons he still wasn't sure about. But this was a whole different ball game. This was off the scale, different planet stuff. His head was swimming, trying to make sense of all the events of the last few days, but he just ended up feeling more confused and panicked.

He wanted to ask Trish about Heather and Akmal but again something stopped him. Instead he heard himself asking her the most unlikely and inappropriate question he could've come up with.

"Who is it that you want me to kill?"

"It'll keep for now," said Trish. "It's on a need to know basis. I'll tell you when you tell me you're going to do it." She got up to show Sam the door. "I'll be in touch soon. Very soon.

"And don't leave the country."

# CHAPTER 55

20 November 2017

Sam could still scarcely believe what had happened and what Trish had said to him. Christ, did she really expect him to kill someone? Was she really serious, or was she testing him out? The more he thought about it, the more he was under no illusions that she was totally serious and that she would be expecting an answer from him sometime soon.

But who did she want him to kill, and why? If his head had hurt before, it was now positively throbbing with bewilderment, disbelief and panic. He also realised that he couldn't keep the development to himself.

He needed to speak to somebody about it, out loud, to help him come to terms with and cope with the reality and utter madness of it all. And the only person he could possibly speak to was Audrey. He was really glad now that he had confided in her regarding the situation, and was reassured that she seemed to have believed his version of events, and that unlike Trish, she hadn't made him feel like a murderer. However, he also realised that, unsurprisingly, it had come as a bit of a shock to her. She was clearly emotionally affected, confused and perhaps even frightened by the whole ludicrousness of the situation.

Sam was also wondering, given the incredulous scenario she was being asked to contend with by a relative stranger, whether she had decided to remove herself from the situation altogether and had perhaps come to the conclusion that her loyalty lay with her friend, Trish.

If that was the case, he reflected, who could blame her? He probably would have felt exactly the same under the circumstances. He suddenly realised that he was beginning to think and feel like he was guilty again.

Sam made his way back to the hotel and on entering the room he realised that this was as low and desperate as he had felt throughout this whole nightmare. He was finding it difficult to think of any positives to hold on to, and to see how and where it was all going to end. As he was considering this, there was a knock on his door.

*Probably the chambermaid with more creative towel arrangements,* he thought. He was just about to discourage her with a "No ahora por favor, vuelve mas tarde," when he heard a voice say, "Room Service for Mr Sam, special VIP service for special customer, me love you long time."

Sam couldn't remember when he'd last felt so happy to hear someone's voice; as he opened the door, he pulled Audrey towards him and hugged her warmly and strongly.

"Now that's what I call a welcome," she said, before kissing him affectionately and softly.

"I wasn't sure if I would see you again," admitted Sam, looking at her with undisguised joy.

Audrey held his gaze and said, "To be honest, I wasn't sure if I could deal with it all, but then I thought, what happened to 'If I want something I go for it'?"

There was a pause, during which she looked deeply into his eyes, before adding, "I hope you're worth the faith and trust I'm about to invest in you."

"I am *so* hot for you right now," said Sam, kissing her back, before stopping himself. "You better sit down."

"Why, what's happened?" she asked in response, looking concerned.

"If you thought that you couldn't deal with the situation before, you better strap yourself in, because it's about to get really fucking mental. And I am about to test the resolve and extent of that faith and trust you are investing in me."

# CHAPTER 56

20 November 2017

As Sam related the details and nature of his earlier discussion with Trish to Audrey, she sat in silence, looking even more unsettled and distressed than she had during their previous conversation. When he had finished, she just sat looking stunned, staring blankly into space.

"Please, say something" said Sam." I swear everything I am telling you is true."

"I . . . I believe you," said Audrey, "but I just don't understand. I mean, why would she ask you to do something like that?"

"I was hoping you might be able to help me out with that."

"What? How? What do you mean?" asked Audrey, puzzled.

"I mean that you know Trish. I only know what she

has told me, which might, or might not be true. But you know her as a person, and you know all about her life and her family. It might help me to understand and work out what this is all about."

Audrey appeared completely overwhelmed by the information and situation that had been presented to her, to the extent that she seemed unable to look at Sam. She'd gone very silent.

"I'm sorry," said Sam, "I shouldn't be asking this of you. I'm sorry for upsetting you. I just don't know what else to do."

"No, it's alright Sam, it's not that." said Audrey, "No need to apologise."

While Sam was relieved that Audrey seemed to be alright and wasn't upset or angry with him, there was also something else in her eyes and her demeanour that seemed to indicate that there was something else that she wanted to say.

"What? What is it?" he asked, intrigued.

"I don't know if I should say, and I don't know if it makes any sense, or has anything to do with it," said Audrey, hesitantly.

"What? What is it that you're thinking about? You need to tell me," Sam said, impatiently, his mind working overtime.

"There was a lot of talk about Heather, and . . ."

"I know about all of that," interrupted Sam, surprisingly curtly. Realising his impatience, he instantly apologised.

Audrey continued, "No, no, I don't mean about Heather and her husband, Rab, I mean about Heather and Trisha's husband, Frank."

"Why? What about him?"

"He had an affair with Heather."

"What?" Sam was completely taken aback, and finding himself feeling very defensive of Heather for some reason. "How do you know that?"

"I just know. A lot of people knew," Audrey answered.

"Did Trish know?" asked Sam, his mind racing, as he started recalling the conversation he had with Heather about the affair she'd had, and realising that Frank fitted the bill. In fact, the more that he thought about it, he knew what Audrey was saying had to be the truth. He just wasn't sure why was she telling him this.

"I think she worked it out eventually. After Frank died," Trish replied.

"Why are you telling me this?" he asked, working out what the answer would be even before she opened her mouth again.

"Because I was already thinking about what happened to Heather, and whether Trish could have had anything to do with it," said Audrey. "Because of . . . you know.

"I didn't think that she could have done something

like that, but now you say that she has asked you to kill someone else, I . . . I just thought I should say something. To you, I mean.

"I haven't said anything to anybody else, only you. Maybe I should have. Do you think I should have, Sam? You don't think that she could have done it, do you Sam?"

Audrey was getting quite emotional now, and Sam didn't know what to think. His mind was full of all different kinds of thoughts and possibilities that were making all sorts of sense and no sense at all.

"I need some air, and a drink," he said, looking at Audrey. "And we need to tell each other everything." He lifted a jacket and asked, "You coming?" Audrey, realising that it wasn't really a question, followed him out.

# CHAPTER 57

20 November 2017

Sam and Audrey found a small bar tucked away behind a restaurant in a small commercial unit; it was almost empty apart from an elderly couple sat in the corner. Sam bought drinks and they took them to the other end of the bar where they could talk, which they did, for some time.

Sam told Audrey what he hadn't told her about Akmal, right down to the Algerian's claim about Trish's involvement. He also went into a lot more detail about the information that both Trish and Heather had given him about their respective lives, some of which Audrey knew and some which she claimed that she didn't.

She seemed particularly surprised to hear Sam outline the details of Heather's reportedly abusive relationship with her husband. Indeed, by contrast, she'd been of the belief, like most people, that they had enjoyed a close relationship, even after they had split up. She was also able to provide Sam with a lot more information about Trish's situation, though, which Trish had clearly either neglected to tell him or deliberately changed to suit her own purposes.

Audrey claimed that what Trish had told Sam in regard to the circumstances of her husband's "failed investment" and reported involvement with a fraudster was factually accurate, up to a point. But – and this was a very significant 'but' – according to Audrey, it wasn't Frank who had been conned, it was Trish herself.

Audrey told Sam how, less than a couple of years after Frank died, Trish had gone on to an online dating website, Plenty of Fish, where she was contacted by and began to exchange messages with a man who would eventually con her out of a large sum of money. As far as Audrey knew from information gleaned from Trish's friends and family – some of whom no longer spoke to her – the man had claimed to be a South African diamond dealer, who, as well as expressing an interest in having a relationship with her, had also offered her the opportunity of benefitting from his involvement in a business deal. He'd told her that it was a sure-fire investment, and stupidly, she believed him. That was until he failed to turn up for a series of meetings and appointments, as agreed, to finalise arrangements and discuss terms.

When she had eventually called her bank, she discovered that she had been the victim of a cruel and heartless deception.

Audrey told Sam that as far as she knew, Trish had also given the fraudster money from her state and works pensions – when pensions were worth something – and had also sold a flat that she had in Torrevieja, Costa Blanca, which she and her husband had bought, shared and enjoyed with their family. The sums of money involved were crazy – Trish had given him over two hundred thousand pounds.

"She only offered me £30,000! To kill somebody, I mean," said Sam. "She must've planned this right from the start, from when she was following me home, or even before. That must've been how she knew that I spent the night with Heather."

This drew a look from Audrey. Sam sheepishly mouthed 'sorry', but she shook her head in polite admonition.

"But why was she following me?" Sam asked nobody in particular, shaking his head. He thought he heard a dog bark, which brought an image back into his head that he had forgotten about. Something else was bothering him, too, something Trish had said, but he couldn't quite bring it to mind and make sense of it. He tried to concentrate, to remember, to think clearly. What was it she said to him the last time they spoke?

Then it came back to him.

She had accused him of already knowing Heather, and of having planned to murder her for some time. It was nonsense, of course. But the more he had thought about it, the more he believed that it had been a strange thing to say, particularly given that she had absolutely no evidence to that effect. But then it occurred to him that, inadvertently or otherwise, Trish had possibly been guilty of projection, and of describing her own intentions and actions. All of a sudden he had a sick, nauseous feeling in the pit of his stomach, as numerous loose ends and unanswered questions seemed to fall into place.

"Oh, Christ. Oh, good God," he said out loud.

Audrey just stared at him. "What?"

Sam had realised that Trish hadn't been following him at all – she had been following Heather.

But why? And was that all she had done?

"Why didn't I see it earlier?" he said out loud. Not waiting for a reply from Audrey, he answered his own question.

"Because I was too wrapped up in my own self-preservation, that's why. What an idiot I am."

"You're being a bit hard on yourself, don't you think?" said Audrey, "I mean . . ."

But Sam was on a roll now. "And that's how she would have known about it being a CCTV blind spot."

"What? Where?" said Audrey, looking even more puzzled.

247

"Remember I asked you if you knew or had heard anybody speaking about the place where Heather was murdered being a CCTV blind spot and you didn't know what I was talking about?"

"Yes, because I didn't," said Audrey.

"I know you didn't, and neither did I. And I still don't. And I'll bet if you ask all the rest of your crowd, none of them will know either. But Trish did. And I'll bet she's right, too."

"Oh, God, so you think that she did kill Heather?" said Audrey.

"I really don't know but it doesn't look good, does it? I mean, you even said that you had thought about it as a possibility yourself."

"I know what I said," Audrey replied, "but I don't think I really believed it. I mean it's like something out of a film."

"I wish it was, but unfortunately it's all too real," said Sam shaking his head in disbelief. And the more he thought about it, the more feasible and likely it was becoming.

"So, what are we going to do?" asked Audrey.

Sam, whist being both surprised and unexpectedly reassured by the "we" in Audrey's response, was silent for what seemed an age before finally answering.

"*We* are going to have another drink," he said, realising that this was becoming his answer to quite a lot of his problems. However, he told himself that it was simply a consequence of the situation he found himself having to deal with, and that it was only a temporary state of affairs. And he was on holiday after all, even if it had long since stopped feeling like one.

"And then what?" asked Audrey, stirring him from his thoughts.

"And then we are going to work out what I am going to say to Trish when I meet up with her tomorrow."

"You're still going to meet with her? Don't you think that you should go to the police? You have to, now."

"You're beginning to sound like Trish," said Sam, half smiling.

"Thanks. But really, you should," Audrey reasoned.

"We'll see. Maybe after I meet with her," he replied, and sensing Audrey's apprehension, adding, "I think I have to, if for no other reason than to find out who it is that she wants killed. Don't you think?"

"But you said that she said she would only tell you if you agreed to do it?"

"Yes, that's right."

"So?"

"Depends who it is," Sam answered.

"What? You can't be seriously thinking about agreeing to do it?" gasped Audrey, astonished.

"Of course not, you eejit, I'm just winding you up."

"I can't believe you are joking about this," said

Audrey,

"Must be a coping strategy, along with drinking copiously," said Sam, raising his glass in an offer of another.

"I'll get it," said Audrey, getting up to go the bar. "I think you're going to need it."

"Why?" asked Sam, intrigued by the comment.

"Because there's something else I haven't told you."

# CHAPTER 58

20 November 2017

"I'm not sure if I can deal with any more surprises right now to be honest," said Sam, although he didn't really seriously believe that there were going to be any more major shocks arising from whatever Audrey was about to tell him.

He could barely have been more wrong.

After she told him, he just stared disbelievingly at her, trying to take in what she had just said. He eventually found his voice, and heard himself repeating what she'd said back to her, as if he needed to say it out loud to process it in his brain.

"*You* had an affair with Frank too?"

Audrey just stared back at him, with a look of such sadness and guilt in her eyes that he knew that she was telling him the truth. *And why would she lie about something like this?* He thought.

"I'm not proud of it," said Audrey, nervously. Sam noticed that she was shaking and he thought that she was about to burst out crying. However, he found himself unable to comfort her, while not being totally sure why. Instead he asked her another question.

"When did this happen?"

"About four and a half years ago," she said, almost apologetically.

"Does Trish know?"

"I didn't think so," she said hesitating, "but now, I'm beginning to think that maybe she does because of all this."

"Has she said or done anything that makes you think that she knows?"

"No. No, not really," said Audrey, looking as if she was still thinking about it.

"Has she been acting differently towards you in any way recently?"

"No, I don't think so. Oh, I don't know. Maybe I'm just being paranoid, because of . . ."

"Because of what?" asked Sam.

"My guilt, probably," said Audrey, and at that point she did break down. However, she recovered sufficiently to continue. "The people I know who have been in her house say it is a shrine to Frank, still filled with all his clothes and belongings; she's been unable to change or move anything, and everything is just exactly the same as it was before he died. All his things have remained untouched. Don't you think that is so sad?"

"It didn't stop her going on a dating site though, did it?" said Sam.

Audrey tried to answer, but became emotional again and couldn't speak. The elderly couple, who were just leaving, looked over. "Are you alright dear?" asked the woman.

"Yes, yes, I'm fine thanks, just a bit upset about something, but I'm OK."

They both looked at Sam accusingly, to the extent that he felt the need to comfort Audrey by putting his arm around her and pulling her closer to him.

This seemed to offer them the reassurance they required, and they made their way out of the bar. The barman, by contrast, looked completely unconcerned, and more interested in closing up.

"I'm fine," said Audrey, gently touching Sam's hand. "I think we should probably go," she added, looking over at the barman; they were now the only people left on the premises. Sam quietly nodded his agreement and they made their way back to the hotel in silence, each with their respective thoughts and feelings. On arriving back at the hotel, Sam noticed that the bar was busy and the thought of being in such a crowded, loud environment didn't appeal to him.

Audrey, as if sensing this, looked at him and asked, "Do you want to come up for a nightcap?"

Sam, who was experiencing a mixture of emotions as a result of the previous discussion, wasn't entirely sure if this was a good idea. However, he also realised that there were other questions that he wanted to ask her, so he decided to take her up on her offer.

On arriving in the room, Audrey poured them a drink, and sat down on the sofa next to Sam.

"I need to ask you something," he said. Audrey didn't respond, but just stared at him with a look of apprehension, wondering what he was about to say.

"Did you know about Heather's affair with Frank when you had the affair with him?" he asked.

"Yes, well, I wasn't sure. At that stage, it was only hearsay."

"At that stage?"

"Yes, I mean, no . . . I mean, we hadn't discussed it."

"You asked him about it?"

"No, he brought it up. He thought I knew about it anyway, and he wanted to be open about it."

"You mean, he wanted it out of the way so that it wouldn't queer the pitch in any way in terms of you being together," retorted Sam, querulously.

"Maybe. Probably. I don't know," said Audrey. "But I was glad he brought it up because I didn't want it to get in the way either. I wanted to be with him. I really liked him."

"So did Heather," said Sam, then realised that he sounded almost protective.

"How do you know that?" asked Audrey, peremptorily.

"She told me."

"Did she say anything else?"

"About what?"

"I don't know, about me, maybe?" said Audrey.

"No. Why would she? Did she know about you and Frank?"

"I . . . eh . . . I don't know, perhaps, maybe, I don't know, that's why I'm asking."

"So what did he tell you?"

"About what? What do you mean? "said Audrey, quite brusquely.

"I mean, what did he tell you about their affair?" said Sam, curious to know and not letting on about any of the details that Heather had told him.

"He told me that he'd ended it."

"Did he say why?" asked Sam, interested in what Frank's version of the situation would be.

"No," said Audrey.

"Didn't you ask? Weren't you curious?" asked Sam, surprised.

Audrey was quiet for a few seconds, appearing to be considering how to respond to the question.

"Yes, but he just said 'circumstances', and I was happy to leave it at that. I didn't want to spend all our time talking about how he felt about someone else."

"Did it bother you when he spoke about her?" asked Sam.

Audrey appeared to be getting increasingly irritated by the questions, but nevertheless responded. "It niggled me a bit, but it was a good few years before we'd met so I didn't let it annoy me too much. There was also the other slight issue of him being a married man that bothered me more, of course."

"Well, it didn't bother you enough to stop seeing him," said Sam, instantly regretting it. "Sorry, I'm just having a bit of a problem getting my head around everything that's happened."

"I know, it's alright, I understand," said Audrey, quite contrite.

Sam didn't ask Audrey who had ended *their* affair because he thought it probably wasn't the time to discuss it, given her apparent emotional fragility and, more pertinently, his already insensitive handling of the situation. He reflected that a few days ago he would never have believed that Audrey could be so vulnerable and brittle. Clearly her mantra of "When I want something, I go for it" hadn't always been the best decision or strategy.

*People in glass houses*, he reflected. *We've all made bad decisions in our life and it's easy to judge others and to be wise after the event. Hindsight is a wonderful thing indeed.*

Unfortunately, he then made things even worse.

"It certainly didn't seem to bother Frank though, did it? He was having a great old time to himself."

Audrey burst out crying again at this, and Sam didn't know what to do or say. "I'm sorry, I'm making things worse. I should go."

Audrey, who was still crying, looked up at him through her tears. "I don't want you to go. But am I damaged goods now? Is that it?"

Sam felt like shit. He hadn't meant to judge Audrey, but he had, and she had sensed it. He hadn't judged Heather in this way. Maybe he had expected more from Audrey, but was that fair? After all, he hardly knew her. In saying that, she seemed to be being very open and honest with him. And she seemed genuinely upset, but more than that, worried almost.

"No, that's not what I meant , I'm sorry, I didn't mean to . . . it must have taken a lot for you to tell me about it. Why *did* you tell me about it? he asked, genuinely curious, whilst also remembering that Heather had also told him very personal details about herself and her unhappy relationship the night that they met. "I don't know, maybe because I wanted to get it out to see how it felt. I don't know. Maybe I needed you to know how I am feeling." She was now sobbing hard and loudly.

"And maybe I also wanted you to know how worried I am and why."

"Worried? About what?" said Sam.

Audrey managed to pull herself together sufficiently to answer.

"I think it might be me that she wants you to kill, Sam."

# CHAPTER 59

21 November 2017

"Do you think Trish knows about us?" Sam asked Audrey as they lay together in her bed in the early hours of the morning. They had not had sex, but Sam had comforted her and reassured her that she was overreacting and mistaken in her thoughts about Trish wanting her dead. While he didn't actually know if that was indeed the case, what he did know was that she needed to hear the words. This was a woman whom, he thought, was struggling to cope with the fact that her past deeds were coming home to roost as a result of the same set of circumstances that had combined serendipitously to bring him to his current predicament.

And her sense of guilt was possibly causing her to feel very vulnerable, emotional and possibly paranoid.

He, however, was guilty of nothing other than being

in the wrong place at the wrong time. He realised that for the first time he had said it and believed it.

"I don't know if she knows we've been together," said Audrey in answer to his question. "But then I don't know anything much anymore," she added, holding him close.

"I know that feeling," said Sam.

"Why do you ask?"

"I wasn't sure if she had caught sight of me at the door of the nightclub when we arrived that night. Or if she had said anything to you."

"No, she hasn't said anything to me," said Audrey, "and obviously she hasn't said anything to you, either."

"Do you think that she will admit to killing Heather?"

"I don't know," said Sam. "It's probably unlikely, although I suppose it depends upon where the conversation goes. I was thinking that I might have to agree to carry out the murder to actually find out who the intended victim is."

"What if it *is* me?" asked Trish, looking at him beseechingly.

"It doesn't matter who it is, I'm not going to do it anyway, silly," said Sam. "But I might have to pretend to go along with it."

"That's a bit risky isn't it, Sam?"

"We'll see, said Sam. "I might just have to play it by ear."

"It just doesn't seem real," said Audrey.

"I know what you mean." Sam had to agree that the whole situation still felt quite surreal.

He changed the subject. "What are you going to do today? Your friends will be missing you. Haven't they been wondering where you are?"

"I've just told them that I was tired and hungover and needing a break from the drink."

"Why didn't you just tell them that you had a hot date?" he asked, genuinely curious about why she had not told them about him, but trying to keep it light.

"I probably would have done if it hadn't been for recent events and the feeling that maybe you wouldn't have been happy with it becoming common knowledge," said Audrey, sounding more like she was asking a question herself.

"The only reason I wouldn't have wanted it known would have been because of Trish, because initially I wasn't sure how she would react; I also wondered whether it would affect her relationship with you. But now we're looking at a different set of circumstances, although I'm sure your theory is wrong," said Sam, trying to reassure her and pulling her close to him.

"Well, hopefully we'll find out soon," said Audrey, before asking him to make love to her again.

# CHAPTER 60

Trish thought back to when she realised that Frank had fabricated the story of the con man and the failed investment to cover up his affair and blackmail that followed, and to explain the need for the money to her and their family. Finding out he'd been unfaithful to her was devastating enough, but she endured much more pain and suffering when she discovered that some of her friends knew about it but had said nothing. She felt betrayed, which might have been what caused her, ironically, to make the catastrophic choices that led to the humiliating situation that followed not long after.

Just over a year after Frank died, Trish went on online dating website Plenty of Fish, and less than a month after that, she was contacted by and began to exchange messages with a man who would ultimately con her out of over a quarter of a million pounds.

His name, he told her, was Adrian Zimmer, and he

claimed to be a South African diamond dealer. As well as apparently wanting a relationship with her, he also offered her the opportunity of benefitting from his involvement in a business deal. He told her that it was guaranteed to bring returns, and stupidly, she believed him, until he stopped returning her calls and emails. Eventually, she called her bank, to discover that she had been the victim of a cruel and callous deception.

Even now, as she recalled the circumstances, she still could not believe that she had been so gullible, not least considering that her own husband had concocted a similarly cautionary tale, albeit to cover his own tracks. Nonetheless, she truly believed that she was investing in something that would set her up for the rest of her life, when in fact she was being played like a fool. When the full sorry details became apparent, she was so ashamed and devastated that she, like her late husband, had also thought about suicide. It was only the thought of her family, some of whom still no longer spoke to her, that had stopped her.

Her deceiver had gained her trust by telling her that he had been left to bring up his daughter on his own, following the death of his wife from cancer. He was so incredibly charming and plausible that she saw no reason to disbelieve him. Once she'd made her initial 'investment', the ruthless fraudster subsequently told her that he had encountered financial problems brokering another deal, and persuaded her to give him more money, this time from her pensions.

He didn't even stop there. Under his influence, she also sold jewellery to get more money on the promise of a share of the deal. Next, he had emailed her the details of an HSBC bank account, supposedly his, with a balance of £50,000 in it that she was apparently entitled to withdraw. She'd attempted to access the account but received a 'security message', advising that she needed to deposit £6,000 to proceed further and access the account. He contacted her again, claiming that this bank account had been frozen for 'security reasons', and that she'd have to wait to get her share of the 'profits'.

It was incredible to think of it now, but she'd gone on to sell a flat in Torrevieja, Costa Blanca, which she and her husband had bought and shared, and given him the profit from this. Then, in the months following that, she gave him further sums of money amounting to tens of thousands of pounds. She started to become suspicious once she'd handed over £100,000, but ignored warnings from a few well-intentioned people including her bank manager, who'd noticed her making large deposits to a foreign bank account and couldn't help but caution her against making so many transfers.

'Adrian' then emailed her to ask for yet more money; this time it was needed so he could book a flight to Bergamo in Italy for her. They would finally meet in person there.

However, when she arrived at the Thomas Cook desk at Edinburgh Airport, she found that there were no tickets waiting for her as promised.

She felt both ashamed and utterly humiliated at her own stupidity. This incident finally confirmed the suspicions she'd been harbouring – he was a cheap and ruthless scam artist. The police agreed, telling her he was probably part of an organised crime gang, possibly based in North or West Africa. When Trish showed them the photo that 'Adrian' had sent her, they recognised him from their files as a Dutch businessman who had been killed the previous year by political activists in South Africa. They informed Trish that it was all too easy for fraudsters to download photos of anyone from the internet these days.

Once Trish realised that she had been duped, she contacted Plenty of Fish, but they informed her that they could not discuss members' details with anyone but the police, while pointing out that they provided clear warnings on the site to people advising them against sending money to anybody they didn't know well. Her bank also tried to trace the account, but ran into a brick wall of misleading data and hidden information protected by a firewall. Incredibly, even after all this, the ruthless perpetrator of this callous and cruel deception continued to contact her to ask her for more money.

Trish experienced terrible guilt in relation to how she

had deceived and ignored the advice of her family and friends, who, on discovering the truth, disowned her, regarding her as having disrespected both them and the memory of her late husband. The sad realization that she had lost their trust and respect because of her actions caused her considerable pain and anguish; she decided that one day she would finally take revenge against the person she viewed as responsible for her husband's death, and everything that had happened since.

# CHAPTER 61

21 November 2017

Sam and Audrey showered together after their lovemaking, which was a less hectic and more tender, intimate experience than previously, while being equally as enjoyable and, in some senses more fulfilling. Sam then went back to his own room to change for breakfast, which they had together for the first time. However, if truth be told not much food was consumed, as they spent most of the time holding hands and just kissing and touching rather than eating, to the amusement, and sometimes consternation, of their fellow residents.

The plan was that after breakfast they would change and then lie together at the pool for a short while as it was a relatively bright and warm day. However, the sun disappeared and the weather and temperature changed, as did the general atmosphere. In contrast to their romantic breakfast, both Sam and Audrey's mood subsequently became very sombre and serious, probably in anticipation of the day ahead.

Sam realised that he still had to give Trish an answer to her "proposition", and if it wasn't the answer she wanted, there was no telling what she would do, aside from what she had threatened. This was a woman who had likely killed someone, after all.

As he was contemplating what the day would bring, his phone rang. It was Trish, asking him to meet her at her hotel room again. Sam agreed to meet her as soon as possible, as he was keen to find out what she had to say to him.

Sam and Audrey took their leave of each other in relative silence, both heading to their respective rooms, with Audrey having previously arranged to get together with a couple of her friends for lunch. However, they both agreed to meet up later.

Sam had arranged to meet Trish at the bar at her hotel and he was there within the hour. When he arrived, she informed him she was hungry and wanted lunch even if he didn't, and headed out of the hotel.

They went to a bar facing on to Levante beach; it made chip butties, which Trish ordered, along with a gin and tonic. The place was quiet both outside and in, and they chose the latter location in order to be able to talk. This time, Trish didn't bother with the pleasantries.

"OK, Sam, have you thought about my proposition?"

Sam wanted to say, "What do you think? I've thought of little else," but he reined himself in.

"I have. But I need to know who you want killed, and why?"

"Nice try, but as I told you, you need to agree to do it, first."

"What if I don't?" said Sam, defiantly.

"Then I would need to give serious thought to going to the police and telling them about your little rendezvous with a certain murder victim."

*This is it,* thought Sam. *It's now or never – time to call her bluff.*

"You won't go to the police, so let's cut to the chase."

"Well, well, we are getting bold in our old age," said Trish. "So pray tell, how can you be so sure?"

Sam told her that he knew all about how she had paid the Algerian guy to 'mug' him, and he also explained how he knew, telling her all about their subsequent encounter. Perhaps surprisingly, she didn't deny this, probably realising that there was no point in doing so now. Even more surprisingly, she went on to describe how she had initially come into contact with him in his capacity as handyman and barman at her hotel.

She also claimed to have noticed that he wasn't shy

in talking about his "other job" as pimp-cum-bouncer to impress people, mainly other men. She had humoured him and his macho posturing, before telling him that she might have another job that he might be interested in and that she would pay him for his troubles.

"So, he agreed to 'mug' or gently rough you up on your way home the next night, for a small fee, no questions asked, probably because he wanted to impress me and not lose face," she said.

When Sam asked her why she'd arranged it, she informed him, unashamedly, that her thinking behind this was for two reasons. First, it would ensure that he was a bit shaken and hopefully amenable to her approach and suggestion of them walking home together. Secondly, she needed him to be short of money and therefore receptive to her offer of assistance and support. This then paved the way for her general friendliness and subsequent suggestion of lunch together, allowing her to lull him into a false sense of trust. However, she acknowledged that she was surprised by his subsequent maverick course of action, not having reckoned upon his pronounced sense of resentment and injustice. She had not anticipated that he would make a point of seeking out his assailant, in order to get both financial and personal retribution. Unfortunately for her, this had also revealed her deceitful and reprehensible actions.

"Why didn't you didn't ask Akmal to murder someone for you?" asked Sam.

"I don't think he's up to it," said Trish.

"Oh and I am?"

"Depends, maybe all you need is a reason."

"But I don't have a reason."

"Yet," said Trish.

"And you think you can give me one?"

"Possibly. And a lot of money"

"Why don't you do it yourself?" said Sam, and nearly added, "I mean, you've already killed one person," but stopped himself, just in time.

"Because I'm not capable of doing it," said Trish, unconvincingly.

"You're not capable of killing someone yourself, but you're quite happy to blackmail someone else to do it for you. That's just as bad, if not worse, for god's sake," said Sam, disbelievingly.

"So, you will do it then?" asked Audrey expectantly, totally ignoring his outburst.

"That's not what I said! And why should I? You won't go to the police now, after all."

"Won't I? It's just your word against mine about the mugging," Audrey retorted. "I'll just deny that I had anything to do with that, along with any suggestion that I asked you to kill anyone. And let's face it, our little Algerian friend isn't going to admit to anything, is he?

"What happened with him doesn't mean you didn't

commit a murder, either. And in fact, from what you've told me about getting your revenge, you might well be just the kind of person who could do just that. And I think the police might just agree."

Sam knew she was right about Akmal and he really didn't want the police asking the Algerian questions anyway, as he might assume that it was Sam who had contacted them.

He wasn't really worried about being charged with assault as it would be his word against Akmal's in the absence of any injuries or witnesses. However, because he had given Akmal his word that he wouldn't go to the police, he couldn't be sure what he would say or do if he felt that he had betrayed him, given his connections. He might even join with Trish in blaming him for Heather's murder. The more that Sam thought about it, the more he wanted to ask, "And what's to stop me going to the police now and telling them that *you* killed Heather or paid somebody to kill her?"

He decided against pushing it. He didn't want to get into a discussion about what her reasons for doing it might be and reveal that he knew about Heather's affair with her husband, as she would want to know how he knew. But he wanted to know who the intended victim was – specifically if it was indeed Audrey.

"Nice try," said Sam. "Your turn to try and push your luck. But let's be honest. You really don't want the police paying you any undue attention or to accidentally incriminate yourself, do you?" He waited for her reaction.

"What do you mean 'incriminate myself'?" Trish asked, sharply.

"Well, they might want to know how you knew that I spent the night with Heather, for a start," said Sam, realising that this was the first time he had used her name when speaking to Trish. He was happy that he had, as it seemed to unsettle her. He decided to seize the moment and take advantage of the situation.

"Were you following Heather on the night that she was killed? And if so, why?"

Trish seemed to be caught off balance even more by that question but nevertheless managed to answer.

"No, I wasn't following her. Why would I have been?"

Sam wasn't sure that he believed her. And something was still annoying him that he hadn't quite come to grips with yet for some reason.

He really wanted to push Trish further, but realised it would probably jeopardise any chance of getting any more information out of her, not least who she wanted him to kill. He decided against it and instead went with a different approach.

"I need to know why you want me to do this . . . this thing," said Sam. "I just need to understand what your reasons are." He hoped this would convince her that there was a remote possibility of him actually carrying out her wishes. Incredibly, it seemed to do the trick.

Trish reiterated that she would simply deny everything if he went to the police, and that she'd tell them about his liaison with Heather as well. He indicated his understanding, and she told him who she wanted him to kill, without providing any explanation.

Sam was shocked by this confirmation of the reality of Trish's intentions, and also realised immediately that it made sense of so much of the other information he had been given previously by Heather, Audrey and Trish herself.

Thankfully, for Audrey at least, it wasn't her that Trish wanted dead. Hopefully, for Audrey's sake, it meant that she was unaware of her affair with her husband, not least as it now seemed increasingly likely that she'd already killed Heather. Now that he knew the name, Sam also realised that by implication, this effectively deprived Trish of any hold over him. There was no reason for blackmail to carry any threat or concern for him. Surely, he thought, she must have realised this? However, he once again decided there was nothing to be gained by pursuing the point any further at this time. It would keep.

As if sensing his train of thought, Trish's response was equally as calm, measured and calculating.

"I'll contact you later tonight for your answer. And there's something else you need to know."

# CHAPTER 62

21 November 2017

As Sam headed back to the hotel, his mind was full of complex thoughts, questions and emotions after his discussion with Trish. He was happy that he would be able to tell Audrey that she was not the intended victim, but at the same time he was shocked and troubled by the information that Trish had given him. It was information that he didn't want to believe, but the more he thought about it the more it rang true. He realised that there were clear reasons why Trish would want to lie to him, but he knew that she hadn't. Then another thought occurred to him.

Had Heather known?

He felt completely lost and desperate now, and wanted to speak to Audrey to hear what she thought about it all, but he wasn't able to think straight yet because of the situation and what the resultant implications might be for himself. His thoughts were interrupted by his phone ringing; it was Audrey asking how things had gone, and where he was. He told her that he would tell her when he got back to the hotel later. He needed time to think. He knew that he could not carry out the task that Trish had asked of him, but that didn't mean that there wasn't another solution, particularly given what he now knew. He just needed time to think things through. Unfortunately, that was the one thing he didn't have. His holiday, if you could still call it that, was due to end within the next four days.

When Sam arrived back at the hotel he went straight to his room and poured himself a drink, and went and sat out on the balcony to consider the information he had amassed and to evaluate how best he should proceed.

After he had cleared his mind he called Audrey to tell her that he was back; she appeared at the room almost immediately, carrying a bottle of Rioja Blanco as though she had anticipated that they were going to need it. Sam poured her a glass and guided her to the sofa. He didn't think that what he had to say should be said out on the balcony where it could be overheard by someone. *You never know who's listening,* he thought. Or was he just being paranoid again?

Being aware that Audrey probably wanted to be put out of her misery, he told her right off that it wasn't her that Trish wanted rid of.

While she was obviously relieved to hear this, she was also naturally curious to discover who the intended target was. She didn't appear surprised or particularly shocked when he told her, just perplexed and intrigued about why.

"She didn't go into her reasons," said Sam, "and I didn't push her."

"To be fair, there could be plenty," said Audrey, half smiling, but still obviously intrigued by the situation.

"Indeed," said Sam, pensively; it made Audrey believe that he was referring to something specific.

She asked him what he meant.

"There's something else," he said, solemnly. "She told me something else."

"What? What else did she say?" replied Audrey, suddenly looking very serious and apprehensive, but at the same time desperate to know just what it was. So Sam told her. As soon as he did, he knew from the look in her eyes that she already knew.

"Are you alright?" asked Audrey.

"How come other people know so much about my private life?" he asked in response.

"It's a small world, full of small-minded people, who all know too much about other people's business. And Calderhall is no different from anywhere else, although you seemed to be blissfully unaware of quite a lot of it."

"I'm always the last to know anything," lamented Sam, "particularly for someone who worked at a newspaper. My colleagues used to tell me that that I must walk around with my eyes and ears closed. It's just that I've never really been into gossip, to be honest."

"Unfortunately, the rest of the world is," said Audrey, "and it's getting worse, on a much grander scale, thanks to social media."

*Too true,* thought Sam, grateful that so far he had managed to contain the situation. He didn't really do Twitter or Facebook, mainly because he found the endless egotistical ramblings both irritating and offensive. The atrociously poor English and grammar in use was, as far as he was concerned, clear evidence of the deterioration in educational standards over recent years. He'd frequently see ridiculous sentences containing phrases like 'would of' instead of 'would have', which, he despaired of – *I mean, it's replacing a verb with a preposition for no reason and thereby robbing it of even basic meaning,* he thought; *these are people who then invariably go on to express very strong and vitriolic social and political opinions and then criticise others for theirs, sometimes quite cruelly.*

Sam realised that he probably qualified as a 'Grammar Nazi', but he genuinely felt that it was harder to take someone seriously when they couldn't even string a coherent sentence together. He regarded the auditory equivalent as equally as offensive and would flinch whenever he overheard others, quite loudly and confidently, delivering such unbelievably inexcusable utterances such as "I have took" or "I have went".

*God give me strength,* he thought. *And earplugs.*

# CHAPTER 63

21 November 2017

"I think we should take ourselves out for a drink and some food to get some respite from all this, if at all possible," Sam said to Audrey, before realising that he hadn't asked if she had other plans and apologising.

"No, that's fine, I managed to catch up with a few people earlier today," she replied. "And I kind of mentioned that I might have a date."

"Did you indeed?"

"Yes! I told you I'd planned to. I think they knew that something was going on because I had been conspicuous by my absence."

"So, how much information did you give them?" asked Sam.

"Just that I had a date. No names, no pack drill, no need for you to worry."

"I'm not worried at all, I mean they wouldn't know who I am anyway." Audrey remained silent. "Would they?" he asked.

"Possibly, because as I said previously, Calderhall isn't such a big place; not everybody goes around with their head in the sand like you do, Sam."

"Well, even so, they're probably more likely to know my ex rather than me because she's actually from there," said Sam. "And I've been away a while," he added.

"People have long memories, Sam, particularly for any kind of gossip or scandal," said Audrey.

*Fuck*, thought Sam, *does everybody know?*

While he really didn't want to think or talk about it anymore, he also realised he did want to do something about it, irrespective of the risks involved.

"Right I'm going to get myself all smart and handsome for our date, so I'm going to be busy. I'll let you go and do what you do to look as beautiful as ever."

"You say the nicest things," said Audrey, as she got up to leave and pecked him on the cheek. "See you at seven."

That gave Sam just over two hours to do everything he needed to do. And what he needed to do was find someone that he had no connection with to carry out a particular task that could not be traced back to him. Unfortunately, he didn't know anyone who could do such a thing. But he knew someone who might be able to put him in touch with someone who did.

# CHAPTER 64

21 November 2017

Akmal was in his usual place, animatedly accosting unsuspecting tourists, male and female, with impressive enthusiasm but no trace of the aggression and violence that he had employed in his initial encounter with Sam. However, his demeanour changed dramatically when he saw Sam making his way towards him.

"Take it easy, Sparky," said Sam, reassuringly, noticing his obvious anxiety. "I just want to talk."

"Talk about what?" said Akmal, warily.

"Business," said Sam, in as firm but friendly a tone as he could manage.

"Business? What business? I don't speak to anyone like you say, so what you want now?"

"I have a proposition for you," said Sam.

# CHAPTER 65

21 November 2017

Detective Inspector Bernardo Costales and Detective Inspector Vanessa Powrie showed their ID to the receptionist at the hotel and asked to see the manager, a young man in his mid-thirties. He asked them to accompany him to his office to talk. After explaining the situation and making the importance and need for discretion and confidentiality abundantly clear, they were advised that they would be granted access to a room for as long as it was necessary. In effect they would be afforded every co-operation with their investigation.

"So what is your thinking, Inspector Powrie?" asked Bernardo Costales of his Scottish counterpart, after they made their farewells and thanked the manager for his help.

"I think that our friend Mr Meredith has a knack for

finding himself in the wrong place, at the wrong time, with the wrong people," said Vanessa.

"Si, te acuerdo mi amigo," said Inspector Costales. "However, it could work out quite well for us."

"What do you mean?" asked Inspector Powrie.

"If he is willing to cooperate, we might be able to get the information required to bring charges against at least one or maybe even both of them," replied Costales.

"Yes, hopefully, we can," replied his Scottish colleague. "But we'll have to proceed carefully and be very mindful of compromising the legality of any conviction."

# CHAPTER 66

11 November 2017

As the Watcher began to follow the Whore, there was an unexpected development to contend with, in the form of someone else approaching from the other direction, who also seemed to be following her with an apparent sense of purpose and intent. Someone that was known and familiar to the Watcher, from the party staying at the hotel very near to the Watcher's own. Initially, the Watcher was enraged at the inconvenience and obstacle to their intended course of action. However, after some deliberation, they decided to observe the situation from a distance and see how it developed.

After a few minutes, both the Whore and her 'shadow' stopped and acknowledged each other, albeit in a rather cold and distant fashion. However, within seconds the situation clearly developed into something of a hostile and confrontational encounter, with the shadow being the clear aggressor. This contretemps lasted only a few minutes, culminating in the shadow storming off, apparently having said their piece, leaving the Whore clearly admonished, and more than a little subdued.

The Watcher surveyed the situation. Apart from them, the street was now deserted. Providing the perfect opportunity for the intended objective.

# CHAPTER 67

21 November 2017

Trish called Sam as he was making his way back to the hotel. He told her that it wasn't a convenient time to talk, but that he would be in touch to arrange a time to meet, rather than agree to anything over the phone. This also bought him some time, while he waited for a phone call. He arrived back at the hotel in time to have drink at the bar and compose himself before calling Audrey to tell her to meet him there, which she did some 15 minutes later, looking uncharacteristically demure. After one drink they took themselves to the Old Town for a change of scenery and found a nice little tapas restaurant just off the main drag.

After their meal and some wine, they decided to go for stroll through the narrow cobbled streets. They walked hand in hand in relative silence before finding a quaintly rustic and relatively quiet bar for a drink. It was only when they went in and sat down that Sam realised that it was the same place he had gone to watch the Ireland game. He was just about to tell Audrey that he didn't want to stay when the barman shouted over to him.

"Senor, senor! Hello, my Irish friend, I am so sorry that you miss the football before, please, I make it up to you. I have a drink for you and your lovely wife," he said smiling and ushering them him to a table and taking their order.

Audrey looked at him quizzically and he explained the situation to her.

The barman, whose name was Luis, brought them their drinks and apologised again, explaining that the Spanish people who had come in on that particular night were the owner and his friends, and that he couldn't refuse them. Sam also apologised for his own annoyance, and thanked him for the drinks. Luis told him that all drinks were on the house, and shook his hand warmly. However, after his complimentary beer, Sam found that he wasn't really in the mood for drinking anymore; he was preoccupied by his thoughts about the events of the day. And maybe it was just his imagination, but he felt that Audrey seemed distracted and distant as well. Certainly, their conversation was quite limited and stilted for the first time, with both of them struggling to be spontaneous and to find anything else to talk about.

They thanked the barman for his kindness and hospitality and said their farewells, while, at his insistence, promising to return to see the Flamenco music and dance show.

As they headed home, Sam sensed a degree of tension in the air but wasn't entirely sure of the reason why. Rather than prolonging it, he decided to confront it head on.

"Are you OK?"

"What? Yes, yes, of course," replied Audrey, smiling weakly.

*Clearly, she isn't*, he thought.

"What's wrong?" he pressed.

"Nothing . . ." Audrey replied, hesitantly.

*Oh god, the dreaded "nothing" response*, thought Sam. *Now I need to work out what "nothing" means. Because, whatever it means, it doesn't mean 'nothing'.*

"Look, I'm shit at this kind of stuff," he said, "which is probably why my relationships never last. So you're probably better off just telling me what it is that's bothering you."

"What? Oh, oh right," said Audrey, probably not expecting such a pragmatic response, but also seeming quite relieved at the same time and sighing deeply.

"I've just been wondering – what happens now?"

Sam wanted to say, "nothing," but thought that such an inappropriate and clumsy attempt at humour probably wouldn't be well received, so decided against it. Instead, he just stated the obvious.

"I really don't know. It's hard to think about anything else other than this fucking crazy situation I find myself in."

"I know, I know," said Audrey. "And that's the other thing I'm worrying about."

"What do you mean?" asked Sam, wondering what she meant, or knew.

"I mean that I'm concerned about what you're planning to do about it."

Sam now knew exactly what he was going to do about it. In fact, he had practically already done it, but he wasn't about to tell Audrey, or anybody else for that matter, what that was. That was between him and his conscience. So, instead, he just looked at her.

"I'm going to sleep on it," he said.

# CHAPTER 68

22 November 2017

Sam spent the night with Audrey and rose early, telling her that he was heading back to his own room before going to breakfast in case she wanted to join him. If not, he would catch up with her later. For whatever reason, he wasn't in the mood to discuss either the future or anything else with her in any great depth; he was preoccupied with the more pressing immediate situation.

He did text her to tell her that he was going to find a pub to watch football, though, explaining that there were several Champions League games being played that night, involving both Manchester City and Liverpool. It was the latter's game with Sevilla that he was interested in, and he told her that if she wasn't into watching football she might want to catch up with her pals.

She didn't appear for breakfast, but texted him – *Enjoy the football, and I'll catch you later.*

Sam was quite happy with this. After having quite a full breakfast, he headed back to his room rather than the pool, as it was an overcast, grey day.

He'd been back in the room for a matter of minutes when his phone rang. There was no caller information on his phone screen, and while he would not normally answer such calls, he felt that he was going to have to make an exception on this occasion. His decision proved to be productive and the call, while brief, was also beneficial.

As Sam was contemplating the task in front of him in the day ahead, his phone rang again. This time it was Trish, asking why he had not been in touch. The conversation between them was equally as brief as the previous phone call, taking only as long as was required for him to pass on the information necessary.

After he ended the second call, Sam suddenly found that he was feeling quite anxious and fragile. He began to hyperventilate. He went out to the balcony for some air and sat down until he had regained his equilibrium and was breathing more evenly. Clearly the full reality and degree of the perilous situation that he now found himself in had just hit home, and he began to wonder if he could really go through with what now seemed a reckless and ill-conceived course of action. However, he very quickly realised that it had gone too far now and he really didn't have a choice.

Sam surveyed the pool area, which was pretty much deserted, while neither the pigeon nor his pals were anywhere to be seen. *Talk about deserting a sinking ship*, he thought. Unfortunately, the weather was also still as dull and it didn't look like improving anytime soon. He hoped that it wasn't a sign.

# CHAPTER 69

22 November 2017

Sam decided that he needed a walk, or a drink, or both, and headed out in the direction of Levante Beach. He bought a newspaper and then walked along the promenade, almost until the end of the beach, where he found a Café/Bar, sat down and had a coffee and checked the newspaper for any updates about the police investigation. It mostly provided a regurgitation of the information previously provided, although interestingly, it included the fact that the area where the body was found was a CCTV blind spot. Sam realised this meant that Trish could have heard about this previously, as she had claimed. However, it didn't significantly alter his thinking about her involvement.

While the weather was still dull and overcast it was not cold, and it reminded Sam of a late spring day in Glasgow. It also made him long for the sanity, sanctity and relative normality of his home town. As he sat there in the relative calm of the Costa Blanca afternoon, he wondered if his life would ever be normal again. Also, the irony of his situation had not escaped him. Here he was, seeking respite and refuge from the strains and stresses of everyday life, and finding more of both than he could ever remember experiencing at any time in his life. All of his previous woes seemed paltry in comparison, and all of a sudden he felt more lost and alone than he had ever felt in his life. He just wanted it all to end.

# CHAPTER 70

22 November 2017

Audrey called Sam as he was making his way back to the hotel, asking how and where he was. He advised of his location, told her that he was fine, and made similar enquiries of her own situation. She told him she had enjoyed a light lunch with some of her girlfriends, and had also made arrangements to meet up later with the larger group, which would likely include Trish. He advised her that he would be in touch at some point later, after the football, which was due to kick off at 6.15 p.m.

As he headed back to the hotel, Sam was still feeling quite overwhelmed by everything that had happened, and all that was going to happen. It still didn't seem real, and he was still trying to come to terms with it.

As he approached his room he noticed that the Chambermaid's trolley was outside. He hoped that she was nearly finished, as he really needed to lie down and try and get some sleep. However, on entering the room, he noticed that it wasn't the maid, but a different woman. She was older, and looked more European than Spanish. She wasn't dressed like a maid, either.

There were no towel origami creations in evidence, the room hadn't been cleaned, and the bed hadn't been made up, either. *Maybe she's a supervisor,* thought Sam, *but what is she doing in my room?*

He was just about to ask her the very same question when she spoke to him.

"Hello, Mr Meredith. You will no doubt have noticed that I am not your chambermaid." She spoke with a Scottish accent, which he was not expecting.

"I am Detective Inspector Vanessa Powrie," she continued, smiling and displaying her police identification. "I'm sorry about all the furtive cloak and dagger stuff, but we didn't want anybody to know that we were speaking to you.

"And we thought that it would be better if I spoke to you first, rather than accosting you as soon as you arrived and then whisking you into a room before you had time to take it all in."

Sam was indeed experiencing difficulty in taking it all in; he was feeling positively vertiginous at the situation that he now found himself confronted with. However, after he recovered from the initial shock, he automatically assumed that the police were there to talk to him about the murder. But then it suddenly occurred to him that maybe they actually were there in regard to the business with Akmal.

*Fuck,* he thought, *I'm absolutely fucking fucked. How could I have been so fucking stupid? What was I thinking?*

But then he realised that, as was the case with Trish, Akmal wouldn't have contacted the police because of his own situation and his job. *Also, it's his word against mine. So, he wouldn't do that. You're just panicking and not thinking straight,* he told himself.

He began to calm down and to gather himself together, and realised that whatever the reason was for the police being here, he needed to mentally prepare himself for the expected interrogation.

"What is it you want to speak to me about?" he asked, hoping that he sounded convincingly ignorant.

Inspector Powrie touched his arm and said, reassuringly, "There's nothing to worry about, Mr Meredith; my colleague and I will explain everything to you."

She advised Sam that a room had been made available for them to meet in and was about to provide him with the necessary details when the hotel manager arrived, indicating that he would accompany him to the room.

Inspector Powrie nodded her assent, telling Sam that she would join him directly. The manager took Sam to the room and left him there in the company of another male, who introduced himself.

"Hello, Mr Meredith. I am Detective Inspector Costales – Bernardo Costales," he said, standing up to greet him and motioning for him to sit down at the table he'd been sitting at himself; it had four chairs placed around it and some equipment on top of it.

He asked Sam if he wanted anything to drink. Sam declined, then immediately cursed himself, because his mouth was as dry as sandpaper. He was also shaking like a leaf, and he doubted that he would be able to string a sentence together. At that point the female detective arrived. DI Costales began proceedings.

"This is my colleague, Inspector Powrie, who I think you have already met?"

Inspector Powrie introduced herself again as Vanessa, asked him to sit down and again asked if he wanted anything to drink. This time, he accepted.

"Yes, could I have some water please?" he asked, earning himself a glance and a wry smile from the Spanish policeman.

A bottle of water was duly obtained from a small fridge at the back of the room, which Sam gratefully accepted and immediately took a large swig from.

"Are you OK?" asked the female cop. Sam nodded, although he was most definitely not OK.

Not by a long shot.

The female inspector, appearing to sense his discomfort, attempted to reassure him again by telling him that they needed to conduct a formal, recorded interview but that he was not suspected of any crime, nor was he being charged with anything. He declined the offer of a lawyer when it was made to him.

Then, with the pleasantries over, and Sam having indicated his willingness and readiness to proceed, Inspector Powrie pressed a button on the recording device on the table.

"Please state your name for the purposes of the recording."

"Sam Meredith," he replied, nervously, realising that he felt both physically and mentally exhausted.

"Can you tell me the name of the woman that you were having lunch with the day before yesterday, Mr Meredith, and the nature of your relationship with her?" asked DI Costales.

"Sorry, what?" said Sam, aghast.

"The name of the woman that you were having lunch with yesterday, Mr Meredith, and the nature of your relationship with her," repeated the Spaniard.

Sam's mind had gone totally blank; he found himself speechless with panic, trying to work out if they meant Audrey or Trish, before finally blurting out "Trish".

"Surname?" said the Spanish cop.

"I . . . I don't know," said Sam, realising for the first time that he really didn't, before adding, "I thought you were here to ask about the woman who was murdered?"

"Yes, we are. Why do you ask? Do you know something about her?" asked the Spanish cop.

"What? No, I don't," said Sam. "What does that have to do with Trish?" he added, wondering if they suspected her or if she had contacted them to tell them about him. But then he remembered that they told him that he wasn't suspected of any crime.

"All in good time, Mr Meredith," said the Scottish cop. "But first, can you tell us about your relationship with 'Trish'?"

"I, eh, we don't have a relationship. We only met just over a week ago. We had lunch, but that's all — nothing more," pleaded Sam. He wondered what they knew and he could feel himself trembling.

"And are you planning to see her again?" asked Inspector Costales.

"What? I, eh, don't know," he said, hoping that he sounded convincing. "We never made any arrangement," he added, defensively, praying that they believed him.

Both officers shared a glance, before the Scottish cop put her hand on Sam's shoulder from behind, causing him nearly to jump out of his skin. She leaned down and said, quietly, "We know that you've only known her for a short period of time, but we also know that you have been spending a lot of time with her since. And that's perfectly fine. We just wondered if there was any particular reason why?"

*God, what do they know?* Thought Sam, *and how do they know it?*

He realised that he was being very naïve and that police authorities knew far more about people than they realised; recalling a story in The Herald and also his own newspaper about a top secret, covert surveillance unit based in Glasgow and run by Strathclyde Police, called the Scottish Recording Centre (SRC).

This resource was used to secretly access data about people's private communications and movements from their smart phones, emails and social media, in fact everything except actually listening to calls, which was still illegal, at least it was, officially.

Sam recalled the outcry that had followed the illegal hacking of various individuals phones by the *News of the World* newspaper, as revealed by the *Guardian*, which had ultimately led to the demise of the former publication and increased scrutiny of the moral behaviour and practices of the press in general. Meanwhile, the SRC and the police were allowed to spy on people without any legal framework, even before this level of invasive surveillance was later authorised under the Investigatory Powers Bill, or 'Snoopers Charter'. Despite concerns being raised in regard to this Bill being a contravention of the Human Rights Act, it was later passed by the House of Commons in

2016, although as far as Sam was aware, it was still being challenged via the Courts.

The bottom line was that if the Glasgow polis had the means to find out anything about anybody, legally, then in these days of global communications networks, it wasn't unreasonable to assume that the same technology existed and was available, legally or otherwise, in other countries, and most probably in a tourist metropolis like Benidorm.

Sam tried to stay calm and to convince himself that he had nothing to worry about. He had been very careful, scrupulous, even, in his planning, and he told himself that he was just being paranoid. However, because he didn't know the extent of the police's intelligence, he wondered if he should just come clean about everything. But he didn't.

"No, there's no particular reason why we met up; we just got on," he lied, instantly realising that it was the wrong thing to say.

"We also know that you spent last night with a totally different woman" said the Spanish cop. "You've been busy, haven't you? I suppose you're going to tell us that you're not in a relationship with her, either?"

Sam found himself unable to speak. *What is this: good cop, bad cop?* He thought. He also thought, *Fuck, your English is good.*

"Do you happen to know *her* name?" asked Inspector Costales.

"Audrey," said Sam, reacting without thinking in response to the jibe.

"And do you happen to know *her* surname?"

"McPherson" replied Sam, adding, "And, we only just met too. So no, I wouldn't call that a relationship, either. Well not yet, anyway." He instantly wished he hadn't spoken so swiftly.

"So, you like her, do you?" said Inspector Powrie.

"You must, if you know her surname," the Spaniard added, before Sam could answer.

"What?" said Sam, taken aback by the cop's cynical attitude.

"Sorry, ignore him," said his female counterpart, giving her colleague a stern look. "He doesn't mean anything by it, we're just trying to work a few things out."

"Sorry, but I don't think it's funny," said Sam.

Both police inspectors looked at one another; they seemed to make an unspoken agreement to adopt a less confrontational approach, as their subsequent line of questioning was less aggressive and consisted of some fairly inconsequential chat about Sam's holiday, his job and his family. Generally speaking there was a more relaxed and friendly feel to their attitude towards him.

"Mr Meredith – Sam – we know that you spent the night with Heather Lindsay, the murdered woman, or most of it, anyway," said Inspector Powrie. Before Sam could reply, the Spanish cop added, "But we also know that you didn't kill her."

Sam felt the knot in his stomach slowly disappear, and found himself involuntarily breaking down, probably because of the release of all the tension he had been experiencing.

The officers allowed him to recover, then went on to explain to Sam that they had seen him and Heather on CCTV making their way to his hotel, and also Heather subsequently leaving on her own.

"So what's all this about, then? If you know that I didn't kill Heather, why are you asking me all these questions?" he asked, once he had got his breath and composure back.

"We have a proposition for you," said the female cop.

*Another proposition – just what I need,* thought Sam.

# CHAPTER 71

22 November 2017

Sam's head was still swimming from all the information that the police had given him. However, after a few minutes of digesting it, if not actually coming to terms with it, he informed them both that that there were things that he needed to tell them. He subsequently told the officers all about his meeting with Trish, about her threatening to go to the police and attempting to blackmail him into killing someone, and about pretending to go along with her in order to buy time, even although he hadn't done anything other than be intimate with Heather on the night she was murdered. He also told them of his belief that Trish had been following Heather on the night of the murder. He had decided not to tell the police about her link with Akmal, because he had agreed with the Algerian that they would keep this information between themselves – it would only complicate things for both of them if it were to come out. And Trish wasn't going to tell, so he was safe there. Or at least he thought he was.

Inspectors Costales and Powrie told Sam that various people had been seen on the CCTV footage within the relative time frame who may have followed Heather. However, the range of the camera ended just prior to where she was murdered. Also, while the images that they did have were very indistinct, the police inspectors strongly suspected that one of the women was Trish, while the other could be Audrey. Sam knew from his professional experience and knowledge that CCTV technology was often of really poor quality and unreliable, particularly when it came to being used as evidence.

After some more discussion he realised that they needed help to obtain evidence, or a confession, preferably provided voluntarily. They considered that given his knowledge of both women, carnal or otherwise, he was the ideal candidate for a bit of casual undercover work. They also figured that his work experience in advertising would make him fairly adept at both planning and following a strategy, not to mention knowing the difference between manipulation and coercion.

Initially, Sam was really very unwilling and anxious

about such a proposition, and tried to get out of it by pointing out to the police that he was due to fly home within the next few days whereas this plan would take longer. However they advised him that they would take care of that and had already secured his room with the hotel manager for as long as was required, with them footing the bill for it along with his rearranged return flights. Unfortunately, this only served to make Sam feel even more under scrutiny and threat, but they again reassured him that he was not under any suspicion or investigation.

They also casually threw in the fact that they would be happy to turn a blind eye in regard to his little tussle with Akmal. Oh yes, they knew about that too— both incidents, in fact. However, they had apparently still not made the connection between Akmal and Trish, and they also didn't ask about his recent conversation with the Algerian, brief as it was. Had they done so, he would have told them that he was just checking that he wasn't going to have to worry about any trouble from anyone.

Sam wondered if Akmal had 'grassed him up', maybe under questioning, but that wasn't the case. In fact, the police had CCTV images of both incidents, which were much clearer than the images of Trish and possibly Audrey, as the location was much better lit.

All things considered, Sam didn't really have any choice other than to co-operate with Benidorm and

Glasgow's finest, with a view to hopefully securing the evidence required to bring one, or both perpetrators to justice.

The plan involved him being fitted with the required equipment or 'wire', which, interestingly, wasn't the complicated or clumsy arrangement or process, as seen in the movies. No, it was in fact a miniature receiver which they planned to hide in his glasses or sunglasses, depending on where and when they decided to meet. All being well, this would hopefully be all that was required.

The police officers advised Sam that they wanted him to arrange to meet up with Trish the next day at her hotel, or, as soon as possible, adding that, given the information already provided by Sam, she was the main suspect. He was briefed about the appropriate protocols and procedures, in order that nothing that he said or did would jeopardise the integrity of the investigation and any evidence obtained.

Inspector Powrie also asked Sam to call Trish from his phone, in her and her fellow officer's presence, which he did. When Trish answered there was a lot of noise and other voices in the background, and he wondered if she was in the same place as Audrey. Trish asked why he was calling, and if there was a problem. Sam obviously didn't want to get into any dialogue with her given the situation and the circumstances, simply saying that they needed to talk about their deal, but not on the phone, and asked to meet her at her hotel the next day. She sounded both wary and suspicious, but agreed to do so.

*Maybe she thinks I'm after more money*, thought Sam.

# CHAPTER 72

22 November 2017

Sam didn't know if he would be able to concentrate on the football at first, but then decided that it might be just the distraction that he needed. He knew for certain that he didn't want to go back to the hotel on his own, and he didn't want to interrupt Audrey on her dinner date with her friends. As a matter of fact, he wasn't sure that he wanted to see her at all, given the most recent developments. He decided that if she didn't call him he wouldn't call her.

He walked along the Calle Ibiza and on to Calle Gerona, finding a bar not far from his hotel which had television screens showing football both inside and outside. It was relatively busy but he was fortunate enough to get a seat outside, which suited him as it was a relatively balmy evening.

The clientele appeared to be a mixed bunch, consisting of Spaniards and other nationalities, the majority of whom appeared to be British. A couple sitting at the table opposite caught his eye in particular. She was black, looked to be in her thirties and was truly stunning; tall, lithe and elegant, and she held herself like a model, with a smile that could light up a room. He was white and also looked to be in his mid-thirties, very athletic and toned in his build, and dressed in matching designer sports attire. However, his left leg twitched constantly, like someone playing drums or keyboard in a rock band.

Sam reckoned that he was mentally rehearsing, or perhaps, alternatively, he'd had a wee pre-match, mind enhancing, chemical hors d'ouvres. Regardless of this, they appeared very happy together and were unquestionably madly in love with each other. *Lucky them*, thought Sam, trying not to feel jealous and failing miserably.

When he eventually managed to tear his attention away from them, or to be more precise, her, to concentrate on the football match, he actually enjoyed it, with Liverpool and Sevilla drawing 3-3 and Manchester City winning 1-0 against Feyenoord. His team, Celtic, were playing Paris San Germain the following night in the Champions League in Paris, and any kind of result other than a heavy defeat would be very welcome. Hopefully he would be able to catch the game, although he realised that he did have other more pressing business to attend to.

# CHAPTER 73

23 November 2017

Sam had a restless and uncomfortable night, punctuated by him waking up several times due to strange and surreal dreams, then struggling to get back to sleep again. In the morning, he felt quite emotionally fraught and anxious. He looked outside to find that it was another clear, bright day, which he felt was totally inappropriate and incongruous with his own mental state and mood. He also felt dizzy and weak: deciding that he needed to eat something, he went to breakfast at around 9.00 a.m.

There was no sign of Audrey, who had called him the previous night when he was making his way back to the hotel after the football. However, he hadn't answered, and neither had he called her back. He had decided that if she mentioned it he would tell her that he missed the call because of the noise in the bar and didn't see the missed call until very late, by which time he was heading to bed and thought she probably was, too.

After breakfast Sam went back to his room and found a note on the bedside table with a number to call to speak to Inspector Powrie, which he did. She arranged to meet with him along with her Spanish counterpart in the same room as before, in an hour's time.

When they met, both officers they gave him a final briefing, and also fitted his tiny microphone in advance of his meeting with Trish at her hotel at midday, as arranged. It was as if, all of a sudden, the seriousness and enormity of what Sam was about to become involved in had just finally hit him; he felt like he was going to be sick.

He knew that he needed to hold it together if he was going to be able to get through this. And there was also another piece of business of his own that he needed to take care of.

He went back to his room, opened the safe, and removed the earring from within it.

Sam arrived at Trish's room at exactly midday; she answered his knock within seconds. *Not playing hard to get, then,* he thought. She wasn't standing on any kind of ceremony, either.

"You wanted to talk to me," she said sharply, not

inviting him to sit down and remaining standing herself.

Sam could feel his heart pounding so hard he thought that the people listening via the concealed microphone would be able to hear it. He also thought that if he didn't sit down he would fall down. So he took the bull by the horns and walked towards the sofa, saying, "I will have a seat, thanks," adding, "Just water will be fine," and marvelling at his composure.

Trish just stared at him with barely disguised disdain and hostility, before going to the fridge and pouring him a glass of water. She brought it over to him and sat down on the sofa opposite, staring directly at him.

"You wanted to talk to me?" she repeated, calmly.

Sam stared directly back at her, holding eye contact.

"I need to know why you want me to kill

Rab Lindsay," he said, equally as calmly. At least, that's how it appeared. Inside he was trembling.

This evidently wasn't what Trish was expecting to hear. She had been fully expecting Sam to tell her that he had "been thinking", and he wasn't prepared to go ahead with the deal unless she made it more worth his while, or something along those lines. So this was a bit of an unexpected development, and she was momentarily blindsided. However, she found her voice enough to say, "That's 'need to know', Sam, and you don't need to know," which she was actually quite pleased with, considering.

*Does that qualify as a confession?* wondered Sam.

Unfortunately his covert communication only worked as a broadcast device, not a receiver, so in the absence of anybody giving him directions, he decided that he needed to keep going.

"I think if somebody is asking you to kill someone, you're entitled to ask why," he said, wondering if he would regret it later.

"In that case, why did you agree to go ahead with it without knowing?" Trish asked, impatiently.

*Back of the net,* thought Sam. There it was— a confession – straight away, simple as that. *Easy peasy, lemon squeezy,* he said to himself.

In all honesty, he hadn't expected such an open and revealing response. Now, he needed to respond in a way that didn't automatically lead to disclosure of the fact that she had offered to pay him £30,000 for the deed. So he changed the subject.

"Is the reason why you killed Heather also on a 'need to know' basis?" he asked.

"What the hell are you talking about?" said Trish, sounding irritated and clearly wondering where this was going.

"Initially, I made the mistake of thinking that you were following *me*, but it wasn't me, was it?" said Sam.

"It was Heather you were following, even if you wouldn't admit it when I asked you before. That's how you knew we went to my hotel the night she was murdered. Sorry, I should say, the night *you* murdered her. Because you were waiting for her, weren't you?" Sam hoped that she wouldn't become suspicious at him going over old ground.

"That's quite an imagination you have, Sam," said Trish, with clear enmity. "I wasn't following either you or her. I knew because I saw you leaving the nightclub with her. Which I thought was hilarious, given that her ex had been shagging your wife."

Sam hadn't been expecting that, and wasn't happy about that particular bit of information being aired again and recorded for posterity. He also really wanted to ask her how the fuck she knew, anyway, but thought better of it, given the situation.

*Least said, soonest mended*, he thought.

Besides, he was still feeling a bit raw and vulnerable about the whole thing. He hadn't felt able to challenge the validity of it when she told him the first time, and if he was honest he still wasn't really up to hearing any gory details.

Anyway, he had already had it confirmed by Audrey as well, and had reluctantly accepted that it was true. It wasn't as if he hadn't suspected something was going on when he and Kim were together, but it didn't stop him from feeling humiliated and at the same time desperate to find out what circumstances had led to that particular situation coming into being. He needed to know how Kim got involved with a scumbag like

Rab Lindsay.

But that could wait for now.

The main thing, for now, was that he had succeeded in getting Trish to admit that she had tried to blackmail him into killing Heather's husband. However, he had to remain focused on the rest of the job in hand.

"So, what's your reason for using a perfectly innocent situation to blackmail me into killing Heather's husband?"

"It was hardly blackmail," she scoffed, "it was practically the opposite. I mean, you were the one that was ending up with £30,000." She was evidently still perplexed by the direction that the discussion was heading.

Sam was glad that she had spoken abstractly, as opposed to definitively stating that the transaction had already taken place between them. He still hadn't got what he needed. And what he needed was to get her to talk some more.

"You threatened to tell the police I murdered Heather if I didn't do what you wanted. That qualifies as blackmail in my book," he said.

"That's some book," said Trish. "You're clearly not happy with just accusing me of blackmail – you're now accusing me of murder, too! Do you have any particular reason or evidence for this obsession of yours?"

"There was something bothering me about

something you said, but I didn't realise what it was until you accused me of knowing Heather before and having had planned it all, which is bollocks, obviously, because I didn't know her. Unlike you. That's what made me realise that it was a projection of your own twisted obsession with Heather."

"Now who's guilty of projection?" said Trish.

"What do you mean?"

"You're the one who's obviously obsessed with blaming me for this murder."

"Aye, right," said Sam. "I mean, seriously? You're having a fucking laugh, right?

*Two words*, he though, *pot and fucking kettle! And it's not an obsession, it's self-fucking-defence.*

"It didn't exactly take rocket science to figure out, either. Otherwise why would you want her husband dead?"

Sam realised that he was in risky territory here, given his own position, but also believed that he couldn't afford to be hesitant. *Fortune favours the brave*, he thought. And he was right.

"Because he brought my husband to his death," said Trish, with considerable emotion.

*Bingo*, thought Sam. *That has definitely got to qualify as an admission of intent and motive.* But he persisted further, out of a genuine need to know more.

"So you admit that you have a reason to want both Heather and her husband dead? That you're the one with the obsession here?"

"When it comes to obsession, I think that you should be looking a little closer to home," said Trish.

"What do you mean by that?" asked Sam, puzzled by her response.

"Your new friend, or should I say, squeeze?" responded Trish, sarcastically.

"What are you talking about?"

"Audrey fucking McPherson, that's what I'm talking about!" barked Trish. "You certainly can pick them!"

Before Sam could reply, she went on.

"I saw you with her at the door of the nightclub; the night that you stood outside and didn't come in. Shame, really, it would have been interesting. I wasn't sure if you had seen me or not, but I guessed you probably had.

"Did you tell her all about me and our little arrangement, Sam? A problem shared and all that. I bet you did, Sam, and I'm sure she managed to seduce you into a bit of pillow talk. And I bet she also gave you my life history and managed to convince you that it was me that killed your slutty friend. I'm guessing that she would be quite happy to have learned that I had asked you to kill Ms Lindsay's scumbag of a husband, too. It would suit her just fine for both of us to carry the can while she walks away Scot free."

That's not the case at all. As a matter of fact, she

was horrified at the thought of me even discussing it with you," said Sam.

"But of course she would say that, wouldn't she? She couldn't have you thinking that she approved of such behaviour. Better to make you think that I was the villain of the piece. How very convenient."

"You're one to talk," said Sam. "You were quite happy to blame me for Heather's murder, or more to the point, to use it to get me to kill her husband for you, whatever your reasons might be. And at the same time you got to cover up the fact that it was you who killed her."

"You have no evidence of that," said Trish. "And as I said, you should be looking elsewhere, even if you don't want to."

*It won't be me who's looking,* thought Sam, but at the same time he was having difficulty in trying to evaluate and make sense of the information and allegations issued by Trish.

"Why would Audrey kill Heather? I mean what reasons does she have? And do you have any evidence?"

"I don't know what her reasons are," said Trish. "But I noticed that on the first couple of days we were here she kept disappearing for long periods, for no good reason. I mean, she wasn't even a smoker. So I followed her a couple of times and realised that she appeared to be stalking Ms Lindsay wherever she went.

Ironically enough, on the night of the murder I nearly bumped into Ms Lindsay myself on my way home, no doubt after she left your hotel. I was a bit drunk, so I decided to get some things off my chest that I had wanted to say to her for years. And I'm glad I did, because it was quite cathartic. But after I left her I realised that there was something else that I wanted to say, so I started to walk back. And that's when I saw that Audrey McPherson was following her, again, so I stopped. That was when I saw her hit her on the head with a bottle before choking her to death. Is that enough evidence for you?"

"You mean that you saw her murder her and you didn't do anything about it?" said Sam, completely stunned.

"What was I supposed to do?" said Trish. "She's a lot younger and stronger than me, and I didn't want to end up on the end of the same treatment as Ms Lindsay. And anyway I wasn't sorry to see the back of her. I didn't lose any sleep over it to be honest, just in case you're wondering."

"But you were perfectly happy to accuse me of the crime," said Sam.

"It was the only way I thought that I could get you to do what I wanted," said Trish, "along with telling you about your wife's affair with him."

So there it was – a further admission that she had attempted to blackmail him into killing Rab Lindsay.

Despite all of this, she was still continuing to deny that she had anything to do with Heather's murder; not only that, but she was claiming that she had witnessed her being killed by Audrey. Sam wondered what the police would make of it all. Then, bang on time, there was a knock on the door. Trish got up, surprised, to answer it, and was met by both Inspector Powrie and Costales along with two other police officers.

Inspector Powrie informed her she was being arrested in connection with the murder of Heather Lindsay, and also with regard to charges of blackmail and incitement to murder in regard to Rab Lindsay. She was then handcuffed by the two other police officers, while Powrie informed her that she was being taken to Police Headquarters for questioning. Inspector Costales assured her that her room would be secured and her possessions kept safe. He also advised that her they would arrange for her to be provided with the services of a lawyer.

As Trish was led away, she looked at Sam quizzically, before realising what had just happened and his role in facilitating it. She began screaming abuse and accusations at him.

Sam's relief at getting it all over with was short-lived. The police told him that they wanted him to do it all over again with Audrey, explaining that even although Trish claimed to have witnessed Heather's murder and identified Audrey as the perpetrator, it was still her word against Audrey's. They needed more evidence, or a confession if possible. Otherwise, it could simply be the case that she was only putting the blame on Audrey, in order to avoid herself being charged with the murder. If they managed to get a confession it would have to be provided without any suspicion of duress, or using any kind of entrapment.

The police even speculated that both women may even have been involved, possibly together, which hadn't even occurred to Sam. But then, a lot of other things also hadn't occurred to him, one of which was that the police had initially suspected that he may have been involved along with either Trish or Audrey.

Inspector Powrie informed Sam that they would be in contact with him after they had interviewed Trish, in order to prepare him for his meeting with Audrey. Sam pointed out that this would have to take place the next day, as she was due to go home the day after.

It was at this point that the police decided to tell him that Rab Lindsay had been found dead in a flat in Finestrat.

# CHAPTER 74

23 November 2017

As Sam was heading back to the hotel, his phone rang. It was Audrey. He told her that he was planning to go and find a pub to watch the Celtic game, but he needed to get some sleep first and was heading to his room for a nap. He told her that he would catch up with her later, hoping that she wouldn't detect something untoward in his manner that would alert her that all was not well.

There was no sign of Audrey when Sam arrived at the hotel, nor was there any when he left later in the evening after some fitful sleep and a shower. She had also not contacted him, which he was happy about, as he was still trying to come to terms with the situation, specifically the claims made by Trish earlier in the day.

He grabbed a bite to eat at the same pub he'd visited to watch the football before, and timed his arrival for the start of the Celtic match. However, he stopped drinking after a couple of beers, as he found, surprisingly, that he wasn't in the mood for drinking, which both intrigued and reassured him. There was a pub quiz on at the same time as the match so the television sound was turned down; this came as something of a relief, as his team were taking a bit of a drubbing. He moved on to soft drinks, and decided to give the quiz a go, but only as a spectator.

A young couple sitting across from him were clearly participating; they were armed with pads and pencils but obviously struggling with the questions, which were being asked in groups of ten. Then he realised that it was the trendy 'loved up' couple he had noticed on his previous visit. He also realised that she was even more beautiful than he had first thought. As Sam knew several of the answers that they were missing, he innocently offered his help to the woman while her husband was at the bar, which she accepted gracefully. However, when he got back to join them her husband was obviously much less grateful for the help. He also appeared , from his demeanour, again to have had a snifter of some substance other than alcohol.

When Sam offered further assistance during the second group of questions, it was abundantly clear that the husband was almost resentful of his intervention, no matter how well intended. Maybe he felt threatened because Sam had, unintentionally, made him feel stupid. Or maybe it was down to whatever chemical substance he had taken. *Bugger this for a game of soldiers,* thought Sam, and he was just about to leave when the guy stood up and aggressively accosted him. "Think you're clever, do you? Well nobody likes a smart arse!" Having fired his opening shot, he then began accusing him of trying to chat up his wife.

His wife was trying to reason with him and apologise to Sam at the same time. Sam was tempted to take out all his pent-up frustration from the previous week on him and just stick one on his chin, when someone pushed between them and manhandled the guy back into his chair.

"Hey, you don't speak to my Irish friend like that! I think you have too much to drink. You leave now."

Sam looked up to see Luis, the barman from the bar in the old town, standing over him.

"It's OK Luis, I was just leaving anyway there's no need for you to get involved, but thanks anyway."

However, the woman was already ushering her husband out of the bar amid his protests that he was only protecting her.

"What are you doing here Luis – are you following me?" Sam asked, jokingly, and then realised that he had asked that question before very recently.

"No, but I will follow your lovely wife, amigo," said Luis, laughing.

*Even more ironic,* thought Sam. "We're not married," he said, prompting a mischievous smile from Luis. "And

327

I'm not Irish, I'm Scottish."

"Oh, sorry, I think you are Irish because…"

"Because I was watching the Irish game, I know. I have Irish ancestry and family in Ireland."

"And you like Celtic, too," added Luis.

"Unfortunately, yes, for my sins," said Sam, "and they must be many, because we are getting a right old gubbing."

"Gubbing?"said Luis, looking perplexed.

"Sorry, Luis – Scottish word," said Sam. "It means we are losing the game."

"I don't know much about football and you can tell my Scottish is not very good," said Luis, laughing mockingly at himself.

"My brother, Fernando, is always make fun of me," he said, gesturing towards an individual at the bar, who waved back. He then explained that this was his brother's bar and it was his night off from working in the other bar in the old town.

"Luckily for me," said Sam. Luis responded by offering to buy him a drink. Sam thanked him but declined, telling him that he had had enough and was heading back to the hotel for an early night.

"Audrey, your 'girl', is there?" asked Luis.

"Not tonight, Luis," said Sam, smiling, as he made his way out of the bar.

"Come to the Flamenco, Senor Sam, and bring your girl!" Luis shouted after him. *What a night*, thought Sam, as he made his way back to the hotel; *so much for a quiet night watching football.*

Celtic's game with PSG, as it turned out, had very little in the way of highlights from Sam's point of view, finishing as it did at 7-1, for the French side. However, he couldn't help feeling that he had at least got some sort of result earlier in the day. Now there was just the small matter of another murder to contend with.

# CHAPTER 75

23 November 2017

When the police interviewed her, Trish openly expressed feelings of hatred for both Rab and Heather Lindsay, because of the Heather's affair with her husband Frank over ten years previously and the subsequent blackmail by Rab, which she believed had ultimately led to her husband's death over three years ago. However, she was unaware that the second blackmail attempt was in relation to his affair with Audrey, assuming that because they were from the same person that they related to the same situation.

Trish did not attribute any blame towards her husband for the affair, instead placing responsibility fairly, or rather unfairly, at Heather's door, despite the fact that she was significantly younger, much less experienced and infinitely more impressionable. However, and understandably, it clearly suited Trish to believe that her husband was seduced by an immoral and ruthless harlot, with no conscience or moral compass, and who led a totally dissolute lifestyle. It had ultimately become more than just a convenient justification, gradually metamorphosing into a complete self-deception, whereby she had convinced herself of her husband's innocence. This way, she could still allow herself to believe that he still loved her and had simply been a victim of a calculated and heartless seduction. Trish also chose, wrongly, to believe that her husband had ended the affair, when it was actually Heather who had done so, due to the increasing difficulty she experienced in sharing her affections for Frank and the shame and guilt arising from the situation.

After further deliberation, Trish also informed the police that she had discovered about her husband's infidelity with Heather not from the blackmailer, but initially, from reading a half-written suicide note, which she had subsequently destroyed, as she did not want anyone to know that her husband had planned to take his own life rather than face up to the truth about his deceitful and clandestine behaviour.

This had followed the second demand for money from Rab Lindsay, which ultimately provoked – in Trish's view – her husband's heart attack, due to the resultant shock and stress. Having concluded that there was no reason to deny or hide the truth from anyone now, she also revealed that she had found text messages to and from Heather on an old phone of her husband's, which he hadn't password-protected. The phone that he had at the time of his death had been locked, but she was able to open that, too, as she knew his password. There she found the incriminating email, which for some reason Frank had kept.

The only other compromising email was a reply that Frank had saved but hadn't sent to Rab Lindsay, stating that he knew him to be responsible for both blackmail demands, even if he couldn't prove it. However, he had finished the email by advising that his intention was to take his chances and ask the police to deal with it, with all their technical and forensic expertise. Unfortunately, his life had tragically been taken from him before he had the opportunity to make the decision to either delete it or send it.

Trish had also found some unsent love letters, written to Heather, which she had also destroyed. There were no messages or letters to Audrey.

She also divulged the details of the story her husband had fabricated about the con man and the failed investment to cover up the fact that he was being blackmailed. Then finally, she spoke quite emotionally about her own guilt in relation to the all too real extortion by a man she had met after Frank died, and who had gone on to con her out of a fortune due to her stupidity. With some considerable difficulty, she related all the sorry details of her encounter with the fraudster and its devastating and humiliating outcome. She became frequently distraught as she spoke about how she had been deceived, and about how she had subsequently deceived her own family and friends and ignored their advice.

But she still maintained that her only crime was to have been extremely naive and gullible. Furthermore, she believed that the situation was ultimately caused by the actions of another equally as ruthless and predatory individual much closer to home. This flawed logic and obsession was what had led to her decision that one day she would finally take revenge against the person that she viewed as the culprit.

Rab Lindsay.

# CHAPTER 76

24 November 2017

Sam had not seen or heard from Audrey the previous night and there was no sign of her when he returned to the hotel. He had gone upstairs to his room and fell asleep in front of the television watching the highlights, or more accurately highlight, of the Celtic vs PSG game, with sound and commentary, on the BBC. He awoke around 3.30 a.m. feeling quite sickly and disorientated, then stripped off and got into bed. Surprisingly he fell asleep again quite quickly and awoke feeling better and less tired than he had in days. The lack of alcohol probably had something to do with it, he concluded.

Sam went to breakfast about 9.30 a.m., but again there was no sign of Audrey. *Obviously having a long lie-in,* he thought. Or maybe not. Maybe she was packing her case? After all, she was meant to be leaving tomorrow. Nevertheless, he was surprised that she had not been in touch; he wondered if she knew about Trish's arrest, and whether it had raised any alarm bells.

After breakfast, Sam went to the supermarket and bought a newspaper to check the reports of Rab Lindsay's murder. The weather wasn't that hot, so he gave the pool a miss and headed back to the room to await a call advising him of the next step in the process, which presumably involved him making contact with Audrey at some point.

He made himself a cup of tea and went out to the balcony, where he was joined by the pigeon, strutting about in quite a 'gallus' fashion, as if it was his balcony and Sam was an intruder.

"Come in, nice to see you," said Sam. "Where were you when I needed you? You don't phone, you don't write and then you just stroll back in like you own the place without so much as a by your leave," he opined, but the bird just jumped on to the table and looked at him like it was expecting something. So he went and fetched some bread, which it was happy to eat from his hand. He poured the crumbs on to the table and let it carry on pecking away while he made himself a cup of coffee, for a change, and then sat down to read his newspaper.

Unsurprisingly, the news of Rab Lindsay's murder was front page news, with all sorts of questions being asked about the possible motive behind the killings, particularly given the connection between the two victims. There were also questions raised in regard to the police and their ability to keep people safe, as well as a suggestion that there may be a serial killer at large.

Predictably, concern was raised about the likely effect on the tourist trade of the resort.

*Aye right* thought Sam, *It'll probably double it!*

# CHAPTER 77

24 November 2017

After further questioning, Trish had disclosed that she only came to the decision to have Rab Lindsay killed after Heather was murdered by Audrey. She believed that it would provide the ideal opportunity, because it would be assumed that the same person was responsible for both deaths, particularly when it was revealed in the press that he was expected to arrive in Benidorm within days. She also considered Sam Meredith to be the perfect candidate to blackmail into carrying out the murder, given his obvious connection with Heather and his understandable reluctance to go to the police.

In her desperate and deluded state of mind, she had perversely reasoned that she could persuade Sam to carry out her request and that he would understand that it was simply justice for the injustice perpetrated against her and her family. She genuinely believed that Sam would agree to do it, particularly given that she was also offering a substantial financial incentive.

Her threat to go to the police was just that – a threat to test his resolve and character, to see how he would react or indeed if he really would go to the police. Once she was convinced that he wouldn't, the money was just a sweetener. It was almost all that was left of the insurance money she got after Frank's death. She had no use for it and regarded it as money well spent if it meant that it ended the life of the man who had ended that of her husband.

However, she believed that the real clincher would be when she told Sam that Rab Lindsay had had an affair with his wife, as this would also provide him with the opportunity to take his revenge– and Rab Lindsay's life.

# CHAPTER 78

24 November 2017

As Sam perused the newspaper, he came across an article about a criminal, Zak Soraya, who had been convicted of extorting money from people online by threatening to expose their use of adult dating and escort websites to their families and friends. Between 2010 and 2016, Soraya was believed to have collected over three million pounds and spent more than one million maintaining a luxury lifestyle that included the purchase of luxury properties, holidays, cars, and prostitutes. Tragically, it was believed that some of his victims had taken their own lives rather than face up to their actions. Sam was delighted to read that Soraya had been sentenced to seven years and ordered to pay back over £500,000 to his victims, or face a further five years in jail.

Maybe there was some justice in the world after all,

pondered Sam. Maybe the chickens, like the pigeon, had come home to roost. However, when he looked up, the pigeon had gone.

The hotel room phone rang as Sam finished his second cup of tea. It was Inspector Powrie, asking him to join her and her colleague in the same room as before.

If anything, Sam was even more anxious and unsettled than he'd been during his first interview. On entering the room, he was asked by Inspector Powrie if he had spoken to Audrey and he advised her accordingly. She and her colleague then informed him that Heather's post mortem had revealed that there was no sign of a struggle, but that the appearance and distribution of the blood was consistent with impact spatter from some form of blunt force trauma. There were also shards of glass embedded in her skull, so she was most likely struck by a bottle, although none was found at the scene.

However, this was not believed to be the cause of death, as there were also pressure marks on the neck and windpipe which had more than likely been caused by strangulation. It appeared that Heather had been disabled by the blow to the head before dying of asphyxiation, caused by being choked to death, probably from an arm around her neck and pressure being applied to the head and neck from behind. There were no fingerprints found, either, so the murderer had obviously worn gloves of some kind, most likely latex, suggesting that the attack had been pre-conceived and planned. It also fitted with the description of what Trish claimed to have seen.

Inspector Costales told Sam that they knew of his whereabouts at the time when Rab Lindsay was estimated to have been murdered, which, ironically, was with Audrey in her room, so he was not a suspect for that murder. However, Inspector Powrie then informed him that they would want to interview him again, as they just needed to "dot some I's and cross some T's."

Both Inspectors again went through the process of preparing and briefing him for his meeting with Audrey, whom they were still hopeful would call Sam, rather than him having to initiate contact. Their wish was granted 20 minutes later when his mobile phone rang. Not surprisingly, the first thing that Audrey asked him was whether he had seen a newspaper, and whether he knew about Rab Lindsay's murder. Without waiting for an answer, she added, "Please tell me you had nothing to do with it?"

Sam assured Audrey that he hadn't, while neglecting to tell her that she was his alibi.

"I am assuming that Trish must have found somebody else to carry out her dirty work," he said, in a very reasoned and matter of fact way. This seemed to reassure her, and she suggested to Sam that they meet up for lunch to catch up. He told her that he'd had a substantial breakfast and also lied that he was severely hung over, and arranged to meet up with her at her room for a coffee instead.

When Sam arrived at Audrey's room she greeted him warmly, told him that she had missed him and asked him how he liked his coffee.

"White with a teaspoon of brown sugar, if you have it," said Sam. Audrey poured and then handed him his coffee, gesturing for him to join her on the sofa. He sat down opposite her.

"So, how was the football?" she asked.

"Mixed," said Sam, relaying the results while wondering if she was checking to see if he really had been watching football.

"I didn't think you were interested in football?" he said.

"I'm not, I'm just interested in you."

"You checking up on me?"

"Maybe – would you mind if I was?"

"Depends."

"On what?"

"On *why* you're checking up on me, if indeed you are," Sam said. "Don't you trust me?"

"I don't know," said Audrey, looking at him quizzically.

"What does that mean?" asked Sam, wondering

where this was going.

"I need to ask you something," replied Audrey.

"Oh, what?" asked Sam, genuinely concerned that she had somehow figured out what was going on.

"Have you seen Trish?"

"Since when?" he replied, cautiously, trying to buy some time. "I thought you were meeting up with her?"

"I did, two days ago, along with some of the others, for part of the night. Then we went our separate ways, as usual."

"Well, I haven't seen her since then," said Sam.

"And neither has anybody else," said Audrey.

"Oh, right," said Sam, as casually as he could manage. "Are you worried?"

"Not really, more intrigued,"

"Maybe she's found a man," suggested Sam, trying to keep it light and low key.

"Mmm, maybe" said Audrey, sounding unconvinced. "It all seems a bit strange."

"In what way?"

"Just that she should go AWOL the same time as you, and also, coincidentally, just before another murder is committed. It's all just a bit convenient, don't you think?"

Sam had not expected a response of this nature from her, but decided to go with it and see where it took them.

"So you *do* think I had something to do with the

murder *and* Trish's disappearance?"

"I don't know what to think" said Audrey.

*Well,* thought Sam; *if she does have anything to do with Heather's murder, she is certainly managing to distract attention away from it by this unexpected tactic.*

Another thought occurred to him.

*She couldn't know that she was being recorded, could she? No, surely not.*

He couldn't help feeling that her dialogue and line of questioning, interestingly, seemed to involve putting him in the frame for Rab's murder and Trish's disappearance. Just like Trish had suggested. No, he was just being paranoid, as he had nothing to worry about on either count– hopefully. Nevertheless, he was now beginning to question everything about Audrey's behaviour, right back to their first meeting in the hotel bar. Was it indeed just coincidence that she ended up in his hotel? And why did she find him so apparently irresistible? *She's a very attractive woman, and a lot younger than me, too*, he thought, *and it's not like we had a lot of time to get to know one another and build up a relationship.*

Notwithstanding that, he couldn't deny that there did seem to have been a connection and mutual attraction, which he was happy to enjoy and benefit from at the time. And who wouldn't have? he reasoned. However, he also realised that Audrey had been the main instigator, the driving force behind all that had happened.

And a lot had happened.

He had wondered then, and he still wondered now, why their liaison had happened, even before hearing the recent revelations and allegations made by Trish.

Also, there was her subsequent unconditional supportive attitude towards him to consider. She'd shown such support to someone whom she didn't really know, a relative stranger, who, amidst possible evidence to the contrary, claimed to have nothing to do with the death of a woman whom she knew and whom he had previously spent the night with, prior to her being found murdered. And there was her willingness, albeit belated (or perhaps premeditated?) to tell him all about Trish and Heather's history and then her affair with Frank, too.

What was the thinking behind it all? he wondered. Was this a case of her keeping her friends close, and her enemies closer?

Or was he still guilty of reading too much into it all?

Then there was the suggestion, from the police, that Audrey and Trish may even be involved together. Was that really possible?

Sam looked around the room and noticed that it was much tidier than normal, with no clothes strewn around, probably because Audrey had packed. Indeed, the wardrobes looked empty, and the suitcases closed and strapped up.

"You all packed and ready to go?" he asked.

"Yes, I'll be glad to get home actually, but not looking forward to going back to work," said Audrey.

*Well, you might not have worry about that,* thought Sam, and then realised that that was most likely dependent upon the outcome of this conversation. He suddenly felt an immense weight of responsibility upon his shoulders.

He also suddenly realised that he didn't know what Audrey did for a living. So he asked her.

"What kind of work do you do?" asked Sam. "You never said."

"You never asked," said Audrey. "I'm a Field Sales Executive with a Medical Supplies Company. It's a peripatetic position with a client base across west central Scotland and north east England."

"Is it a local business?" enquired Sam, who could not think of any such company in Calderhall.

"No, the main office is in Glasgow, in the City Centre."

"Have you always worked there?"

"No," said Audrey, hesitating before adding, "I used to work in the Boots factory before it closed, mainly doing financial administration and book keeping work."

"And then, presumably, you got a better offer with more money in the job in Glasgow?" asked Sam.

"Well no, not initially. I went to work for a local construction company in an administrative position for a while. But it didn't work out, so I applied for the job in the town."

Sam sensed unease in Audrey's demeanour, then realised the possible reason behind her hesitancy.

"How long have you been in your current post?" he asked.

"Just under six years. Why do you ask?"

"It was Frank's company, wasn't it, Audrey?" said Sam. "Did you leave the job during or after the affair with him?" he continued, not waiting for her answer.

"What does it matter?" Audrey replied, tersely. Responding to Sam's piercing stare, she continued.

"I left during the affair. It was becoming too awkward and difficult to work there at the same time as we were seeing each other, so he encouraged me to look for another job, telling me I was over qualified for the admin job anyway, which I was."

"Who ended the affair, Audrey? Was it you or Frank ?"

"What difference does it make?" replied Audrey impatiently. Sam said nothing.

"He did," she finally admitted, with some apparent difficulty.

"So, how long had it lasted?"

"Just under two years."

"Were you still with your husband? Did your marriage end because he found out about you and Frank?"

"What? No, that wasn't what happened at all," she answered, defensively.

"My marriage ended because I didn't love my husband anymore, mainly because he was a jealous, possessive maniac who was too handy with his fists. That's why I ended up going to self- defence classes.

"Anyway, why did your marriage end, Sam? Was it because you found out about your wife's affair with Rab Lindsay? Oh no, I forgot, you were totally oblivious to that."

Sam still wanted to ask how she and apparently half of Calderhall appeared to know what he hadn't, but he still wasn't up to it, and he reminded himself that this was not why he was there. He needed to focus.

"Can I ask you something?" he said.

"What?" said Audrey, looking drained and wondering what was coming next.

"Where were you when Heather was killed?"

"I was, eh . . . why are you asking me that?"

"Because it's a need to know situation, Audrey, and I need to know."

"I was out with the girls. Trish was there too. But then we split up again, as per usual."

"So were you with someone the whole night?"

"Yes, until I went home," replied Audrey,

"Did you walk home alone?"

"What? Yes, eh, no, eh, I'm not sure. Yes, I think so, but only for part of the way."

"You don't seem sure," said Sam.

"Why are you speaking to me like this, Sam?" Why are you asking me all these questions?

"Same reason you were asking me all the questions you did," said Sam. "To find out if I can trust you."

"Trust me about what?"

"About everything, really," said Sam. He wanted to ask her all the questions he had about everything that had happened but decided to stick to the script.

"Where were you when Rab Lindsay was killed?"

Audrey seemed momentarily disorientated and she paused, as if thinking about the question before answering.

"I don't know. I don't know what time he was killed," she replied.

"But you seem to know when Heather was murdered," said Sam.

Audrey again appeared taken aback and surprised by the question and was initially hesitant and uncertain in her response.

"I, eh . . . must have read it in the papers or social media, probably" she replied, hesitantly.

Sam didn't think he had ever seen Audrey reading a newspaper but, like a lot of people, she was on her phone a lot. Nevertheless, it made no difference.

"You couldn't have read it anywhere. The police have never released that information to the papers."

"Well maybe there was speculation about it on

social media. Or maybe I was thinking about when she was found rather than when she was murdered.

"And how do you know the police never released that information, anyway? You seem to know an awful lot of information all of a sudden."

"There's something I haven't told you," said Sam.

"What?" asked Audrey, looking genuinely anxious and worried.

"Do you remember when I met with Trish and she asked me to murder Rab Lindsay?"

"Uh huh, what about it?"

"Well, I never told you, but during the course of the conversation, I asked her, quite reasonably, if she had killed Heather, or arranged to have her killed," lied Sam.

"And?" said Audrey, seeming remarkably calm and unconcerned.

"She was quite up front about how much she hated Heather and her husband, but she was also adamant that she had nothing to do with her murder," said Sam, searching Audrey's face for any kind of reaction.

"Well, she is going to say that, isn't she? For god's sake – you didn't expect her to just hold her hands up and come out and admit to it, did you?" said Audrey.

"No, I didn't. But I also wasn't expecting or prepared for what she did say."

"And what was that?" asked Audrey, all of a sudden appearing hesitant and anxious.

"She claimed that it was _you_ that killed her, Audrey," said Sam, as dispassionately as he could manage.

"She's a liar!" said Audrey, without missing a beat. "She's obviously just saying that to cover up the fact that she did it!"

"Did you see her kill Heather?" asked Sam, conscious that Audrey did not seem particularly shocked or upset at the allegation.

"No," said Audrey, defiantly.

Sam left a deliberately long pause before speaking again.

"Trish says that she saw _you_ kill her," he said.

"Well she would say that, wouldn't she? I mean, this is a woman who asked you to kill Heather's husband, remember, or have you forgotten that? I told you that I thought she wanted to kill me too, and she was clearly following me."

"I was actually convinced that she was following Heather, too, but now I know that it was you who had been following her, Audrey.

"But, you're right. Trish _had_ been following you, because she thought you were behaving suspiciously. That was when she worked out that you were following Heather.

"However – and ironically – on the night in question, she wasn't following you," he explained. "She was actually on her way back to her hotel from the bar she had been at with her friends when she saw Heather and decided to tell her what she thought of her."

"I know. I saw her," said Audrey, and clearly immediately wished she hadn't.

"So you admit that you were there; that it was *you* that was following Heather?" said Sam.

"I admit that I saw Trish talking to Heather the Whore, but then she walked away, so she couldn't have seen anything. Not that there was anything to see," she added hastily.

"But there was, and she did," said Sam. "You see, she turned back because there was something else that she had forgotten to say to her, and that's when she saw you kill her."

"How very convenient. And what was it that she so desperately wanted to tell her?"

"I don't know, I never asked her," said Sam, realising that he should have checked this. He moved on.

"Why would she want to kill Heather anyway?" he asked

"I don't know. Maybe she found out about the affair?" answered Audrey.

"Yes, she did find out about the affair and she stated openly that she hated Heather," said Sam. "But her anger and wrath wasn't directed at Heather. It was Rab Lindsay she wanted dead, because she blamed him for her husband's death."

"You seem to know an awful lot about how she felt

and why she wanted Rab Lindsay dead," said Audrey. I thought you said that she never gave you her reasons?"

"I lied," said Sam, now finding the whole experience extremely stressful and unpleasant, and wishing it would just stop. However, he needed to keep going as he felt that if he continued to press Audrey she would let something else slip.

"If you think that Trish knowing about the affair was reason enough for her to murder Heather, then maybe it was reason enough for you?" he said. "You were clearly jealous of her."

"I wasn't jealous of her" said Audrey, angrily. "And I never killed anybody, I couldn't do that. I'm not strong enough to strangle anyone."

Back of the net!

Sam stared at Audrey, deliberately letting her words hang in the air before eventually asking;

"How did you know that she was strangled?"

"I . . . I don't know," she replied, clearly struggling to explain. "Like I said before, it must have been in the papers or the news."

"No, it wasn't," said Sam. "The details of how she was killed and the findings of the post mortem have also never been released to the media."

Again, he looked at Audrey for any sign of uncertainty.

"In that case, how do *you* know how she was killed,

and how do *you* know all about the post mortem, Sam? You're beginning to sound like the bloody police."

"As I said before, Trish told me, and remember I work for a newspaper so I am in touch with people in the media," he replied, hoping that this would satisfy her, but realising that he needed to be more careful, as he was becoming a bit reckless. He decided that the best form of defence was attack.

"The only people who would know how she was killed other than the police and forensic staff would be Heather's sister, brother and her ex-husband, as they would have been advised by the police. Along with Trish – if she's telling the truth – and the murderer. And you clearly know when and how she was killed."

Audrey just stared at Sam and said nothing.

He decided to continue with the direct, confrontational approach.

"Please tell me you didn't murder Heather because of her affair with Frank?"

"What? No, I didn't care about that," Audrey retorted. "I had accepted that and the fact that he loved her. It was long before we met. But *she* couldn't accept it. She couldn't let it go, couldn't accept the fact that he was happy without her. That *we* were happy."

"But he was a married man, married to Trish."

"Oh, for god's sake, he wasn't happy with her," said Audrey. "He hadn't been for years, otherwise why would he be looking elsewhere? He only stayed with her because of the family and the financial situation."

"Or maybe he just liked a bit on the side," said Sam, being deliberately provocative.

"It wasn't like that. I told you, we loved each other," protested Audrey. "I loved him more than either Heather or Trish did. I mean he was hardly cold when Trish was off looking for another man on a seedy dating site.

"She couldn't wait, as far as I am led to believe. So she got what she deserved. And so did the Whore."

"It annoyed you that he had told you that he loved Heather but he hadn't told you that he loved you, didn't it?" said Sam.

Audrey hesitated, and stared at Sam before finally answering. "Yes, but he would've told me. I know he would have, it was only a matter of time. But we weren't allowed to have the time, because that bitch and her husband wouldn't allow it. Because she had decided that if she couldn't have him, no one would. So she used her thug of a husband to make sure that it couldn't continue."

"I don't think he needed any encouragement from Heather; he was perfectly capable of doing something like that on his own," countered Sam.

"Is that what Heather the Whore told you was it, while you were fucking her? She probably only shagged you because your wife shagged her husband. It was most likely a revenge fuck."

*So is this the real Audrey finally showing herself?* thought Sam. *Trish was right all along, then – it was all just cynical pillow talk to get the information she needed to set us both up. How could he have been so gullible?* He answered his own question. *Because she was so clever and devious, and I was thinking with my dick instead of my brain. Down there for dancing indeed.*

It may have been a pride thing, but for whatever reason, he decided that he would play her at her own game.

"Thanks for that. You really are a piece of work. And to think that I almost believed all your lies. Anyway, just so you know – from what I can gather, Frank was happy to use the blackmail as an excuse to finish it with you," he said, deliberately lying to be antagonistic, and looking for a reaction.

However, he really wasn't sure what was allowable and what wasn't, as far as the police were concerned. He was half expecting the whole thing to be brought to an end at any minute.

"You don't know that – it's a fucking lie! Why are you saying it?" Audrey retorted angrily.

"Come on," said Sam, "I'm sure that you must've considered it as a possibility?"

"No, I hadn't, ever," said Audrey, curtly. "He finished it because he wanted to protect me in the event of the threat to reveal our affair being carried out, which was likely, because he couldn't afford to pay the money.

"Rab Lindsay was probably also blackmailing other married men that his slut of a wife had slept with at his behest. She was a whore who would do anything that he asked as long as he kept her sweet."

Sam realised that Audrey was clearly in denial, having chosen to believe Frank's flimsy and senseless reasoning and to blame Heather for her own relationship with Frank ending , rather than accepting that their relationship was coming to an end. And also that Rab Lindsay had acted totally independently and his actions were nothing to do with Heather.

"So, after almost five years of obsessive stalking and planning, you followed Heather to Benidorm to finally carry out your retribution," said Sam. And then, remembering the police's previous comments; "Were you and Trish in it together?"

"What? No, why would I be involved with her? She couldn't even kill somebody by herself. She had to ask somebody else to do it for her. Or maybe she did, because she was fed up waiting on you? Or maybe you did do it, Sam, and you're not letting on?"

"There's only one of us here who is murderer. And it isn't me," said Sam.

"I don't regret what I did. She deserved it. I had wanted to do it for years. I just never had the opportunity before.

"So, what are you going to do about it, Sam? Tell

the police? Maybe they would like to hear about how Trish asked you to kill Rab Lindsay?"

There was a knock on the door. Sam stood up and looked at Audrey.

"Well now's your chance to tell them yourself," he said.

# CHAPTER 79

2014

Frank Roy was not given to a lot of soul searching or reproaching himself for past misdeeds, even after his selfish, indulgent behaviour five years ago had led to such traumatic consequences for both himself and his family. However for some reason, on this particular day he found himself in a quite reflective, if pragmatic state of mind.

He had been with his wife for over forty years and he supposed that he still loved her; she was the mother of his children after all, and he would never leave her because of both the personal and practical effects that would have on both of them, and the family as a whole.

For some reason, his marriage was not enough for him; he needed to have his other relationships. He didn't feel good about it; he didn't feel anything about it, in fact, it was just the way it was – the way *he* was –

he enjoyed having affairs, even though it had been difficult and stressful to keep them hidden from his family and friends. He had, however, confided in a select few of the latter out of necessity; he needed support and alibis for his unfaithful behaviour from time to time. As far as he knew, none of these confidantes had betrayed his trust, although you could never be completely sure, because people liked to talk. What's the point in knowing a secret if you can't tell someone else? He was well aware that some people liked nothing better than a bit of gossip and scandal.

One of the unfortunate consequences of infidelity is that the participants in that particular activity are constantly trying to find or fabricate reasons and construct situations that will allow them to see the object of their affections without arousing undue suspicion. While such opportunities can prove to be extremely rare and difficult to come by, necessity is without doubt the mother of invention in that particular scenario.

Sometimes Frank wondered if his wife knew about his affairs, and had just turned a blind eye. Whenever he thought about it, he found it difficult to believe that the sinned against spouses or partners of people involved in illicit relationships did not suspect anything or recognise the signs, when their errant partners were behaving suspiciously or out of character.

This would typically involve out of character,

altruistic behaviour, like offering to go to the supermarket or anywhere else that got them out of the house for a brief but precious period of time. But there's only so many times that you can take your car for petrol or to the car wash. He mused that men who are having affairs invariably either have the cleanest cars in the street, or the most problematic – vehicles which seem to break down constantly, requiring the attention of their own personal mechanic, who just happens to be female, blonde and invariably almost half their age.

Then there would be the partners who claimed to be going to the pub and returned several hours later in a remarkably sober state. Or the ones *in* the pub, who were so easy to spot as they whispered into their mobiles, while nervously exiting the premises.

He had met Audrey, as he recalled, when she came to work for him at his building firm. She was everything that Heather hadn't been, but not in a good way. Initially she was good fun and very passionate and adventurous, and she seemed to enjoy the clandestine side of their affair, unlike Heather. However, as things progressed she also became much more demanding, possessive and jealous; strangely, this wasn't directed at his wife so much, but at Heather.

He came to regret telling her about that previous affair, and had only done so in the first place because he thought she already knew – she'd once made some comments which he had misinterpreted because of his paranoia. He also wished that he hadn't told her that he loved Heather, as this seemed to prey on her insecurity. She'd also started to ask questions about his marriage, specifically whether he still had sex with his wife, how often they did it, and if he enjoyed it.

The truth of it was that she was becoming increasingly intolerant of his situation; he was also beginning to get the feeling that she would have been happy if their relationship had been discovered. Frank became increasingly irritated by her clingy, jealous behaviour, and realised there were in fact quite a lot of things about her that he had begun to find more and more objectionable and difficult to deal with. All these factors had ultimately combined to cast the death knell on their relationship for him, more or less, and he was glad when she took his advice, applying for and accepting another, better-paid job elsewhere, which was genuinely more suited to her abilities. If nothing else, he could not deny that she had been very efficient and professional in her job when she'd worked for him.

Perhaps not surprisingly, he soon found himself making excuses for not being able to see her. In retrospect, he realised that he probably should have ended it long before he did, but it had been too convenient to stop. By the time they split up, she had moved in to a rented flat with a friend, which was relatively close to where he lived, following the break-up of her marriage. After just a few months, her flat-mate had unexpectedly decided to move back home to be with her parents when her father took unwell, leaving her with an 'empty'. He was almost happy to have the excuse of a blackmail threat to use as a 'get out of jail' card when it came. What he hadn't bargained on, however, was the extent of her anger and resentment at their relationship coming to an end. And for some reason that he couldn't fathom, she was obsessed with the idea that Heather was behind it all. At one stage he was actually worried about what she might do, such was the level of her ire. But by then, he had something else much more concerning to worry about, which, in the end, arguably and tragically, brought him to his death.

# CHAPTER 80

24 November 2017

The Watcher stared at the wall of the cell, almost as if she was trying to look through it, and beyond it, to try to find some answers and understanding of everything that had happened to her. How had it all gone so wrong? She had planned it all so well, and for so long. And how had that bastard Sam managed to outsmart and out-manoeuvre both her and Trish – the police having told her of the latter's fate? Even more amazing was the fact that he apparently seemed to have managed to strike some sort of deal with the police to avoid being charged with anything himself. How the fuck had he managed that? He had clearly been involved, along with Trish, in killing Rab Lindsay, and he'd been paid handsomely for it.

She had underestimated him, and she was now paying the price.

When questioned by the police, she presented as extremely febrile and indignant, particularly in response to any suggestion that she was in any way responsible or involved in Heather's murder. However, after they told her that they had clear CCTV footage (which they didn't), and her own testimony on tape from the wire worn by Sam (which while not totally conclusive, was considered sufficient to justify charging her), she decided that there was nothing to be gained by further denials. She wasn't even emotional or distressed in the end.

On the contrary, she was very voluble, and answered the police's questions without rancour, calmly divulging all the details of the "evil" destruction of her life by "the Whore". She also revealed everything she knew about Rab Lindsay's blackmail of Frank, which he had reluctantly told her about prior to ending their affair.

Audrey wasn't aware, however, that he had also been blackmailed years previously as a result of his affair with Heather. Unsurprisingly, Frank hadn't confided in her about that particular situation. While Heather had had nothing to do with the blackmail, or indeed Frank ending their relationship, Audrey would never accept that to be the case.

Heather had undoubtedly loved Frank, however, she had moved on. On the other hand, Audrey was clearly still obsessively jealous and resentful of Heather, convinced that she, along with her husband, had deliberately and systematically destroyed both their lives. At one point, she also actually suspected that Frank was still seeing Heather, but that was just jealousy and paranoia. However, the truth of it was that Frank simply didn't love her and had already decided that their affair was coming to an end. Unfortunately, very soon after, so did his life.

The other consequence of the situation was that Audrey hadn't really achieved any emotional closure or resolution, with feelings of anger and hurt continuing to fester and gnaw away at her, culminating in an obsessive need for revenge and what she perceived as justice.

While it was arguable that Rab Lindsay's criminal and callous actions had led indirectly to Frank's death, all of Audrey's hatred and anger was reserved for Heather. This was a much more personal and painful matter altogether, because of how it had made her feel. And how it had made her feel was both humiliated and scorned.

Hell hath no fury, indeed.

# CHAPTER 81

24 November 2017

During her interview with the police, Audrey told them that when she saw Sam in their hotel she recognised him as being "the man whose wife, Kim, had had an affair with Rab Lindsay," which, ironically, was also the last thing that she said to Heather before she killed her. Ironic, because it was also what Trish had forgotten to tell Heather and had intended to reveal to her, if what she told the police was to be believed. She wasn't sure if Heather knew, but she wanted to make sure that she understood the irony of her just having been with Kim's estranged husband.

Audrey also said she couldn't believe it when she saw Sam and Heather together in the night club on that fateful night, when she had firstly chanced upon, followed and then finally murdered her. Calmly and dispassionately, she described to the police how she had put on a lightweight, all in one waterproof polythene suit, like the ones worn by Forensic Pathologists or Scenes of Crime Officers, to protect her clothes from any spatters of blood, simply folding it back into a small pouch before washing it in the shower and then ditching it in a bin some distance away. She had put the remainder of the broken bottle into a bottle bank.

After Audrey had subsequently manipulated and seduced her way into Sam's bed and confidence, she was also surprised that he'd not known about his wife's affair with Rab Lindsay, until Trish told him.

"If he doesn't know, he's the only person from Calderhall who doesn't," Trish had said to her and everyone in the company when they had been discussing the issue, earlier on in the evening of the murder. Audrey realised the irony of that coming from Trish, but she wasn't about to say anything.

After discovering that Sam and Trish were spending quite a bit of time together, Audrey decided to find out why, particularly as she was unsure if Trish suspected or had inadvertently found out anything about Heather's death.

She already suspected that Trish had been suspicious of her and had perhaps even been following her. So she had decided, as Sam ultimately suspected, to make sure that she was in a position to be kept informed of developments. She was quite happy to use her feminine wiles and sexuality to achieve it. She only told Sam about her affair with Frank Roy because she wanted to find out whether Trish knew and had told Sam about it. If that was the case, there was indeed a genuine possibility that she did in fact want Sam to kill her.

On learning that she was not the target of Trish's homicidal intentions, Audrey was both relieved and happy to use the situation in any way she could to her advantage. Also, despite her claims to the contrary, she would have been quite happy for Sam to carry out Trish's wishes. And she still wasn't sure that he hadn't.

Audrey had orchestrated and exacted her own revenge against the person she perceived, quite misguidedly, as being the person responsible for destroying her life, by taking her life. And now the rest of her own life would be the price she would have to pay.

# CHAPTER 82

24 November 2017

Following Audrey's arrest, Sam was debriefed, relieved of his wire, and thanked by the police for his efforts and co-operation. They reminded him that they would still need to interview him, most probably the next day, and that they would be in touch. When they left and he was on his own, Sam felt as though a huge weight had been lifted from his shoulders. He also realised that he was completely exhausted, both physically and mentally, but he knew that he wouldn't sleep a wink because he was completely wired (a pun which made him smile), before suddenly becoming quite emotional.

Sam headed back to his room, where he freshened up and changed, deciding to make the best of what remained of his holiday. As he was removing the shorts that he was wearing something fell on the floor.

He looked down and was surprised to see Heather's

earring. The earring that he had decided to plant in Trish's room as insurance, in the event of insufficient evidence being obtained. However, thankfully, he had forgotten all about it; he realised now just how stupid he had been in even considering it, and was very glad that he hadn't carried out his ill-conceived plan. He placed it on the dresser and changed into a pair of denims. As he did so, the doorbell rang, and the maid used the key to open the door, asking if he wanted the room cleaned. He told her that he was just on his way out, and beckoned for her to come in.

As she came in, she walked over to the dresser and said something loud in Spanish, before picking up the earring and turning to Sam.

"My earring! You find my earring! I think I lose it, they were my mother's. Thank you so much Senor, I am so happy you have found it."

She definitely was happy, so much so that he thought that she was going to kiss him. So he moved towards the door, as he had had quite enough of that nonsense to last him a lifetime. He realised that it must've fallen off when she was making the bed. He also realised what an absolute tit he would've made of himself if he had remembered to execute his ridiculous 'plan'.

God, he needed a drink! And he was quite happy to admit it to himself. His phone had been switched off, for obvious reasons, and when he switched it back on it began beeping and ringing off the scale. The messages were coming from colleagues at the newspaper, who were obviously desperate for information from their "man on the scene", following the news of the second murder being released. He let it ring. He was on holiday, after all. And he had an appointment with a man and a monkey.

Sam had considered the Flamenco at Luis' bar, but he realised that his barman amigo was more interested in Audrey; he'd probably be disappointed that she was not with him and want an explanation.

He would be able to hear and read about her in the media soon enough.

# CHAPTER 83

Sam's 'proposition' to Akmal had been to tell him that he needed to ask him to "speak to someone". Akmal misunderstood initially, protesting, "You say that I don't speak to anyone about what happened."

"No, sorry, I need you to speak to someone for me," said Sam, before correcting himself. "Actually, not for me," he clarified, "for Trish."

"Trish? You speak to Trish? But you say to me not to speak to her about what happened," replied Akmal, becoming even more confused and agitated.

Sam explained to Akmal what was required, emphasising that this was what Trish had wanted, and about the price she was prepared to pay for it. Akmal, who seemed quite relieved and not unduly concerned about the nature of the request, said he would make the appropriate inquiries. Sam also gave him his mobile number, in order that he could contact him to confirm the arrangements if he needed to, but he was very clear that he should only call from a payphone so that there was nothing to formally connect them.

Sam had also arranged to meet Akmal at Trish's hotel to give him the photo of Rab Lindsay from the newspaper along with the address of a flat in Finestrat which had been given to him by Trish. Akmal had called him to confirm that the terms and task were indeed acceptable, and provided details of a bank account that the money could be paid into, in one instalment. Sam then simply gave the information to Trish when she called, at the same time agreeing to carry out the murder. While Trish assumed that they were his bank details, not surprisingly, the account was untraceable and like the account of the fraudster who had conned her previously, it was protected by an impenetrable firewall. Consequently there was nothing to link Sam with either the transaction, or the money.

# CHAPTER 84

25 November 2017

Sam awoke with an erection, a full bladder and a thirst you could photograph – the legacy of his over indulgence from the previous night, when he had drank far too much and had also succeeded, finally in being entertained by a man and a monkey, which he had to admit was worth waiting for. The act had been very user friendly, polished and professional, and he, along with everybody else had clearly enjoyed it. Sam thought that there was an originality and a freshness about it which raised it above the rest of the fare on offer in this latter day Sodom and Gomorrah. He recalled the Beatles song, *Everybody's Got Something To Hide Except For Me And My Monkey*, which seemed strangely apt for the unfolding drama he had found himself involved in.

Sam made his way to the bathroom and emptied his

bladder by standing like a giraffe having a drink. He then slated his thirst with a bottle of 'Agua con Gas' from the fridge, which was a life-saver. He couldn't face going to breakfast, so instead made some tea and toast and took himself out to the balcony for some much-needed air and reflection.

It was a particularly grey, bleak day. There was no sign of the pigeon, or anybody else for that matter. The outdoor pool was pretty much empty, with only the most optimistic and determined sun seekers in attendance.

Sam found himself reflecting on the revelations and circumstances that had led to the events of the last few days, and recalled that Heather had told him that after she had left Rab Lindsay he had continued to stalk her and to inundate her with abusive and threatening phone calls and texts, making it known that he knew where she had been, and who she'd been with. When Heather had tried to block his calls, he had changed the settings on his phone to circumvent the problem. He would also turn up at her house uninvited, refusing to leave until she threatened to call the police, which often made him worse, on occasion resorting to violence. He subjected her to a persistent regime of terror, to the extent that she was constantly in a state of fear and too terrified to do anything.

Sam believed, without a shadow of a doubt, that Heather's murder was a consequence, albeit indirectly, of her husband's pathologically selfish, ruthless and evil behaviour. Also, whist Frank Roy had certainly been unfaithful and betrayed his wife, on at least two occasions, and possibly more, Sam didn't believe that he deserved to be tortured for it to the point where it had at the very least contributed to his death.

The similarity between the circumstances of the blackmail threats made to himself and Frank were also not lost on Sam, from the threats and language used, and the use of crypto-currency. However, the threats had clearly emanated from completely different sources, with the former being of a much more personal nature, borne originally of anger, resentment and revenge for what Rab Lindsay had perceived as a slight and a threat to his position, power, control, and, as he saw it, his 'property'.

After Heather had told Rab Lindsay she was leaving him and that she knew that he had been seeing someone else, which he denied, she'd initially thought she sensed a softening in his attitude. However, the truth was that he was too proud to admit that he did not want her to go. Not because he loved her – he was far too much of a narcissist and a control freak to really understand what true love was. No, it was more to do an erosion of the power that he had over her.

The likelihood was that he hadn't really accepted that he had lost her, and saw it as merely an interlude, a minor blip and an irritant that would eventually resolve itself once she came to her senses.

Sure, Heather had had an affair with Trish's husband Frank, but that was years before she married Rab Lindsay, and it had been over for years. Just a painful memory of something that she would rather have forgotten about and which she wished had never happened. And Trish might never have found out if Heather hadn't foolishly and tragically confided in her controlling, abusive monster of a husband, who had then subsequently used the information to extort money and gain perverse and twisted revenge.

He was an immoral, greedy, ruthless sociopath, whose attitude towards life meant that he had little or no regard for the consequences of his actions for others, merely regarding it all as collateral damage.

Sam realised that in the absence of an actual tangible entity to blame and strike out at for the blackmail threats and menace that he had suffered over recent months, he was perfectly happy to regard Rab Lindsay as an acceptable manifestation of all that, and more. He certainly merited it, thought Sam, because of the suffering and tragedy he had been responsible for causing to so many people.

From the information available, Sam considered it probable that the second blackmail attempt had stemmed from Rab Lindsay's anger and resentment at Heather leaving him, in conjunction with him finding out about Frank's affair with Audrey, presumably from some redoubtable local source. While Rab Lindsay did not specify this in the email, Frank would have known what it referred to. Less than a month later, he was dead.

And now so was Rab Lindsay.

# CHAPTER 85

26 November 2017

Detective Inspector Vanessa Powrie poured a coffee for herself and her colleague, Bernardo, placing them on the latter's desk, before sitting down in the chair at the desk adjacent to him.

"So, Senora Powrie, when are we going to interview our little Algerian friend, Senor Samir?"

"Unfortunately, Senor Costales, we're not. He appears to have vanished off the face of the earth."

"What do you mean?" asked Bernardo. "Surely he is still working at the hotel?"

"That's just it, Bernardo mi amigo, he isn't. Apparently he just left, saying that he had to return to Algeria as a matter of some urgency. I also got the impression that they were happy to see the back of him."

"Algeria?" said Bernardo, disbelievingly.

"How very coincidental. And convenient! When did he leave? The hotel must . . ."

"Before you ask, Bernardo, no, he did not leave a forwarding address or any other contact details. They did have a mobile number for him, but I tried it and it is now unavailable.

"Also, he is not on our system, which would suggest that it is not his real name and that he was here illegally – surprise, surprise – and his other 'employers' are unlikely to be too happy about any approach from us, either."

"Mierda!"exclaimed Bernardo. "We should have spoken to him before now."

"Yes, you're probably right, but maybe it's for the best, Bernardo. This way it brings the investigation to a close, because without him we have no other evidence."

"But Senor Meredith doesn't know that, does he, Vanessa?"

"No, you're right – let's see what he has to tell us," she said, lifting the telephone.

# CHAPTER 86

26 November 2017

Sam's hotel room phone rang and on answering it he found that it was Inspector Costales, asking him to make his way to the same room as before to be interviewed by him and his colleague. Sam happily agreed.

On arriving at the room, Sam found both Inspectors sitting at the same table, recording equipment at the ready, looking fairly serious and solemn. Inspector Costales gestured for him to join them. When he sat opposite them at the table, Inspector Powrie looked at him, pressed a button and said, "The time is 10.15 a.m. on the 26th November, and Inspector Vanessa Powrie and Inspector Bernardo Costales are commencing an interview with Mr Sam Meredith."

She looked at Sam.

"Please state your name for the purpose of the recording," she said, in a very serious and formal manner, with no hint of the small talk they'd shared previously.

Sam, acknowledging the significant change in mood and the seriousness of the situation, did as he was told and responded, wondering what was going on.

He didn't have to wait long to find out.

"Were you responsible for arranging or conspiring to arrange the murder of Rab Lindsay, husband of Heather Lindsay, who was also murdered on the 11th of November?" asked Inspector Costales.

Sam was not expecting this, having previously been assured that he was not believed to be involved in or of having committed any crime. He was completely thrown and unsettled by this unforeseen turn of events, and wondered where it was going. However, he managed to remain calm.

"No, I was not, and I thought we were agreed on that," said Sam, looking at both detectives enquiringly.

"No, Mr Meredith, we agreed that we would need to interview you again, particularly in the event of any further information coming to light," said Inspector Costales.

*What further information?* thought Sam, and then asked the same question of the inspector.

"What new information? And from who? Trish? Audrey? Surely you don't believe anything they've said, do you? They're only trying to save their own skin. You must know that? What have they said?"

"Did you pay Akmal Samir £30,000 to make arrangements to have Rab Lindsay killed?" asked Inspector Powrie, ignoring his previous questions.

Sam thought that he was going to pass out with panic. How the fuck did they know that?

Then he realised; the obvious answer was that they had questioned Akmal and he had confessed under pressure.

*Fuck, what am I going to do?* he thought, then realised that in the absence of any actual evidence it was still Akmal's word against his. So he did the only thing he could think of; he lied through his teeth.

"I have no idea what you are talking about and you have no evidence to the contrary, so why are you asking me this?"

"Because it is our job, Mr Meredith," said the Spanish Inspector, "and because we know what you did. We just wanted to give you the chance to confess."

"It would be better if you did, Mr Meredith," added his Scottish colleague, looking at Sam.

"Oh, it's Mr Meredith now, is it? What happened to 'Sam, don't worry, we know you didn't do anything'?"

"We didn't say you didn't do anything. We said that we knew you didn't kill Heather Lindsay," she replied.

"And I didn't kill Rab Lindsay, either," said Sam.

"No, but you asked Akmal Samir to arrange it and

used Trish's money to pay for it, didn't you, Sam?

"Oh, it's Sam again now, is it? That's some imagination you have, Inspector. Well, nice try but forget it, both of you, I am not confessing to anything, not today, not to you, not to anybody, ever."

"We didn't think you would, but we just wanted to tell you that it might be better if you did," said Inspector Powrie.

"Why, what do you mean?" replied Sam, perplexed.

"Rab Lindsay isn't dead, Sam."

"What? But it was in the papers, in the news, everywhere. He must be!"

"He was left for dead, certainly, but he survived. We just allowed the media to say that he was deceased."

"But . . . why?" asked Sam, trembling.

"So that we could wait until he was well enough to tell us what happened to him and to tell him who we think is responsible."

"What do you mean? What did you tell him?" said Sam, having difficulty believing what he was hearing.

"Just what we believe. That you made arrangements with Akmal Samir to have him killed, paid for with £30,000 of Trish Roy's money," continued Inspector Powrie with a sinister smile.

"He's not going to be too happy with you or Trish, when he's out of hospital and up and running again."

"You told him my name? You can't do that! It's not right, it's unprofessional . . . and unethical!"

"We didn't tell him anything, Mr Meredith, but it's amazing what gets leaked to the media and other 'interested parties'."

"You said you would keep my name out of it!" Sam protested.

"No, we said that we would try," replied Inspector Powrie. "But that was before we spent some time talking to your little Algerian friend. He was very helpful."

So he was right, the little reprobate had indeed given him up, even although he had honoured their arrangement.

Sam could hardly believe what he was hearing, but he tried to remain calm and to evaluate the predicament he now found himself in. After what seemed an age but was in fact only a matter of seconds, he spoke again.

"I think I need to speak to a lawyer, and you have no evidence that I did anything."

"Ah, yes, sorry to burst your bubble, but that's where you're wrong," said Inspector Powrie, looking at her colleague. Inspector Costales took a mobile phone from his pocket, placed it on the desk and proceeded to play a message, or more precisely, *the* message that he had left for Trish, advising her that he agreed to carry out Rab Lindsay's murder for the terms agreed.

Sam thought his head was about to explode, then

he saw something out of the corner of his eye that made him doubt his sanity; he saw both Trish and Audrey smiling at him through the glass panel in the door.

"What the fuck? I thought that they were both in custody?" he said, looking at Inspector Powrie.

"They were, but we had to let them go, Sam," she replied.

"But, why? asked Sam, his head reeling.

"Because of you, Sam," said Inspector Powrie, "and the part you played in securing the evidence and confessions. As you're a suspect now, all the evidence obtained using you, and any subsequent conviction resulting from its use, would be inadmissible and unsafe. You're also free to go too now, Sam. So you'll all just have to take your chances with Rab Lindsay."

"Should be interesting. Best of luck with that, Senor Meredith," said Inspector Costales.

At that, both police Inspectors got up and left the room, as Rab Lindsay entered it.

# CHAPTER 87

26 November 2017

Sam awoke with a start and sat bolt upright, in a cold sweat, shaking and shivering uncontrollably, unable to breathe properly, and experiencing chest pains. He tried to relax, to regulate his breathing and gather his thoughts, running into the bathroom and throwing cold water on his face with his hands, which helped calm him a little.

"What the fuck was that all about?" he said out loud, which also helped to orientate him and restore his equilibrium. He knew what the answer to that question was; obviously he had had a nightmare.

It was more than that, though; much more – it was a glimpse of the guilt and the demons that he would have to contend with for the rest of his life. He poured himself a glass of water, swallowing it greedily in a single gulp, before filling the glass again. His hotel room phone rang. Sam answered it hesitantly.

"Hello, Sam, it's Vanessa. We're in the room downstairs if you would like to join us, please?"

*You have got to be fucking kidding me,* he thought, *that's the last thing I want to be doing right now.* But instead, he heard himself say, "I'm on my way".

Sam made his way to the makeshift interview room again, still feeling traumatised by his deeply disturbing dream and not surprisingly, in a state of apprehension and anxiety.

Nevertheless, he found himself thinking, *Whatever happens, it can't be any worse than what happened in that dream.*

# CHAPTER 88

26 November 2017

The two officers' demeanour and attitude could not have been any more different from their nightmarish alter egos, as they greeted Sam in a warm and friendly manner.

After some coffee and inconsequential conversation, Sam was interviewed about both deaths by Vanessa and Bernardo, who focused specifically on Trish's claims that she had paid him the sum of £30,000 to murder Rab Lindsay. Sam, unsurprisingly of course, denied the accusation, and there was no evidence to prove otherwise, either in the form of cash or any other type of financial transaction.

Sam's hotel room and possessions were searched, while his bank was contacted and his accounts checked. His phone was also scrutinised, revealing that all calls between him and Trish, and him and Audrey came from them rather than Sam, apart from the one he had made at the request of the police. The phone call from Akmal had no contact details, and Sam advised that it was a cold calling company asking about an accident that they'd erroneously claimed he'd had.

In the absence of any evidence to the contrary, the official view taken by the police was that Trish's claims were vindictive, and borne of anger and revenge. Sam was the good guy, after all, and he'd been happy to co-operate with the police to help them secure enough evidence to hopefully convict her for conspiring to have someone killed.

The police assured Sam that his cooperation in establishing who had committed the crime(s) and securing the necessary evidence to bring them to justice would be made public. They also reassured him that they would attempt to ensure that his intimate relationship with Heather was kept out of the news, as it was not considered to be in any way relevant to the commission of the murder. However, they could not guarantee it, and Sam wasn't really hopeful that they would be able to do this, given the high profile nature of the case and the thirst for information from the press. He also realised that there was nothing that anybody could do to prevent people from judging Heather's character and supposed sexual promiscuity, either. Unfortunately, everybody likes a good gossip and a scandal. Meanwhile, Heather's character had already been scrutinised and maligned by the media, through association with her husband, along with a healthy dose of misinformation and fake news.

Sam was thanked for his co-operation by both Bernardo and Vanessa, and they told him he was free to return home at his leisure. However, Vanessa, who advised that she was also hoping to be returning to Glasgow within the week, also cautioned Sam that he may be required to be available at a later date, in the event of "any further evidence" coming to light in regard to the murder of Rab Lindsay. She pointed out that they still had to speak to the Algerian man that Sam had the disagreement with – but "just as a formality".

"Routine procedure you understand, Senor," added Bernardo, holding Sam's gaze as he spoke.

"Unless . . . is there anything else that you wish to tell us now?" added Vanessa, quite pointedly.

"No, nothing," said Sam, as calmly as he could, while also reiterating his willingness to assist and co-operate with any subsequent enquiries and proceedings.

Whether it was because the trauma of the dream had passed, Sam found that he wasn't unduly concerned, believing that there was nothing to cause him any concern and that the outcome they'd arrived at appeared to be satisfactory to all concerned, apart from both perpetrators, obviously.

Also, rightly or wrongly, and after some rational evaluation of the situation, he wasn't concerned about Akmal talking to the police; he reasoned that if Trish had recorded their telephone call, he was certain that this would have been brought to the attention of the police by now, and they'd have brought it to his attention, just not in quite as dramatic a fashion as they had in his dream.

Trish had been right, of course. Sam had indeed accepted the offer of money from her to murder Heather's husband, even though he knew that he was not capable of carrying out such a crime for even ten times that amount. Trish should have known that, too. But she was too desperate for revenge to see it.

It wasn't about the money for Sam. It was about justice. But not for Trish, even although he had been instrumental in ensuring the desired outcome of her 'proposition' was achieved. No, Sam wanted justice and retribution for Heather and the others whose lives Rab Lindsay had wrecked and ultimately ended. But, he asked himself, was it really for Heather and the others? Or was that perhaps just a convenient excuse to gain revenge for the fact that Rab Lindsay had been intimate with his wife?

Whatever the truth was, and however the experience of the past two weeks had affected him, Sam was also surprised and slightly shocked by how little remorse and guilt he felt for his actions.

Indeed, he chose to see himself as someone who had played his part in ridding the world of an evil and morally corrupt and controlling scumbag who had contributed nothing worthwhile to society, and who would not be missed. If there was anything in the saying that the dead needed closure, then maybe Rab Lindsay's death would provide that for Heather. At least that's what he told himself.

# CHAPTER 89

26 November 2017

As Sam reflected upon the events of the previous two weeks, he found himself evaluating his relationships and life to date. As he did so, he experienced a deep sense of failure and disappointment. He began to ponder whether his recent decision making and actions, however flawed and immoral, had been borne of a need to compensate for, or perhaps ameliorate, a sense that he'd wasted his own life and that of the others that he had promised so much to, but had ultimately disappointed. Also, now that the dust had settled, Sam was able to contemplate the 'normal' issues of everyday life outside the claustrophobic and oppressive cocoon that he had been functioning within.

Interestingly, and unexpectedly, he found himself thinking about Kim. He found himself worrying about how she would be feeling about the recent dramatic and tragic events and how they, undoubtedly, would have affected her. He imagined that like him, she would be experiencing many feelings and emotions about the revelations, particularly given her alleged involvement with Rab Lindsay.

Sam still wasn't entirely certain what information and details about Kim's involvement would be made public by the media, but he imagined she would not be happy about any of it. He also speculated that she would probably be interested to know more about his own part in the whole sordid business, irrespective of their current alienation from one another.

The other irrefutable fact was that he still hadn't come to terms with losing her; to make matters worse, now there was her alleged infidelity with Rab Lindsay to contend with. But he needed to deal with it; he needed to know how it had happened. He needed to understand how his wife had become involved with a man like that – and while she was married to him. Assistance with all these issues was soon forthcoming, from the most unlikely of sources.

# CHAPTER 90

27 November 2017

As Sam was packing his case, his phone rang; he was extremely surprised to see that it was Kim. This was certainly not something that he had been expecting, as he had not spoken to her since they had broken up over nine months previously. She sounded weak and almost apologetic, asking him how he was and telling him that she knew about the events of the past weeks. She asked him if he was still in Benidorm and he told her he was on his way home soon. She then asked him if they could meet up when he returned, stating that there were some things that she needed to talk to him about. Sam said he would be in touch when he landed.

# CHAPTER 91

29 November 2017

By the time Sam met up with Kim at her home, the papers had published a story which contained much more detail under the redoubtable headline, 'Benidormicide'. All the background to it was there in black and white, including Sam's liaison with Heather and his subsequent co-operation with the police. Reference was also made to Kim's involvement with Rab Lindsay, with the circumstances being described as 'tragic serendipity'. Kim was the unfaithful wife who had had an affair with the murdered businessman with gangland connections. The businessman's own wife had gone on holiday and, after having a sexual liaison with the unfaithful wife's husband, had also been murdered. A Hollywood scriptwriter couldn't have written it better.

Sam had done well to be the only survivor of the

bizarre but all too real scenario. It was pure journalistic gold. And obviously it didn't stop there, with Trish and Audrey's roles being fully documented and dramatised, while Frank's role in the drama was certainly not omitted from proceedings. So much for letting sleeping dogs lie. Kim told Sam that she had read the stuff in the newspapers and even more on social media, which was a lot more toxic.

Sam was surprised that Kim had agreed to meet at her home, as he'd understood that her partner had moved in and wasn't sure how he would feel about him being there. However, she soon told him that they had split up and that he had moved out. Sam felt as if he should have said that he was sorry to hear this, but didn't; he couldn't bring himself to say it and mean it.

However, he did ask her how she was dealing with the situation, and her response was surprisingly pragmatic and honest.

"I suppose I brought it on myself, and I probably deserved it," she said. "But I wanted to say sorry to you for the way I treated you. You didn't deserve it."

Sam wasn't expecting such contrition, and didn't quite know what to say in response. He sighed.

"You said that there were some things you wanted to tell me?"

Kim told him that she had met Rab Lindsay at a funeral, initially finding him quite interesting and charming. At that point she knew very little about him, although he told her early on that he was separated from his wife.

He had then pestered her with phone calls – she had stupidly given him her mobile number – and wouldn't take no for an answer. As she and Sam weren't getting on at the time, she had agreed to meet him. He was very supportive to begin with, and made her feel appreciated and special. So they began to see one another whenever they could, and for a while, Kim said that it was "quite exciting", while apologising to Sam for her insensitivity. As the affair had developed, however, he had become more possessive, jealous and demanding of her. She didn't go into detail but she didn't need to – Sam had already read the CV.

Kim realised then that she needed to end the affair; however, he had made it very difficult, becoming aggressive and threatening to make everything public, even publishing photos that he had taken of her. This wasn't easy for Sam to hear, and apparently it was even harder for Kim to tell, as at that point she broke down, apologising profusely for deceiving and hurting him so.

"I just pretended that I didn't care what he did, and told him that he had more to lose than I did, in terms of his public profile. I even threatened to go to the police, and thankfully that finally seemed to work."

"I wish you had told me," said Sam, "I could've helped." He realised that he meant it. Apparently so did Kim, as she broke down again.

"I couldn't have told you Sam, how could I?" she said, struggling to speak.

Sam just nodded, feeling himself becoming emotional and saying nothing. Kim took his hand.

"And then I pushed you away after my mother died, when I should've done the opposite, but there were reasons, reasons that . . . that I never told you about."

"It's OK, you don't need to say any more," said Sam, but despite her tears, Kim insisted that there was more that she needed to tell him and that if she didn't do it now she never would.

"The service I met Rab Lindsay at was Frank Roy's funeral," she said.

"He went to Frank's funeral?" said Sam, disbelievingly.

"I know. Knowing what I know now, it's just sick. I'm not sorry that he's dead," said Kim, choking with emotion and having no idea of the significance of this for Sam. "But I feel so bad about Frank."

"I didn't know you knew him," said Sam.

"My mother did, and I went to the funeral with her," said Kim. "She didn't want to go there alone. Don't you remember, Sam?"

On reflection Sam had a vague recollection of her attending a funeral with her mother, but he clearly had no knowledge of or interest in who it was at the time. That was probably a fair reflection of his involvement in the relationship at that time, he realised. If he was honest, things probably hadn't been good between them even then, and indeed for some time before.

"My mother told me something before she died Sam," said Kim. "Something I have never told anyone."

Sam looked at Kim. He could not recall ever seeing such sadness and pain in her, or anyone else's eyes. He squeezed her hand softly and held her gaze.

"What is it, Kim? Tell me, what did she say?"

"She told me that she had had an affair many years before, about five years into her marriage with my dad," said Kim, tearfully. "They had been told that they couldn't have children, because of my dad's infertility, rather than my mum's. I don't know the exact details. She said that it affected their relationship, and she found herself feeling differently towards him. So she did what I did, and went looking for affection and god knows what else, elsewhere. The apple doesn't fall too far from the tree, does it, eh Sam?"

Without waiting for a response, she went on.

"Anyway she found it, obviously, and then she got pregnant – with me. However, there was no question of the putative father becoming involved, and despite my 'dad' obviously knowing that the child wasn't his, he was happy to go along with the charade. Amazingly, he and mum stayed together until he died, and I couldn't have loved him any more than if he had been my real dad."

Struggling to hold back her tears, she looked down at the floor.

"Sam, Frank Roy was my father."

# CHAPTER 92

Sam held Kim in his arms as she broke down in floods of tears, sobbing and shaking uncontrollably for a long time. When her emotion subsided, she continued talking, explaining that after her mother died she felt lost and emotionally devastated, because as well as losing her mother she had also just discovered who her natural father was, but found that she had nowhere to go with her feelings. She was unable to obtain any closure or resolution. And now she had also discovered that he was a serial adulterer.

A thought flashed into Sam's mind, and while he was conscious of Kim's fragility, there was a question that he had to ask her.

"Did you tell Rab Lindsay about this?"

"God, no! I had managed to get away from him by then, thank God. The thought of him knowing anything like that about me is just horrific, Sam, knowing what he is capable of now. He is — was — a monster. What he did to Frank . . . my father . . . I hate myself for ever having anything to do with him."

Sam thought she was about to break down again, but she gathered herself together sufficiently to speak further.

"You're the only person I have told, Sam. But when I found out what had happened in Benidorm and that you were involved, I needed to tell you everything,"

She then seemed to take a minute to think before adding, "I don't know who else might have the information, but I don't want anybody else to know, Sam.

"You can't tell anybody Sam, please . . ." she was shaking with emotion, now.

"It's OK, Kim, your secret's safe with me, you know that," Sam said, putting his arm around her comfortingly.

"I know that, Sam," she replied, "I know that I can trust you."

Sam found himself thinking about what she had said about not knowing who already knew. If his recent experience was anything to go by, you just never knew who knew what about you. Sometimes you find out that people know more about you than you do yourself, which he found to be really scary. But he thought that was something for the future,  for now, Kim had nobody that she could turn to, and Sam knew that she needed a friend. He hoped that maybe he could be that friend. The friend that he had failed to be previously.

Thankfully, she felt able to confide in him now, and hopefully she had also eased her troubled heart and mind by telling him her secret. Maybe one day he would tell her his, or then again maybe not.

# EPILOGUE

It was a lovely clear, fresh winter's day in Glasgow. Sam had gone for a walk in the park and was now sitting on a bench with a newspaper which informed him that hackers who had publicly threatened to reveal the names of people who had subscribed to the adult dating site Madison Avenue had done exactly that, with several high profile names featuring in the sizeable list. Needless to say, his was nowhere to be seen, however. "And why would it?" he said to himself. "I never did anything wrong." And this time he meant it.

He then noticed an article about his favourite company, 'Missed Bus', stating that they would be giving up the franchise in Scotland and moving their business to England.

*Good riddance*, he thought, *they'll probably not manage to do that on time either! It'll probably take them as long as it's taking for Brexit to be negotiated.* Not that he supported that development; no, he, like 62% of the Scottish people wanted to remain, but of course, as always, Scotland's views were not deemed important and therefore had been ignored by Westminster.

As he was contemplating the prospect of leaving Europe under a Conservative government, Sam thought that he heard an owl hooting somewhere. Then he realised that he had heard, or *thought* he had heard, a lot of owls hooting over the years. However, he had never actually seen one, other than in a zoo or sanctuary, or as part of a special display event. Still listening carefully, he heard a magpie's distinctive call and, as usual, waited for maybe another one, two, or more to appear. However, on this particular day, after getting up from his bench and walking through a stretch of woodland, he wandered into a clearing and found himself looking at a group of exactly seven Magpies for the very first time.

End.

# ABOUT THE AUTHOR

John Gillick is a retired social worker and former standup comedian and comedy writer. He is widowed, and has two children and grandchildren. He lives in Glasgow.

Printed in Great Britain
by Amazon